The Driftwood Girls

Mark Douglas-Home is a journalist turned author, who was editor of the *Herald* and the *Sunday Times Scotland*. His career in journalism began as a student in South Africa where he edited the newspaper at the University of the Witwatersrand, Johannesburg. After the apartheid government banned a number of editions of the paper, he was deported from the country. He is married with two children and lives in Edinburgh.

By the same author

The Sea Detective
The Woman who Walked into the Sea
The Malice of Waves

The Driftwood Girls

MARK DOUGLAS-HOME

PENGUIN BOOKS

PENGUIN BOOKS

UK | USA | Canada | Ireland | Australia
India | New Zealand | South Africa

Penguin Books is part of the Penguin Random House group of companies
whose addresses can be found at global.penguinrandomhouse.com

First published 2020
001

Copyright © Mark Douglas-Home, 2020

The moral right of the author has been asserted

Set in 12.5/14.75 pt Garamond MT Std
Typeset by Jouve (UK), Milton Keynes
Printed and bound in Great Britain by Clays Ltd, Elcograf S.p.A.

A CIP catalogue record for this book is available from the British Library

ISBN: 978–1–405–92363–7

www.greenpenguin.co.uk

For Colette

Twenty-three years ago

Her glower was as scornful as any sixteen-year-old girl had directed at a boy all that long summer. 'Go with you? On a boat? You kidding me?'

'No,' he replied coolly. 'I'm serious. I don't joke.'

'Is that right?'

He lit a cigarette, exhaled instead of answering.

'Tell you what . . .' she said, turning away, the crowds on the seafront appearing to interest her more than him.

'What?' he asked eventually.

'Fuck off, yeah?'

If he was disappointed at her rejection, he was encouraged by the thought that here, at this exact place, other teenaged boys had danced this same dance, this clumsy choreography, and some had been successful. He would try again.

'Why, what else are you doing?'

Her head jerked backwards. 'I'm going to the gig.' Behind her, on an empty shop window, a poster announced 'Carter Emery Entertainments presents Crazy Stupid Dreams'. Tickets were three pounds fifty. The start was seven thirty.

He checked his watch: seven thirty-eight. 'Going with someone?'

'What do you think?'

'I think he's late.'

'*She.*'

'What?'

'Not he, *she*. Her name's Sarah.'

'OK, *she*'s late.'

For a few moments neither spoke. They stood side by side, a study in opposites: the white-blond, curly-haired, muscular boy with the broad, suntanned face and the lean, pale-skinned girl with long, lustrous auburn hair, big eyes and wide mouth.

'I thought . . .' he said at length, coughing to clear his throat. 'I thought you looked nice. That's why I asked you on my boat.'

Another glower from her: 'What age are you? Eighteen?'

'Seventeen, yesterday.'

'And you've got a boat?'

'We could go to France.' He gave her a sideways glance. 'We could go tonight.' His voice lifted at the prospect.

'Sure we could, if you had a boat and I wasn't going to the gig.'

He nodded, seeming to acknowledge a problem.

'Have you,' he said, after consideration, as if proposing a solution, 'ever had a crazy, stupid dream that, one day, someone will take you from here, will ask you to run away?'

'*Run away?*' She frowned at the question, also at not knowing whether to engage with him or to rebuff him again. 'Why would I?'

'It'd be an adventure. That's what I'm doing, running away, running away from home in a boat. Come with me.' He added, 'I dare you,' which made him sound younger than seventeen.

To look older, he sucked his cigarette and blew smoke.

'I don't dream about that,' she said.

'What then?'

Her eyes narrowed. She watched him, making up her mind about him, noticing how a curl of hair tucked behind his right ear, how his eyebrows and lashes were also white-blond. 'Why am I telling you this?'

'Go on,' he said.

She took a deep breath. 'I dream I'm on a beach with my mum. There's sand stretching for miles and miles and a beach hut with a blue door and windows. It's just me and her. She's in a deckchair. I'm making sandcastles.'

A twist of her mouth: 'My mum's dead.'

'Mine too,' he lied before realizing he had.

He should have said, *might as well be dead; was dead to him.* He would have corrected himself except for the difference he sensed in her now their lives were joined by tragedy.

'Hello, I'm Thomas.'

He held out a hand.

So, hesitantly, did she.

Her fingers stubbed against his before they managed a handshake; each, it turned out, as awkward as the other.

'I'm Ruth.'

'Hi, Ruth.'

Instead of a glower, her expression, he noticed, was curious, amused.

'You're an odd boy, Thomas,' she said, 'with all your questions, handshakes and stuff.'

He smiled.

'Are you serious?' she asked.

'About what?'

'Having a boat? About France?'

'I don't joke.'

'No, you said.'

She turned towards the seafront, looking for Sarah. 'Where is she? She's never late.' After searching the crowds for someone hurrying she found her eyes lifting to the horizon. 'This boat of yours . . . You *do* have a boat, right? You'll bring me back?'

'If that's what you want?'

'Tomorrow night or I'll be missed.'

'Tomorrow night, I promise.'

First a lie, then a promise he would break.

I

The television camera went close up, lingering on Kirsty Fowler's rubbed-red eyes, a nervous flickering of her mouth and her blotched face framed by lank, mousy-brown hair: a study in misery.

A male voice said, 'I can't imagine the state I'd be in if that was my father. Do you know if he's been in touch with anyone, anyone at all?'

Kirsty's expression changed from abject to accusing. Her eyes flashed in the lights of the studio and with something else, something feral and fierce. 'A man called Cal McGill,' she replied. 'He talked to Daddy. He spoke to Daddy on that bridge. He drove Daddy's car.'

'They went to a café. Do you know what was discussed?'

'No,' Kirsty wailed. 'McGill won't say.'

The camera zoomed out as Greg Lane, the show's host, leaned closer to his guest and said something inaudible, apparently reassuring because she mumbled, 'I'll try.'

Their proximity accentuated their differences: Greg, tanned, with short-cut black hair, neatly parted, wearing a pink shirt and dark blue trousers; and Kirsty, whose clothes were as messy as her emotions. She wore an oversized moss-green sweater, blue-denim skirt and scuffed white ankle boots.

'Before he went missing,' Greg continued, 'your father had some very bad news about his health?'

'Yes.'

'It's important he has medical treatment as soon as possible. That's right, isn't it?'

Kirsty nodded.

'And your father going off like that, telling no one in the family, that's totally out of character, yes?'

'Yes.'

Greg turned to the camera. 'Kirsty's done all she can to find her father. Now it's over to you, our wonderful and, more to the point, vigilant viewers.'

On a large screen behind Kirsty flashed a photograph of a silver-haired, stooped man in a tweed jacket. Greg said, 'As you know, Kirsty's father is called Harry Fowler. He's seventy-six and this is what he looks like.'

Beside the picture of Harry appeared a maroon-coloured Vauxhall with the registration number enlarged. 'And this is his car. It hasn't been found, has it, Kirsty?'

'No.'

'If you see this car or Harry, please ring the phone number at the bottom of your screens.'

Kirsty blurted, 'We're so frightened. Please come home, Daddy.' She paused and looked straight at the camera. 'Please help us find him.'

Greg squeezed Kirsty's hand and said, 'On Kirsty's behalf we tracked Cal McGill to a light industrial estate in the east of Edinburgh where he appears to be based. Here's what happened.'

On the same screen a youngish man with short, dark brown hair, wearing jeans and a white T-shirt, opened then quickly closed a door. It banged shut.

'As you can see, he's not exactly helpful . . .'

6

Greg picked up a sheet of paper from the sofa. 'This is what Cal McGill said when one of our researchers reached him by phone. "I have assisted the police to the best of my ability. Any questions about Mr Fowler should be addressed to Mr Fowler himself. He is, after all, an adult, has every right to privacy and, when we parted company, was in full command of his faculties."'

Greg let out an exaggerated sigh. 'Isn't that the point, Cal McGill? We can't ask Mr Fowler. Nor can Kirsty, nor the police. No one has the faintest idea where he is, with the exception, perhaps, of you.'

He referred again to the printed sheet. 'You might be interested to know more about Mr McGill, or should I say *Dr* Cal McGill? He runs a rather unusual business called the Sea Detective Agency.' One of Greg's black eyebrows arched like a crow swooping on rotting carrion. 'I'll say it is . . .'

Newspaper headlines flashed behind Kirsty. 'Sea detective tracks body of drowned schoolgirl'. 'Hebridean murder mystery solved by oceanographer detective'. 'Marine scientist joins hunt for missing fishermen'.

Greg said, 'Apparently, Dr McGill finds bodies which are lost at sea by being able to calculate the different effects of tides, currents and winds on their speed and direction of travel. He's been involved in murder inquiries, marine accidents . . .' He glanced at Kirsty. 'And suicides.'

Kirsty blurted, 'If Daddy's dead, it'll be that man's fault.'

Greg's mouth twisted in sympathy. 'Your father isn't the kind of man who'd cause anyone unnecessary trouble or distress, is he?'

'No.'

'He said as much to you before this latest diagnosis. What did he say, Kirsty?'

She blinked.

'Take your time, Kirsty.'

'He said if he was ill, seriously ill, he'd go off and hide himself away . . .' Kirsty sniffled, wiped her eyes.

'That must have been difficult for you to hear.'

Kirsty nodded.

'You told him you'd look after him?'

'Yes, yes . . .'

'Of course you did.' Greg waited before carrying on. 'Kirsty, you have a particular worry about this Dr McGill. Would you share it with our viewers?'

'I think Daddy might have . . . I'm worried he might be . . .' The final words of the sentence were too hard to say.

Greg prompted, 'You think your father might take his own life? Is that right?'

'Yes, yes.'

'And, knowing your father as you do, you think he arranged to meet McGill?'

'Yes.'

'Why would he have done that, Kirsty?'

'I . . . I . . .' A tear rolled down her cheek, followed by another.

'Correct me, Kirsty, but you think your father met Dr McGill on that bridge for advice . . .'

Kirsty nodded.

'The river was in flood that night . . .'

'Yes, yes,' Kirsty wailed.

'That part of the river is also tidal, isn't it?'

Kirsty nodded.

'You think your father was asking Dr McGill when or where he should jump into the water so his body would be carried out to sea and wouldn't ever be found, wouldn't cause anyone distress. You think that's why they were together on the bridge. Is that right?'

Another tremulous 'yes' emerged from Kirsty.

'And you think that's why McGill is unwilling to talk, because he was giving a sick old man advice on how to kill himself?'

Her eyes flashed wide. 'What other reason could there be?'

'Kirsty, do you have a message for your father, in case he's watching?'

'I love you, Daddy.'

The camera closed on Kirsty's doleful face as Greg announced, 'Time's up, I'm afraid. Tune in next week and let's hope there's good news about Harry Fowler. This is the show which lets the missing know their families still love them and want them back. Isn't that right, Kirsty? Thanks, folks, for watching *Missing Not Forgotten*.'

Cal slammed shut his laptop, swore. The next time he drove across a bridge at night and saw someone staring into a river he'd be the one shouting, 'Jump, you mad old bastard.' He wouldn't park on the far bank, return on foot and talk to the man. He wouldn't play the Good Samaritan or concerned citizen.

He clicked on his inbox. New emails were arriving by the second.

He read two.

He deleted both before scrolling from one screen of bile and invective to the next, 427 unread emails since Kirsty Fowler's Facebook appeal for her father, which included the Sea Detective Agency's email address and an invitation to 'Let McGill know what you think of his refusal to say what he and Daddy discussed and why they met.'

Cal's phone rang. He glanced at the screen – the caller was Alex Lauder, a friend from Cal's student days. Like Cal, Alex was a marine scientist. Unlike Cal, Alex was sociable. He enjoyed long 'catch-ups', inquiring about Cal's work, telling Cal about his. Cal, increasingly, preferred not talking. Recently, he'd ducked Alex's calls. He did the same now. He'd ring Alex later, he told himself: his usual, insincere get-out. Too much else was going on.

His attention returned to the angry emails, mesmerized by their rush to judgement and, worse, hatred. He paused at a familiar name: Jim Arthur. Jim was a retired head teacher, who'd asked Cal to look for his missing daughter, Maureen. A fortnight ago, after a storm, her dinghy had been found abandoned and empty off Portsoy, north-east Scotland. Her body hadn't been recovered.

Dear Cal (if I may),

In view of the publicity about Mr Fowler, I would be grateful if you did not involve yourself in trying to find Maureen. I am

concerned about your sudden and, I am sure unjustified,
notoriety drawing the wrong kind of attention to your search.

With sadness,
Jim

Jim was the fifth client lost in the last thirty-six hours.
Only one remained. Her name was Elaine Mawhinney.
Her sister, Cath, had been on holiday on the Scottish
island of Islay and had gone night swimming as the tide
ebbed. She'd been carried away.

As Cal refreshed his inbox, an email from Elaine
appeared with the other new arrivals.

I think it will complicate matters for you to be involved in looking
for Cath right now. The police assure me her remains are likely
to appear in their own time. In the circumstances, I've decided to
let nature take its course. For all I know, Cath might prefer not
to be found since she was always so in love with swimming and
the sea.

Cal's final client had gone.
He leaned back in his chair. Under his breath he said,
'Fuck, fuck, fuck.' Then, throwing himself forward, he
crossed his office, stopping by the door and pressing his
eye to the spyhole: was another gang of accusers gathering
outside? All he could see was bare tarmac and brick-built
shuttered units opposite. Moments later, in the dim yellow
glow of a streetlamp, he was hurrying from the industrial
estate to stone steps which descended to a long-disused
rail line. By day it was busy with walkers and cyclists.
By night it was a netherworld, sunk between deep and
overgrown cuttings, a haunt of foxes, owls and, when

the walls of his office appeared to be closing in, of Cal. Sometimes he would stay out until sunrise, traversing the city unseen. This night, as he walked beneath a dome of skeletal branches interlocking like bare, bony fingers, he thought of Harry Fowler (he couldn't have killed himself, could he?) and how arbitrary life was. A virtual mob was baying for his blood because he'd shown consideration for another human being. Yet Alex Lauder, who had reason to complain about Cal's evasive, probably hurtful behaviour, was never critical, always dependable.

Guilty conscience made Cal turn back. Even though it was late, past midnight, he would contact Alex. Cal would apologize for being a stranger. He'd let Alex talk, even if the prospect made Cal resentful, then reflective. Was he becoming more solitary in his habits, too comfortable in his own company and silence? He thought so.

After opening his office door, he noticed a light on his worktable: someone ringing his mobile phone. The call ended as Cal approached. One of five during his absence, he discovered. Three were from Alex, one from Helen Jamieson, a detective sergeant with Police Scotland who was another friend – his only other friend – and the last from Olaf Haugen, a beachcomber, Norwegian by origin, who lived on the island of Texel off the Dutch coast. Olaf was a mutual acquaintance of Alex's and Cal's. The sea was their connection; for Cal and Olaf there was also a particular interest in the movement of flotsam.

Cal thought that perhaps a body had washed up somewhere. Were Alex and Olaf alerting him to a potential case? Alternatively, more likely, they were ringing to commiserate about his monstering on television and Facebook. That would also explain Helen's call.

On ringing Alex's number, Cal was surprised at a woman answering, especially as the rasp in her voice made her sound older than Alex's girlfriend. 'Is that Flora?' he asked doubtfully.

'Caladh?' was the brusque reply.

Apart from Alex and Olaf, no one referred to him by the longer version of his name, which, in Gaelic, meant 'harbour' or 'haven'. Alex used to protest at the abbreviation 'Cal' because, he said, Caladh was such a resonant, characterful name that anyone lucky enough to be born with it would be bound to be a haven in a storm or at a time of crisis. Whenever Alex called him 'Caladh' – recently in phone messages – he was jolted into realizing how much the opposite of a haven he'd been.

'Yes,' Cal replied hesitantly. 'Sorry, who are you? Is Alex there?'

'I'm Alex's mother, Rosemary Lauder.'

'Oh, hello, Mrs Lauder, how are you?' Cal remembered a severe-looking woman with hair turned prematurely grey. 'Is Alex there? He rang me just now. I'm sorry for ringing so late.'

'It wasn't Alex. It was me. I'm borrowing his phone. It's easier for contacting his friends.' Her voice was monotone, lifeless.

'Mrs Lauder, what's wrong? Has something happened?'

'Alex is dying.'

'Dying?' Cal repeated, shocked. 'Dying how? What's happened?'

'The cancer's returned. He can't fight it, doesn't want to

fight, he's given up. There's no hope, none. Two days, possibly three, possibly one.' She gasped at that unbearable and imminent prospect.

'I didn't know,' Cal managed to reply, a response as inadequate as the conduct of his friendship. 'He had cancer years ago, didn't he . . . before we met . . . ? Dying, God, that's awful . . .' He gabbled in the hope of hitting on some appropriate words or sentiment. 'I thought it was dealt with then . . . Oh, I'm so sorry, Mrs Lauder. Two days, did you say? Poor Alex. What can I do? Is there something? Anything?'

Mrs Lauder, in contrast, was precise, matter-of-fact. 'You made a promise to Alex once . . . about where Alex would like to be buried. Can I tell him you'll do that for him?'

Do that for him at least.

Cal heard himself say uncertainly, 'If that's what Alex wants, yes.' He was thinking: *Does Mrs Lauder know what she's asking? It's a criminal offence.*

'Do I have your word?'

Should Cal warn her? He decided not to because, being a minister's wife, she would know the regulations about burial. Also, she sounded implacable; nothing would be allowed to frustrate her dying son's wish, not even the law. Cal replied, 'Yes, yes, of course.'

'You won't let me down? You won't let Alex down?'

'No. I promise.'

Silence.

Then Mrs Lauder said, 'It was a pity you two drifted apart. I don't know what happened. As far as I'm aware, Alex didn't either, but he missed you, you know. He was a

14

good friend to you, even if you weren't ever really one to him.'

Mrs Lauder ended the call and Cal swore.

What was wrong with him? He thought of Alex's unanswered calls. Why didn't he ever feel the need of friends, the company of other people, even someone as loyal as Alex?

2

Her complaint entered the kitchen before she did. 'Hopeless,' Kate Tolmie declared on leaving her bedroom and crossing the passage. After wrapping herself in a dressing gown she slumped into the armchair by the table, yawned and inquired of Maria, the cleaner, 'I haven't held you up, have I?'

Maria Fuentes, who was ironing by the open door to the utility room, muttered in Spanish at the waste: a beautiful young woman like Kate lying in bed all day, depressed.

'What?' Kate said indignantly, tying her long red hair in a loose knot at the back. 'It's not my fault I don't sleep at night and can't wake up in the morning.'

Maria said nothing. The iron hissed steam.

'Well,' Kate insisted, 'is it?'

'You know my opinion . . .' Maria paused while she folded a shirt. 'You need a new job and a nice uncomplicated boy, someone your age. We talked about that last week, didn't we?'

Last week, the week before, the one before that. Maria had become Kate's amateur life coach following her breakup with Pete. He was forty-five, sixteen years older than Kate, separated from his wife and – the reason for Kate walking out on him – controlling. The same day, she resigned from her gallery job designing exhibition flyers and catalogues. Pete owned the gallery.

'So, what I need now,' Kate sighed, 'is a job, a boyfriend and my sister to speak to me.' She put on an apologetic expression. 'The list's getting longer, Maria.'

'You've fallen out with Flora?' Maria stopped ironing.

Kate nodded.

'When Alex is ill?' Maria was disapproving. 'When Flora needs your support more than ever? Kate, you're her big sister!' Maria muttered again in Spanish and crossed herself, as though a blasphemy had been uttered.

'Flora won't answer my calls or reply to texts or emails,' Kate said. 'She's blanked me for three days. I don't think she'll ever speak to me again. I'm so worried, Maria.'

Maria sighed and carried on ironing.

As usual, she wore a daisy-patterned housecoat with matching scarf tied around her head from which only a few stray mousy wisps of hair escaped. In six years, in all the time Maria had cleaned the flat which Kate and Flora shared, this had been her uniform. Completing her ensemble were yellow rubber gloves to protect her hands (according to Maria, her 'only good feature'), navy tracksuit bottoms, pale blue trainers and rimless spectacles which slid to the end of her nose, leaving a track in her make-up.

After finishing another shirt, Maria said, 'I don't suppose I have to guess.'

Kate said, 'No.'

Maria softened. 'Losing your mother like that, it's difficult for both of you.'

'I didn't ever *have* her, Maria,' Kate protested. 'My mother thought looking after children in another country was more interesting than staying at home with me and Flora.

I don't want to remember her. I don't want to be known as Christina Tolmie's daughter. I had enough of that growing up. So what does my sister do? She sets up the Christina Tolmie Foundation, which is *exactly* what I asked her *not* to do. I don't think my mother should be celebrated or made out to be some kind of role model. She wasn't one.'

'You want Flora to stop her work?' Maria frowned, puzzled. 'What she's doing is marvellous, helping unfortunate children, just like your mother.'

'No, Flora's stirring everything up again,' Kate replied, becoming exasperated. 'Every time she's interviewed about the foundation, she invites every crank to come up with theories about our mother's disappearance. The woman hasn't been heard of for twenty-three years! What's the point?' She looked out of the window.

After a few moments, Maria said, 'You know what stops Flora from sleeping at night, don't you?'

Kate said nothing.

Maria continued in the same gentle tone. 'Well, there's Alex obviously, but Flora also worries about your mother. She thinks she might have spent the last twenty-three years locked in a cellar and all that keeps her alive is the thought that you and Flora will never give up on her.'

'What,' Kate snapped, 'like she didn't give up on us?'

Maria waited before saying quietly, 'Flora's your sister. She's family, your only family. Don't fight with her.'

Kate sighed. 'It's a bit late for that.' Then she shuddered, imagining their mother held captive in a dungeon, a covered-up hole in the ground, a basement, a container, somewhere cold and dark, ever since Flora was four and Kate six.

3

'One word? To describe Olaf?' Sarah Allison peered through the beach restaurant's window. One hundred metres away, Olaf Haugen's dark bulk and wild mane of silvery-white curly hair were silhouetted against a gluey-looking grey sea. He was ambling, occasionally stopping, sometimes bending as he searched for driftwood and other usable flotsam; as familiar a part of the scenery on the island of Texel as uninterrupted beaches or Texelhopper buses.

'*Solitary*,' Sarah tried. '*Dependable*. Oh, I know!' Turning to Lotte Rouhof, her friend and next-door neighbour, she announced, '*Reassuring.*' Sarah dipped her head, emphasizing her certainty. 'Yes, that's it. I find Olaf's presence very reassuring.'

'*How* reassuring?' Lotte frowned, teasing. 'In what way reassuring? Reassuring because he's hard-wearing, tough-as-old-boots reassuring? Are you sure you don't mean *durable*?'

'Durable.' Sarah tasted the word along with a sip of wine. 'No, durable makes him sound boring. A stone's durable.' She glanced once more at Olaf, then to his left where the beach gave way to a high, unbroken and grassy dune. 'You asked "*How* reassuring?"' Sarah said. 'Reassuring in the same way I sleep at night knowing the sea can't break through that dune. In *that* way reassuring: like sea

19

defences are reassuring if you live, as we do, in a village close to the coast on a low-lying island.'

Lotte gave Sarah an amused look. 'Have you told him?'

'Told him what?'

'You sleep better at night because of him.'

'That's not what I said.'

'Isn't it?' Lotte lifted her glass, tilting it slightly towards Sarah, being playful. 'Because that's definitely what I heard. You and Olaf, that's a surprise.'

'Oh, stop it, Lotte. Don't,' Sarah said, annoyed. 'Don't ever say that. If he heard you, you'd frighten him away. And I'd mind. I like Olaf. I like his habits. I like knowing he'll be out here, beachcombing, after high tide, and if he's passing near the hut when I'm there, he'll just go slower, without looking up. He'll give me the choice whether to say hello or not. I like it when he sits with me. Heaven knows I must bore him, but he's never restless or in a hurry to go. And sometimes –' Sarah turned wistful – 'I look at him and I think *Oh, you poor man, something's troubling you*, and I'm sure he'd like to talk too. But he never does and I don't think I can say, *It's all right, Olaf, trust me – you can tell me anything*, because I'd hate him to think I was prying and to scare him away.'

Sarah smiled self-consciously, then shrugged at Lotte. 'Well, you asked. That's how. I feel safe with him. And now, since he's moved into your annexe, I like knowing that, when it's not high tide, he'll be in the passageway between your house and mine, at his bench, making his driftwood men. I like his predictability.'

An interlude followed. The waiter arrived with their orders: spinach quiche for Sarah and Asian chicken salad for Lotte. Each took a mouthful.

Lotte said, 'This is *good*.'

Sarah washed hers down with water because her throat felt dry. 'Anyway,' Sarah continued, giving Lotte a sideways glance, her turn to be playful, 'I'm not the only one who likes Olaf's company, am I? I've heard you.'

'I know!' Lotte's blue eyes opened wide. 'If Olaf's working when I'm having breakfast, I'll open the kitchen window, sit on the sill with my coffee and I'll talk to him, say whatever comes into my head. Imagine that: me talking to someone who smokes cigarettes, doesn't possess more than two pairs of trousers and whose hair is knotted and hasn't been cut for years! Do you know, sometimes he'll stop sawing or hammering, whatever he's doing, and he'll pay attention? Like you say, he listens even if he isn't exactly conversational. Well, not yet, he isn't.' She laughed. 'But there's definitely progress, thanks to you.'

'What did I do?'

Lotte appeared nonplussed. 'Don't you remember? Before Olaf moved in, you said it was important for us to be neighbourly, to make sure we talked to him, because he'd lived on his own for so long in that horrible farmstead of his that he probably wouldn't be comfortable around people or know how to interact with them. You know, to make Olaf our project.'

'Our *project*?' Sarah put down her fork. 'Really, Lotte, I don't remember saying that. What sort of project?'

'Why,' Lotte said, puzzled, 'to bring Olaf out of himself, to find out why a Norwegian like him is living at the wrong end of the North Sea, whether he has any family, why he appears to be so alone.' Lotte watched Sarah as if expecting her to say, *Oh that, yes*.

'Surely you remember,' Lotte prompted. 'To solve the mystery.'

'I'm sorry?' Sarah experienced a sinking sensation at the glint in her friend's eyes. 'What mystery? *We* live on Texel and I'm English and you're French. That isn't mysterious. Why's Olaf living here a mystery?'

Lotte frowned. 'Because you and I know why we're here. What's Olaf's reason? No one has any idea, not even you.'

4

Cal McGill expected a middle-aged man with a long face, graveyard pallor and dandruff, a living cadaver. Instead the funeral director was a forty-something female with shiny chestnut-coloured hair and flushed, plumped skin, the opposite of death's harbinger. She smiled, all white teeth and glistening pink lips: 'Can I help?'

'Oh . . .' Cal said, adjusting. 'Do you have a coffin? What I mean is, do you have a coffin I can take away?'

'Today? Right now?' The smile faded.

'Preferably,' he replied.

'Well, that's a bit unusual.' She studied Cal as if drawing conclusions about this stranger, registering his age, early thirties or possibly younger; his height, five ten; his short, dark hair; his nose which skewed to the right; his clothes, black jersey, olive jeans and walking boots – and the way he didn't quite look at her. 'Are you,' she asked doubtfully, 'familiar with our range of coffins?'

'I'm not, but my grandmother is.' Cal spoke to her shoes, which were flesh-coloured and high-heeled. 'She's been looking at your website. It's for her, the coffin.'

'Oh, your grandmother!' The exclamation was accompanied by a short, brittle laugh of relief. 'For a moment there I thought you might be organizing a stag party. A funeral theme's the fashion at the moment. You know, the groom being carried from pub to pub in a coffin to represent the living death of marriage.' Her head shook. 'Arthur Dirleton and Daughter is a family company. We don't want to be associated with anything, well, gross like that, or disrespectful.'

Cal managed to arrange his features into a similar expression of disapproval: the unreasonable behaviour of others affected them both, it suggested. 'No, nothing of that kind,' he said, glancing at her. 'Just a ninety-two-year-old waking up this morning and deciding she had to organize her funeral . . .'

He left the sentence hanging to imply other times she'd woken with other peculiar notions and of Cal being put-upon and dutiful.

The funeral director's lips pressed together in approval as well as sympathy. Cal looked for any sign of recognition. Seeing none, he relaxed a little, pushing to the back of his mind the thought of Greg Lane, the host of *Missing Not Forgotten*, updating his audience about Harry Fowler's disappearance, saying, 'There's been an interesting development. Cal McGill, the Sea Detective, has been reported shopping for a coffin.'

Cal imagined one of Greg's black eyebrows arching, a crow swooping once again on carrion.

'Anyway,' Cal said hurriedly, 'my grandmother tells me you have a solid pine coffin, which is butt-jointed – she's very particular about that because a butt-jointed coffin will be stronger than one that isn't and security matters to her. Apparently, the coffin has a name, the Caithness, and the price on your website is six hundred and fifty pounds. She knows there's another twenty per cent VAT if she doesn't also buy a funeral package from you, but she's not going to, definitely not. I said to her, "I can't buy a coffin like take-away chips from McDonald's," and she replied, "If I give you the money, why on earth not? You drive a pick-up, don't you?"'

Cal sighed. 'I said I supposed I could try.' His right cheek flinched at having allowed himself to be browbeaten again and wishing he hadn't.

'So I'd like a coffin, the Caithness, to take away for a rather headstrong woman who's five feet nine and a size twelve. It doesn't matter if the coffin isn't a perfect fit. In fact, she'd rather it was a bit roomy because she's worried about becoming claustrophobic.' Cal rolled his eyes. 'And no name, she was emphatic about that. She'd rather be dead than risk any gossip about her buying a coffin.'

Cal knew he was over-explaining. But he was nervous, still worried about being suddenly recognized. Also, because of his solitary existence, he was out of practice at the minor dishonesties and half-truths that most people uttered routinely. As a result, when he had to deceive, he found himself saying too much, too quickly, or the wrong thing, often all three together. 'You must think me odd,' he carried on, 'it's just I didn't wake up this morning expecting to be standing here, in an undertaker's.'

'No, I imagine not.' She flashed that smile. 'I'm Julia by the way, Julia Dirleton, the daughter, as in Dirleton and Daughter. Let's see what I can do for you.' She went to a glass-topped trestle table where an iPad lay beside a telephone and a large jasmine in flower. After tapping the screen, she made hopeful noises about a Caithness being available but Cal was distracted by the plant's cloying scent, the vigorousness of its growth and this woman's (it seemed to him now) inappropriate vitality: *their* exuberance.

The temperature of the room – Cal's skin was becoming prickly and hot – provided another contrast to the images suddenly flashing in his head: his experience of death, bodies washed up on beaches and rocks, gashed, swollen and putrefying, hardly human at all by the time Cal found them. That was death, brutal and cold, not this masquerade of flowers, sweet smells and Julia's pinked skin.

Unaware of Cal's mood change, she said, 'Well, that's good news, we have a Caithness in stock, more or less the right dimensions, a little big . . . but if you're sure that's what your grandmother would like?'

'It is,' Cal said abruptly.

'And she was right about the price, six fifty plus VAT. So that'll be seven hundred and eighty pounds.'

Without speaking, Cal brought a roll of money from his back pocket. After removing a rubber band, he peeled off thirty-nine twenty-pound notes.

'Perfect,' she said, now with a faintly puzzled expression at Cal having been effusive one moment, reticent the next. 'I'll have the coffin brought round to the front. If that's where you're parked? Or there's the back lane. You could drive round. It's more private.'

'The back,' Cal said quietly, rolling up his remaining money, securing it again with the band. Then, 'You enjoy your work, don't you?'

She recoiled a little, as if in the distance she heard a faint detonation, a warning of approaching trouble. 'I do, yes. I don't suppose it would be everyone's cup of tea, but

I was born into it. Yes, it suits me. I like helping people through a difficult time.'

'Do you talk to everyone?'

'Sometimes people need to talk, sometimes they don't. I leave it up to them. It's always important to be approachable, which means, I think, being friendly and open.'

'The dead too?'

'Sorry?' Her frown deepened.

'Do you talk to the dead?'

'Why would I . . . dead people?' She seemed startled; the detonation now rumbling closer. 'What would be the point? The dead . . . well, they're dead, after all. What would I say?'

'Wouldn't you want to hear a human voice before that lid was shut?' Cal turned for the door. 'I know I would.'

Outside, he swore.

Later, dragging a tarpaulin over the coffin, he looked up and saw his reflection in the funeral director's windows. He imagined Daughter Dirleton watching him. Would she make a connection with Harry Fowler? If she did, would she contact Greg Lane, even the police, or would she stay silent because of her dread at being 'associated with anything, well, gross . . . or disrespectful'.

Cal hoped the latter. Why, he wondered as he drove off, had he found her objectionable?

In their different ways both were in the business of death. She thrived on the association, whereas he did not. He had no clients. Was that why, suddenly, he found her offensive? She was managing more successfully than him.

*

27

He made two stops before leaving Edinburgh. The first was at his office-cum-bedsit where he collected his RIB, a twelve-foot rigid-inflatable boat bought third-hand, and trailer. To avoid adding unnecessarily to the evidence trail, he left his phone behind.

The second stop was at a DIY and garden store on the north-west side of the city. Wearing a baseball cap low, he bought a spade, two softwood planks three metres long, strong nylon rope, eight right-angled metal brackets, two steel bands, a hand-drill and bit to make holes of 20mm, a screwdriver and two packs of screws of different lengths, 25mm and 32mm. He paid in cash, £153.40, and left the receipt at the check-out.

At an adjacent supermarket service station he filled up with diesel. Again he paid cash, £63. He declined a receipt.

Driving north on the M90 and A9, Cal paid little attention to the changing scenery: the fields of arable lowland Scotland turning to moorland and mountain. He was distracted by two recurring, nagging worries: what if Harry Fowler was found dead? The other concern became more urgent the further north he travelled: what if the coffin didn't sink?

Having bypassed Aviemore in the Cairngorms National Park, he left the A9. A mile or so later, at a signpost advertising 'Woodland for Sale', he turned up a rough track. Once the pickup and trailer were sheltered from the road by trees, he parked, climbed into the back and uncovered the coffin. He worked efficiently, attaching brackets internally for extra strength, drilling twelve holes in each side and the top, three in either end board, just as the regulations stipulated.

Then, to stifle his worry about the coffin floating, he drilled four more holes in each end.

It set him wondering. If he was caught, what would the charge be? Desecration? Grave robbing? He preferred 'desecration', which was more all-encompassing and iconoclastic, whereas 'grave robbing' sounded grubbier, rootling around six feet under in the mud for cash or jewellery.

At seven forty-three p.m. he was back on the A9. After Inverness, he followed the A835, going north-west, passing Garve, a village on the rail line to Kyle of Lochalsh. The sign jolted Cal. At first glance he misread it as 'Grave', an unexpected reminder of the unpleasant job he had to do. Less than a mile later, he stopped in a lay-by where he slept for two hours. At eleven p.m., he was driving again, branching left on the A832 towards the west coast and left again on the A896, in the direction of Torridon.

A few minutes after midnight, the darkness appearing solid because of the mountains it concealed, Cal was reversing his trailer on to a slipway by a sea loch. Once the RIB was in the water and tied up, he threw a stone into the darkness. The splash was like a signature on a contract.

Whatever his reservations, whatever the law, whatever the consequences or penalty, he'd made a promise to Alex.

Notification of Alex's death came three mornings after Cal's phone conversation with Mrs Lauder. Its arrival in an unaddressed envelope slipped under Cal's door was as unexpected as it was mysterious. Had Mrs Lauder driven to Edinburgh during the night and delivered it herself or had she entrusted the task to someone else? If the latter, who?

Did someone else know about Cal and what he had to do? The thought made him feel uneasy, wary. On opening the envelope, Cal discovered a hand-drawn diagram of the graveyard, an 'X' to mark where Alex's grave would be and a map reference for the slipway.

The date and time of the funeral were handwritten, as were the instructions: *Alex must be reburied the night following the funeral service and his grave left as you found it, the flowers replaced. A new coffin will be required, otherwise the replaced earth will settle and sink. Also, there'll be a risk of the grave being found to be empty when the neighbouring lair is dug in due course for Alex's father.*

Going along the single-track road from the slipway to the graveyard, Cal drove slowly with only sidelights illuminated, and pictured the landscape, as if rehearsing. Having studied aerial photographs, he knew the graveyard was walled and rectangular and was on the southern flank of a promontory jutting out into the sea loch. Alex Lauder had been buried there that afternoon.

Cal imagined a lowering sky and shuffling mourners at the graveside. There, upright, apparently unaffected, his faith intact, would have been Alex's father, the Rev. William Lauder, accompanied by his wife, similarly steadfast in appearance despite the death of her son, her only child. Her steeliness would have owed little to religion or faith but to a different calling – carrying out Alex's last wish without raising suspicion in the community and particularly in her traditionalist of a husband, who insisted the dead be buried in holy ground and in a grave over which prayers could be recited.

Even so, in Cal's make-believe funeral, Rosemary Lauder flinched as the first granules of earth rattled on Alex's coffin, her anguish heightened by the fear of Cal proving to be as unreliable in his promises to Alex as he had been in friendship.

Cal clenched his right hand into a fist and thumped his steering wheel, a sudden fit of anger at Rosemary Lauder for failing to acknowledge the difficulty for him if he was caught, also of frustration at Harry Fowler. Why hadn't he reappeared? He must be deaf and blind not to be aware of the fuss caused by his vanishing act. Why hadn't he come to Cal's rescue?

Cal muttered, 'Fuck, he wouldn't have gone and killed himself, would he?' Another thump on the steering wheel followed when, on his left, in the dim glow of his lights, he saw the gravelled approach to the graveyard's shut metal gates. *Concentrate*, he told himself. He'd made a promise to Alex and Alex's mother.

He had to violate holy ground and steal a body.

5

Kate prowled the passage, going one way then another, counting her steps, twenty-five in each direction, backwards and forwards, again and again obsessively, or circling the kitchen table, a dozen, two dozen times in an effort to exhaust herself. Instead she became wider awake, unhappier and more alone: would Flora *never* speak to her? Having worked through her night-time repertoire, which also involved drinking too much coffee and white wine, Kate retreated to Flora's room, her refuge until daylight when she would return to her own bed and sleep, hopefully, miraculously, would engulf her.

Until then, she would be surrounded by the cause of their acrimony. On the chest of drawers to Kate's left and on the wall above the bureau were photographs: Flora with Christina, her mother, *their* mother; Flora with her boyfriend, Alex; Kate with Flora. On the wall behind the bed was a blown-up poster-sized print of their mother, red hair blowing, kneeling, her arms around two young girls, as though each was loved as much as the other, their similar looks, colouring and clothes superficial evidence of that bond.

That had never been Kate's experience.

As her eyes travelled the room, Kate attempted to stem her bitterness at the difference between her life and Flora's, which all these years later displayed itself in one sister believing herself to be unlovable – Kate – whereas the other, obviously, considered herself to be the opposite. Kate was jealous *and* curious; what would it be like to be Flora, to have had a loving mother?

On other nights Kate passed the time by trying on Flora's clothes or lying under Flora's bedcover and reading the books on her bedside table. This night, feeling more disconnected from her sister than ever, abandoned, Kate removed letters and papers from the bureau's pigeon holes. After reading them, she explored the drawers below. Systematically she examined bank statements, letters, photographs, birth certificate, insurance policies, mortgage documents, even Flora's old school reports; everything was read and returned to its proper place.

After going through the top three drawers, Kate pulled on the handles of the fourth and was surprised to find it locked; surprised and, having had too much wine, offended. As if it wasn't hurtful enough of Flora to have blanked her calls and messages for heaven knows how long – days and days now – here was further evidence of Flora shutting Kate out.

Kate went to the kitchen, poured more wine and retrieved the storage box which contained an assortment of screwdrivers as well as paintbrushes, sandpaper and a hammer. A full glass in one hand, the box balanced on the other, Kate returned to Flora's bedroom. After taking another gulp of wine, she removed the biggest screwdriver and stared at the drawer, as if giving herself a moment to make a different decision. Then, tentatively, she poked the tip of the screwdriver into the lock and wiggled it about while pulling at the same time on the drawer handle. It was stuck fast. She pulled harder: still stuck. In sudden anger at its stubborn resistance – too much alcohol had the effect of making her short-tempered and volatile – she took the hammer from the storage box and hit the screwdriver. The lock shifted. The wood surround cracked and splintered.

Kate pulled on the drawer. It moved. The lock fell inside with a metallic clunk.

Her shock at having caused such damage, which would be difficult to hide, was quickly overtaken by curiosity. Inside the drawer were three fat box files, one beside the other. The left-hand one, according to a label, contained documents about charity law and the responsibilities of trustees. Kate's attention moved to the middle one: 'The Christina Tolmie Foundation – fundraising and projects'. She glanced at the right-hand box file; its label promised 'Christina Tolmie, disappearance, investigation and leads'. Beneath was a list of entries and dates. Kate was surprised to see five recent additions all in the last month.

In Flora's handwriting were the same two words five times over: 'Unsigned card'.

Kate opened the lid. Clipped together and lying on top of files and newspaper cuttings were a number of identical envelopes.

On each, in black ink, was written: *For the urgent attention of Flora Tolmie, chief executive of the Christina Tolmie Foundation.* None had stamps or postmarks. Each, apparently, had been hand-delivered. And inside each, Kate discovered, was a single white postcard with a similar instruction.

The first said: *Wait outside the Market Street entrance to Waverley Station at six p.m. on Thursday if you're interested in discovering the truth about your mother.*

Different dates and times were on the other cards, also different meeting places, but all in Edinburgh and at busy locations.

The handwriting on each card was the same.

All five promised 'the truth about your mother'.

Kate laid the postcards side by side on the top of the bureau. Her eyes flicked from one to the next. *The truth about your mother.* The phrasing rattled her. Why not, Kate wondered, *if you are interested in discovering what happened to your mother?*

Was a threat implicit in the anonymous writer's choice of words? Kate thought so.

She glanced again at the lid of the box file. According to the log, the first card arrived after Flora's interview on BBC Radio when she'd appealed for information about their mother's disappearance. Afterwards, Kate had been angry and Flora tight-lipped. Why hadn't Flora asked her? Other flare-ups and tense silences followed. The last happened as Flora was packing to drive north to be with Alex. As she was leaving, Flora said, 'Sometimes, Kate, you might try being supportive instead of finding fault with me. She's your mother too.' She didn't look at Kate, nor did she say goodbye. She slammed the front door so hard the flat shuddered and so did Kate.

Had Flora kept the postcards a secret to avoid another fight with her sister? As Kate studied them, she thought the writer was likely to be some fuck-up who saw Flora on television or in the newspapers and had some fantasy about her, a potential stalker.

'Honestly, Flora,' Kate said out loud, exasperated, 'why didn't you tell me?'

Having gone into Flora's room to feel closer to her sister, she'd never felt more distant or more alarmed for her safety. At another time, in her rational, sober mind, she'd imagined she and Flora being reconciled; they'd had worse rows before, hadn't they? If so, she couldn't remember such a long-lasting rift between them. A voice in Kate's head – until then her occasional companion as she prowled the flat at night – became loud, persistent and, because of the wine, slurred. *You're unlovable, Kate; your mother abandoned you – now it's happened again. You've driven Flora away just when she needs you. Her boyfriend is ill. A creep, some stalker, is playing games with her. If something terrible happens to Flora, it'll be your fault.*

And Kate shuddered again, just as she had after Flora slammed the door.

6

In preparation for disinterring and stealing a body, Cal had read a valedictory letter from a retiring minister of the parish in the penultimate decade of the nineteenth century. It included a passage commending the graveyard's situation. Being bounded on three sides by the sea loch, it had, in the opinion of the Rev. Archibald Walker, 'the characteristic of being removed from the living but nevertheless within reach . . . a staging post between this life and the next'. From a Christian perspective 'the symbolism was appropriate, reassuring as well as uplifting.' The graveyard, he insisted, was an example of 'Our Lord's infinite wisdom, because he saw fit not to make the soil of sufficient depth for burials any closer to the village.'

Cal's appreciation of the graveyard's position on a southwesterly sloping headland was practical rather than spiritual. Rising ground and half a mile separated it from both the church and the nearest houses, decreasing the risk of him being observed or interrupted. However, another unexpected hazard presented itself as he opened its iron entrance gates.

The grass strip through the middle of graveyard was spongey. Even in the dark, deep imprints were visible in the ground, left eleven hours earlier by the hearse bearing Alex's coffin. Cal would have to follow in its tracks or else there would be questions. Why had another vehicle entered the cemetery? What had been its business?

Dare he turn on his lights, even sidelights, to be certain of the pickup's tyres exactly fitting the hearse's? He decided not, the danger of someone across the sea loch seeing the glow and alerting the village too great. In an area like this odd lights late at night were noticed and reported, especially those in a graveyard.

The pickup edged forward.

Cal stared bug-eyed, head over the steering wheel, attempting to discern the darker shade of the hearse's tracks against the lighter black of the grass and the black-blackness of the night. Differentiation was difficult, sometimes imagined.

Progress was slow, the slope and the weight of the pickup providing forward movement which Cal controlled with the clutch and, manually, by his handbrake to avoid his rear brake lights flashing on. Half a dozen times he stopped, opened his door and leaned out to check whether the pickup's wheels were following the existing tracks – the first occasion, a heart-stopping moment, as he'd forgotten to disable the internal light.

By the time he reached Alex's grave, twenty minutes had been lost.

Cal worried now about sunrise. Was five hours long enough to dig out and fill up a grave and exit the graveyard?

The forecast was for a calm, dry day. Cal wished for strong winds, weather to pin the community indoors at least until eight or nine in the morning, to provide a reassuring margin of safety. One local, in particular, was on his mind.

Alex's father was an early riser, who, if the day was fine, might be in the habit of walking before breakfast to witness the blessings his good Lord had bestowed on the earth. That might involve a circuit of the graveyard, almost certainly would the day after his son's funeral.

As Cal dug the freshly turned, loose peaty earth and deposited each spadeful on to a spread-out tarpaulin, he experienced a variety of anxieties: the Rev. Lauder's bony fingers tightening on his shoulder, the dead rising up against Cal and burying him alive with Alex, even Harry Fowler's body being in the coffin instead of Alex's. On such a still night, in such a place, with a pale quarter moon, the nightmarish or grotesque seemed possible, even likely.

When finally, after an hour of digging, his spade clunked against wood, he was jarred back to reality. How was he going to transfer Alex from one coffin to the other?

His mood turned exasperated at the inadequacy of his preparation, also at Rosemary Lauder's failure to show any consideration – she hadn't inquired whether Cal had the stomach for digging up and handling a dead body. Not just any body but Alex's body, for God's sake, Alex's. Nor did she appear to care about the risk Cal was taking. Apart from grave robbing, he would also be contravening the regulations for burials at sea. There were only two 'authorized' sites off Scotland. One was 210 nautical miles due west of Oban, at 56° 45'N 009° 15'W, the other about 15 nautical miles west of John O'Groats, off the north coast, at 58° 42.70'N 003° 23.30'W. Neither was anywhere near where Cal's RIB was moored – the sea loch which had been Alex's favourite place on earth.

Resentment of Rosemary Lauder for holding him to an old promise so casually given was further stimulated by her failure to pay for a suitable coffin, even to offer. Until yesterday Cal's savings (his so-called survival fund) of £1,250 were sufficient for subsistence living, his preferred kind, by the coast, fishing, foraging, for a year, perhaps longer given his abstemious habits. Only £253.60 remained after visits to the funeral director, the DIY store and the service station for diesel. Thanks to Harry Fowler and now Rosemary Lauder, money was a worry. Such anxieties and indignations proved to be short-lived distractions standing in a grave, fleeting indulgences. Other, more immediate worries pressed in on Cal. How would he behave towards Alex? Should he touch him as though he was alive, warm and breathing? If so, would Cal experience distaste? Worse, would it show?

Also, the question he had been avoiding until now: how was he to move Alex? Would he be able to lift him? Cal doubted weight would be a problem, though dead weight was different. But Alex wasn't ever heavy, about ten and a half stones. By his death, he would have been lighter, perhaps skeletal. No: the question was *how* Cal should lift him, a combination of the best and most dignified method.

After running his hands across the coffin lid, sweeping away grit and earth, Cal thought he might straddle Alex and lift him in an improvised bear hug. Then what? Manoeuvre Alex over his shoulder, in a kind of fireman's lift perhaps. The depth of the grave being a few inches more than Cal's height was another difficulty. He would have to raise Alex above his head. A possibility was to lift the body in two stages. Since there was already a gap between the coffin and grave on one side, perhaps he could widen it by digging two boot-sized niches at the base of the grave's wall, sufficient for a firm and stable footing. Then, broadside-on, he'd squat, put one arm under Alex's torso, the other under his legs, and raise him from the coffin. Next he'd change grip, brace and, like a weightlifter, he'd thrust, lock knees, extend his arms and raise Alex above ground.

Would that work?

Another worry: what should Cal say to Alex? Unlike Julia, the daughter of Arthur Dirleton, funeral director, his habit was to talk to the dead.

Should he say sorry?

Sorry Alex was dead.

Sorry the cancer had come back.

Sorry Cal hadn't seen him for so long, had been a neglectful friend.

Wasn't sorry too late?

About what to say, if not how to carry Alex, Cal made a decision.

As he moved Alex from one coffin to the other, Cal would describe what was going on, what would happen next. He'd provide a commentary, informing Alex about the communities of creatures he would encounter in the sea loch, the seaweeds, the varying depths and temperatures, the rocky sills at the loch mouth, those glacial relics which had interested Alex ever since they'd been students together at SAMS, the Scottish Marine Institute, near Oban, and, later, in his academic research.

At least having to talk, having Alex to talk to, would

take Cal's mind off other troubles, also what he was doing, the grim ghastliness of it.

After digging the niches for his feet, Cal changed position. Instead of standing on the coffin, he was at its side, leaning over. He switched on a pocket torch – safe enough now since he was deep in a grave – and directed its narrow beam at the coffin lid. With a screwdriver in the other hand, he removed ten brass screws. After the last, Cal turned off the light before prising the lid – a vague feeling of not wanting to blind Alex, also of not wanting to see him, of remembering him alive not dead, of not seeing his deathly expression set in reproach.

Raising the lid, Cal said, 'Alex, don't be alarmed. It's me, Cal. I think you were expecting me.'

Then: 'Look, I'm sorry. I haven't been much of a friend, have I? Are you all right with this, putting you in the sea loch? There'll be time to talk later but right at the moment we're in a bit of a hurry.' Cal bent down and worked his hands under Alex's back and thighs. 'Ready?'

He braced, lifted up Alex – he was lighter, stiffer, colder than Cal expected, smellier but not unpleasantly so; not really Alex or human. After steadying himself, Cal stepped into the now empty coffin, placing his feet apart. Then, adjusting his grip, he thrust upwards until Alex protruded above the grave; a levitation in slow motion. Suddenly Cal's legs and arms, already tired from digging, began to shake and wobble. And so did Alex. Both toppled together, Cal against the damp, compacted wall of the grave and Alex, propelled by a final, desperate shove, on to grass beyond the grave's rim. The body made a series of noises: a soft thump, then a moan followed by a loud fart.

Cal laughed through his breathlessness. 'Sorry about the landing, Alex. Did you feel that? It sounded like you did. Uhhh . . .' His heart pounded, his lungs hurt as he climbed from the grave. 'You fart away,' he said, collapsing beside his former friend, gasping. 'You know, they say the hearing's the last sense to go, so if you can hear me it's a beautiful, awesome night. As soon as I've tidied up here we're going to the loch. Do you remember that promise I made? Can you see those stars, Alex? I hope you can. They're amazing, dazzling. If they were the last things I saw, I think I'd be satisfied. I know you can't talk, so fart if you agree.'

If Alex had been alive, if they'd been having coffee or a drink, Cal would probably have been awkward, self-conscious and reticent. Yet, in a cemetery, lying beside a corpse, Alex's corpse, Cal was being talkative, unguarded, unaware and free of the urge to escape, to be on his own. The same happened when his work led him to a body washed up on the beach or broken on rocks. He'd always talk, be conversational, finding the dead easier, better company, than the living.

'You'll probably laugh, Alex,' Cal said, 'but I think I have a sixth sense around the dead. I know when they . . . you . . . have heard enough, when I can be of no further use, when talk's more of an irritation than a comfort, when the dead . . . you . . . become dead to me, deaf to me, if that makes any sense. When I'm working and that happens, I shut up and ring the police and tell them to come and collect the body.'

He watched the stars again. 'Usually that feeling of the dead . . . you . . . not listening any more happens after I've talked about how loved, how desperately missed the person has been. That seems to be what they want to hear. By the way, Alex, that's true of you too. You're missed. You're loved. You don't have the faintest idea how much you're missed and loved, always will be.'

Cal rolled towards Alex. 'Though obviously, on this occasion, when you don't want me to talk any more, I won't ring the police.'

He waited as though Alex might answer.

Cal lay back again. 'Look at those stars. You're not shut in any more. That must be amazing, to be out again, in fresh air, on a starry night.'

Then: 'I'm going to check if you've left anything behind and screw down the lid. OK? Won't be long.'

Cal dropped into the grave, shone his torch into the open coffin. He saw some photographs of Alex at different stages: a sallow-skinned, dark-haired boy hugging his mother; a teenager standing tall between his parents; Alex in a football team; Alex with a mixed group of young men and women – Cal recognized his year group at SAMS. Cal was back row, third left. Alex was in front. Alex was always in front. Despite the passage of years, in whatever pose, Alex was Alex, smiling, though Cal was surprised that in every photograph his dark brown eyes appeared to look out at the world with suspicion.

Cal hadn't noticed that before.

An absence in the later photographic record of Alex's too short life also occurred to Cal. There was no photograph of Alex and his girlfriend, Flora. He wondered why not: had they split up? Cal had met her briefly once. His recollection was of a couple who were happy, in love – *had been* happy, in love.

What was her other name? Flora what? Talmie? Tolmie? Tollamy? He couldn't remember exactly.

After screwing down the lid, Cal climbed out of the grave.

He reassured Alex about the photographs. He'd collected them, would lay them out in the new coffin, and found himself saying, 'Though I was surprised there wasn't one of you and Flora because when I met her – when was it? Last year sometime – she appeared to be in love with you, and you seemed, well, to be joined together, partners.'

Straight away the atmosphere changed. 'Oh,' he said to Alex, 'you don't want to talk about Flora. Not my business. I understand. I'm sorry if it didn't work out.'

Cal put the photographs into his anorak pocket, moved Alex further from the grave's edge and bent over him. 'I'm going to have to lift you again, OK?'

He heaved, steadied himself before waddling awkwardly with Alex lying in his arms. Following his mistake of mentioning Flora, he thought he would shift to safer subjects, the sea loch, 'Not that I can tell you anything you don't know already', and what would happen next. When Alex was prone and stiff in the back of the pickup beside the new coffin, Cal said, 'Would you like me to put you inside? If you do, I'll leave the lid open for now. Apparently, the coffin should be weighted with iron, steel or a weak concrete mix, a minimum of 100kg, and evenly distributed. But I thought you'd prefer stones from the sea loch. Don't worry, Alex, you'll sink. To reassure you, I've done everything according to the regulations, the holes drilled in the top and sides of the coffin, and the brackets and steel bands for reinforcement.'

He climbed beside Alex, lifted him into the coffin. 'There, you look at the sky while I shovel the earth back into your grave – bet you're glad to be out of there.'

After half an hour, the hole had been filled in, the wreaths and flowers returned. Cal hunkered down and shone the torch: a sudden bright shaft, then darkness again. The grave was more or less the same as he'd found it.

'OK, we're leaving,' Cal told Alex as he put the folded tarpaulin beside the coffin in the pickup.

Exiting the graveyard was as difficult as entering, the black beyond Cal's windscreen growing lighter and darker, playing tricks with his vision. The track of the hearse, now deeper than before, was similarly elusive, evident one moment, not the next. He swore quietly, not wanting Alex to hear his anxiety.

The return journey passed without further incident. Closing the gates, Cal looked back and hoped he hadn't left a separate set of tracks.

'Alex, you all right?' He banged his hand lightly against the pickup as he returned to the driver's door. He had the feeling of being alone, of Alex having left him, of no one listening.

Where the road ran out by the slipway, a wraith dressed for a funeral waited. The pickup's headlights turned her hair, face and hands luminous white. She looked as though she had no body, her black funeral clothes blending with the night.

Cal lowered his window as he stopped beside her. 'Mrs Lauder, you shouldn't be here. We agreed I'd do this on my own. You can't be involved.'

She stared at Cal. 'Where else should I be?'

Cal nodded. 'Yeah.' The word was breathy, infused with resignation, understanding as well as worry. 'You know you can't risk being caught with me.'

Rosemary Lauder turned towards the sea loch, where her son would finally be buried. She listened to the slow, rhythmic slap of water. 'I've hardly slept since Alex told me he was going to die,' she said. 'Most nights I've just driven; it hasn't mattered where. My husband's not going to miss me tonight. Who else will look for me?'

Cal thought that explained his instructions and the map of the graveyard being slid under his door at night. 'No one's seen you?'

She didn't answer.

Cal said, 'OK.'

Then: 'Well, you're here now.'

Another pause: 'I'd better get on.'

She didn't look round or speak.

Cal reversed down the slipway, imagining the worst that could go wrong. What if he dropped the coffin? What if Alex fell out and farted again? Improvisation didn't seem such a good idea with Alex's mother as spectator.

He started with the planks, making a slide between the rear of the pickup and the RIB. He'd been concerned about the slope being too steep. It wasn't; the gradient was just right for gravity to exert sufficient pull and for the coffin's broadside descent to be controllable. Next he cut the rope in two, tied each length around the coffin, one at either end. Checking the strength of the knots, he whispered an apology to Alex for any bumps or jolts he might experience. After manoeuvring the coffin so that it lay at the top of the planks, he let it slide, a restraining rope in each hand, until it rested against the RIB. Jumping down, he shoved and lifted the coffin until it straddled the 'V' of the RIB's bow. Cal's remaining anxiety was having the strength to tip the coffin into the loch once extra weight – the stones – had been added and the lid attached. His plan was to use the RIB's hull as a pivot. All he had to do was lift up one end and push. His plan (*plan?* hope) was that the RIB would take the weight as the polished coffin slipped into the water.

'Mrs Lauder?' he called out softly.

Her face flashed white by the shore as she turned towards Cal.

'You can sit with Alex, if you like. The coffin's open.' He dug his hand in his pocket. 'Here. I removed the photographs. Why don't you arrange them?'

'You mean, I can see him, hold him?' Life returned to her voice, at the unexpected and precious opportunity to be a mother again.

'You won't have long,' Cal said. 'Just while I collect stones from the shore of the loch. I thought they'd be best to weigh the coffin down . . . Well, I thought Alex might prefer that to concrete blocks. The regulations . . .' He stopped because Mrs Lauder wouldn't want to know about regulations.

'Go and sit with him,' Cal said. 'The coffin's steady enough on the RIB. I won't be long.'

On his return, carrying a large stone in each hand, he found Mrs Lauder stroking Alex's hair. He gave her his torch. 'You can turn it on for a second or two, not longer.'

Cal noticed the photographs in the torch's glow. They were lying on Alex's torso.

'None with Flora,' Cal observed. 'I was surprised.'

'Why should she be with him?' Rosemary Lauder was suddenly defiant, protective, a mother with her talons out. 'She abandoned him. He should still have been alive but for her.'

Cal said, 'Flora? Flora left him?'

'I think she decided not to waste any more time or emotion on Alex. He was dying; what might have been was worthless to her. Her interest was the future, not Alex.' She touched her fingertips against Alex's cheek. 'My poor darling, you were heartbroken. You had nothing left. You gave up when she left, didn't you? You lost your will to live, lost your fight.'

She looked at Cal. 'Alex's father rang her afterwards and told her never to contact us again or to attend the funeral or send flowers.'

'You should turn off the torch now,' was all Cal said.

After bringing up more stones and wedging them around Alex's head and legs, he said, 'Mrs Lauder, I'm sorry, you'll have to say goodbye.'

She leaned forward, kissed her son's forehead. 'My sweet, my darling, I love you.'

Cal attached the lid and, for reinforcement, fixed two steel bands around the coffin's ends before swinging the RIB side-on and helping Mrs Lauder to board.

Darkness, the engine's throbbing and the necessity to be as quiet as possible inhibited talk on the sea loch. After Cal dropped overboard the spade, hand-drill and screwdriver – disposing of incriminating evidence – he glanced at Alex's mother. She was seated behind him, restless, lifting her head, letting it fall again, folding and unfolding her arms. When Cal cut the engine – the RIB almost in position – she whispered, 'Did Alex really want this?'

Cal thought, *She's going to change her mind and it's too late.*

He sat beside her. 'The evening Alex and I came here, the sun was setting, the water as calm as tonight, with the lightest of breezes blowing. Alex said to me, "Isn't this the perfect place?" I paddled further on, but Alex stayed back, roughly where we are now. He shouted after me, "This is where I want to be buried."'

Rosemary put her hands to her face as she listened.

Cal continued. 'I turned round and said, "Here, in the sea loch?" Alex said, "Yes, right here."

'I said, "OK," and started to paddle again, but Alex shouted after me, "Promise."

'"Promise what?"

'"That you'll bury me here."

'"What if I die first?"

'"Then *I'll* bury *you* here."

'I said, "But I don't want to be buried here. I want to be buried in the North Atlantic. I want my coffin to float so that it travels towards the Arctic."

'"I'll promise to do that for you, if you promise to bury me here."

'So I promised and Alex promised. Alex never forgot, did he?'

Rosemary Lauder whispered, 'No.' A pause. 'Show me where the sun was when you were with him.'

Cal pointed into the night. 'Over there.'

She turned in that direction. 'When I told him I'd spoken to you, and you'd remembered your promise, he

. . . well . . . seemed to settle. For those last few hours . . . he didn't feel so alone, the thought of you doing that for him.' She glanced back at Cal. 'It was important for him to know that this was where he would be buried, that you had kept your promise, that you hadn't abandoned him.'

Hadn't abandoned him *too*, like Flora, she meant.

Cal said nothing.

Mrs Lauder asked, 'Is this where you were?'

'Yes, more or less,' Cal replied.

'Then we must imagine him as he was, the setting sun lighting up the water, lighting up him.' For the first time she seemed composed, reconciled.

'Are you ready?'

She whispered, 'Yes.'

Cal went to the coffin.

'He would want to be buried here, wouldn't he?'

Cal said, 'The Alex I knew would, yes.'

He raised one end of the coffin, adjusted to its weight and shoved hard. It slid off the RIB's hull, splashed, sank, reappeared and sank again. The only noise on such a still night was the sound of bubbles rising to the surface and a mother's sobbing.

7

Going downstairs, Sarah stopped at the half-landing and opened the small window overlooking the passageway between her house and Lotte's. A conversation was going on below: Lotte and Olaf talking. Sarah listened in, her new habit following that supper in the beach restaurant when Lotte's eyes glinted at the prospect of solving 'the mystery of Olaf'. That had rung alarm bells for Sarah. She feared Lotte being too inquisitive and Olaf feeling got at, hemmed in. She dreaded an eruption and Olaf having to vacate Lotte's annexe. What a disaster that would be!

Sarah blamed herself. She should have taken into account the differences between Lotte and Olaf, one effusive, the other not, before asking about the empty room at the back of Lotte's house. But at the time, February, her concern had been Olaf's welfare. It was winter. He had nowhere to live. Having run out of money, he'd put his farmstead on the market. Then, as a condition of sale, he'd paid for the one-hectare site to be cleared of a decade's accumulation of driftwood and other flotsam, including his self-built shack. The cost of hiring lorries, a bulldozer and a gang of men for two weeks had been considerable and Olaf had insufficient money left after paying off debts to buy another plot or a roof over his head. And who, on Texel, wanted him as a long-term tenant?

Olaf came as an undesirable package. Driftwood,

flotsam, hammering and a trike with a barrow on the front were his non-negotiable accompaniments.

Sarah felt impelled to help him, even though Olaf and she weren't friends in a conventional sense. Their encounters over the years had been haphazard if numerous and had taken place only on the beach. But on those occasions when she had been overwhelmed by guilt and regret, usually anniversaries and birthdays, Olaf always seemed to be close by. He would sit with her in a deckchair by the hut and listen. He would let her talk and talk. When it mattered, when the past closed in on her, he'd helped her. Her obligation was to reciprocate, if she could.

She'd offered her spare room 'until you sort yourself out'. Olaf had been grateful but had declined; he couldn't live with anyone else, nor, he doubted, could anyone live with him (Sarah's concern too). His habits were antisocial and ingrained. He wasn't domestic. He didn't do bedtimes or mealtimes. The tides dictated his life. After high tide, he went beachcombing, night or day, winter or summer, stormy or not, for hour after hour. Also, he had to have outside space, where he could assemble and store his driftwood men for selling to holidaymakers in summer. No, he'd said, he'd make a shelter among the dunes at the north of the island and take his chances on the tail-end of winter being short and kind.

She'd told him to wait there on the beach. She ran to Lotte's house and asked 'as a kindness for a few months' if Olaf could move into her empty annexe. It was suitable for him: it had its own front door; he could come and go as he pleased; and, in the passageway to the street, was an unused lean-to shed which could be Olaf's work area and store. It might also help Lotte since Olaf was good with his hands. He could do gardening or odd jobs. Hadn't she been talking of finding someone?

Lotte, to Sarah's relief, was enthusiastic. 'Three months to begin with,' she'd said, 'and Olaf doesn't need to pay rent if there's a quid pro quo.' Sarah had been delighted; a barter arrangement was perfect for Olaf and, on inspection of the annexe – one large room, a small kitchen and bathroom – he'd accepted straight away. Apparently, he wasn't quite as reconciled to winter in the dunes as he'd pretended.

What had never occurred to Sarah was that Lotte would find Olaf the slightest bit interesting. They were so different, from such different worlds. If anything, she'd thought Lotte might be aloof, speaking to Olaf only when something needed doing in the house or garden. Hence Sarah's suggestion to Lotte to be neighbourly; it mattered, Sarah thought, after living apart for so long, that Olaf should feel accepted in the village.

After Lotte made that remark about Olaf being 'our project', Sarah wished she hadn't said a word. Poor Olaf! She anticipated Olaf being interrogated by Lotte in her search for clues to the so-called mystery. As it turned out, she appeared to be wrong about that too.

After eavesdropping for the past four mornings, Sarah was surprised by how revelatory Lotte was being. Lotte treated Olaf like a confessor, talking frankly about the life she used to have – a flat in Paris, a wealthy financier for a husband who was serially unfaithful and how miserable it made her. Then, after these and other complaints, she would often exclaim how much happier she was living in

De Koog, a seaside resort of not even a thousand full-time residents on the west coast of Texel, the largest and most southerly of the West Frisian Islands, as distant from a fashionable Paris suburb as could be imagined.

At first, Sarah was suspicious of Lotte. Was she being tactical in her revelations about her private life? After, say, an intimate admission about 'hating' her husband's mistresses, her reluctance to start another relationship or regret at not having had a child, she'd ask Olaf a personal question, for example whether or not he'd been married or was a father.

Sarah wondered if Lotte was trying to entice Olaf into similar disclosures: *I've told you a confidence, Olaf, now it's your turn.*

If it was a ploy, Olaf was equal to it. He deflected intrusive questions with responses like, 'It's too long a story', 'Another time', or 'I'd prefer not.' What struck Sarah was Olaf's patience, his reasonableness. Yesterday, for example, Sarah was listening when Lotte described her husband's heart attack and premature death as 'a blessing' because it was freeing. 'That's a terrible thing to say, isn't it, Olaf?' Olaf's reply was typically brief while managing also to be understanding. 'No,' he said simply, 'it's a fact.'

Rather than be worried about a falling-out between Lotte and Olaf, Sarah came to the conclusion these morning encounters were companionable. The two of them, so Sarah was beginning to think, were an improbable support for each other: Lotte, forty-nine, a refugee from infidelity but, unlike most refugees, one with money and a fashionable wardrobe; and Olaf, forty-ish, square-built, rough-edged, a beach scavenger, who lived hand-to-mouth by making strange-looking driftwood men to sell for one hundred euros each. They were the oddest of odd couples, Lotte sitting at her kitchen window talking to Olaf's back as he worked at his bench, but surprisingly easy in each other's company. Thank goodness!

This morning, after carrying on downstairs to her kitchen, Sarah thought perhaps she should be congratulated for having brought Lotte and Olaf together. Wasn't it peculiar how things turned out? In that calmer frame of mind she had breakfast – poached eggs, toast and coffee – while checking the forecast. As grey chilly weather was set to continue, Sarah decided to postpone the reopening of her shop, Sarah's Beach Fashions. She amended the dates on its website, a delay of a week, and notified her two assistants, emailing with 'many apologies for not giving more warning but until the sun shines there really isn't any point. We won't have any customers.'

After clearing away the dishes, she glanced at the window to check on the tree outside. Since the branches weren't moving, she thought she'd take the opportunity to clean the beach hut – on a blustery, windy day more sand was blown in than she could sweep out.

In the hall, she slid her feet into her boots, tied the laces and was taking her coat from the hook when a loud knocking startled her. 'Sarah, Sarah!' a familiar voice shouted excitedly. She opened the door to Lotte, who, as usual, looked younger and more stylish than Sarah despite being ten years older: her ash-blonde hair was cut in a fashionable short bob and she wore a smoky-blue cashmere jersey, black wool trousers and flat shoes. By contrast

Sarah felt scruffy; her black hard-to-control, wiry hair was tied severely back; she wore jeans, a comfortable cotton shirt and a cardigan.

Another dissimilarity was the rush of words emerging from Lotte about a 'discovery', 'a breakthrough'.

'Look,' she commanded, pointing into Sarah's hall. 'Look at him.'

Him was a driftwood man, which had been a gift from Olaf. 'Tell me what's unusual about him.'

To indulge her friend, Sarah studied the man who was about four feet tall. His arms were made from wooden poles, his hands from squared-off planking and his fingers, nailed-on plastic tubes. His hair was dishevelled like Olaf's, a tangle of blue fishing net. His eyes were made from sea glass, one a red fragment and one milky-white, and his nose was a small crimson-coloured medicine bottle. His legs, tied-together bundles of sticks, were bent more at the leading knee than the back. His feet were made of flattened fizzy drink cans bound by wire. The general attitude of his limbs and forward tilt of his body gave an impression of vigorous motion.

'Tell me, what's not unusual about him?' Sarah answered, smiling because Lotte's opinion of Olaf's driftwood men was familiar to her. Lotte thought them 'creepy' but Sarah liked how hers leaned forward, right arm extended. Whenever she arrived home, her driftwood man seemed to be welcoming her back. Sometimes she would even shake his hand and tell him her news. *Well, that dinner party was a waste of time* or *I met a lovely woman at the beach hut who wanted to know everything.*

'Look again,' Lotte said. 'Please.'

'It would help,' Sarah said, 'if I knew what I was looking for.'

'His mouth.'

'He doesn't have a mouth.'

'Exactly,' Lotte replied, as if her point had been proved, whatever her point was. 'Nothing. Not even a slash of paint or some glued-on plastic strip. Everything else but not a mouth. Why not?'

'I don't know. None of Olaf's men have mouths, do they?'

Lotte looked triumphant. 'Don't you see? They're all little Olafs. They have wild hair like Olaf and like Olaf they're silent. They don't have mouths because there's something they can't talk about, something *Olaf* can't talk about, a secret, something that's not very nice.'

'Really?' Sarah studied the driftwood man, hearing alarm bells once again. 'Are you sure the lack of a mouth signifies anything . . . ?' She chose her words carefully, hoping to steer Lotte in a different direction. 'If it does mean anything, couldn't it just be that Olaf's making a comment? He's always saying how little we know about flotsam. A piece of driftwood might have come from a shipwreck, from a spilt cargo in a storm. It might have witnessed murder or tragedy. It might have been dumped with someone's rubbish and been washed down a river.' Sarah glanced at Lotte. 'Don't you think the reason Olaf hasn't given his men mouths is because flotsam can't tell its story?'

'No, Sarah.' Lotte shook her head, sounding and looking frustrated. 'There's a reason why Olaf's like he is. Why he's here. Why he's alone. Why he won't talk about the past, about anything private.' Lotte paused. 'It won't be a good reason. It never is with men like him. Sarah, be careful.'

Sarah was as shocked by Lotte's warning as by the intensity with which it was delivered. Far from getting on with Olaf, as Sarah thought, she was accusing, antagonistic. Nothing Sarah had overheard supported Lotte's bad opinion of Olaf. *Did Lotte just not trust men, any men, after her husband's betrayals?* In recoil, Sarah said, '*Me* be careful? *Me!* I'm not the one who talks to Olaf every morning. I'm not the one who tells him everything about my dead ex-husband, about his affairs, *everything*. Lotte, I've heard you.'

'Oh, Sarah.' Lotte sounded pitying. 'Please. If you don't believe me, ask Olaf why he doesn't put mouths on his driftwood men.'

8

Late April, ten a.m: the Scottish landscape caught between winter and spring; frosted grass on the verges; mist draped across the hills. A low sun slanted into Cal's eyes. Having stopped at the junction of the A832 and the A835, he was almost as still as his surroundings. Apart from the pickup's vibrations, the only movement was a slight turn of Cal's head, right then left.

There was no traffic approaching from either direction.

Again, right then left.

Which way to go? Right led south, to Edinburgh; left to the far north-west, to a remote coast.

The reasons for going right – the state of his business (did he have a business?), worry about Harry Fowler – were also, to Cal's way of thinking, the reasons for going in the opposite direction, for running away to the coast, for giving in to his reflex.

Right led to the possibility, *likelihood*, of aggravation, a catch-all description for situations where Cal was at risk of being put-upon by other people and confrontation. Left led to a distant beach and solitariness.

He went left.

Forty-five minutes later, he arrived in Ullapool, a ferry and fishing town beside Loch Broom. In a convenience store on Shore Street opposite the pier, Cal bought a litre-bottle of water, two bars of chocolate, six bread rolls, three packs of tomatoes, some apples. He registered the cost, £7.48. On the way out, at the newspaper stand, he flicked over the pages of the *Scotsman*, stopping on page seven. Harry Fowler was still missing.

Driving back along Shore Street, he stopped at another junction. Right or left? He turned left, carried on going north, eventually reaching the scattered crofting community of Oldshoremore, two miles beyond Kinlochbervie, the most northerly port on Scotland's west coast. At the next settlement, Blairmore, Cal drove past white-painted cottages before slowing at a gravel parking area. His spirits lifted at there being no other cars. Late breakfast was a roll, three over-ripe tomatoes and a bar of chocolate.

After filling his backpack with food, water and a change of clothes, he crossed the road to a gravel track. For almost four miles he walked as though a wind was at his back, pausing only when Sandwood Bay came into view. Cal squinted at the long expanse of beach where once Vikings had hauled up their longboats.

It was deserted.

Cal experienced the closest he ever came to elation. He was on a wild coast alone and no one knew where he was.

That first night, unable to sleep, he walked the cliffs all the way to Cape Wrath, a distance of five miles. His thoughts turned to an old case. A fourteen-year-old boy had gone missing from an uninhabited Hebridean island more than a hundred miles to the south-west. The boy's father was certain his son had been killed, murdered and his body thrown into the sea. To calculate where currents might have taken the boy, Cal used a proxy, a dead pig called Millie. He recalled his annoyance at having to skulk at night because he was contravening regulations about the disposal of dead farm animals. Other scientists, researchers, used pig corpses to learn about decomposition and to advance forensics. They didn't have to creep about in the dark like a Victorian bodysnatcher. Why should he?

Yet last night he *was* being a bodysnatcher and skulking.

On the second night Cal crawled on to a natural cantilever of rock above the sea. He watched the light of the moon make diamond sparkles on the breaking crests of waves and recalled a similar, if different-coloured, effect of the streetlights on the river when Cal parked his pickup, walked back across the bridge and inquired of Harry Fowler, 'Are you all right?'

'You know all that's the matter with me,' Harry had replied, continuing to stare into the water, 'is that I've never been sufficiently wholehearted or passionate.'

'No, I didn't know that,' Cal said, 'but then I don't know you.'

'Well,' Harry continued, 'it's as well to understand that about me from the get-go because you won't find out anything more significant on longer acquaintance.'

'A shortcut to you?' Cal suggested.

'An essence,' Harry countered. 'Harry Fowler in a sentence, a little long-winded for an epitaph, but it'll do. That's another thing you should know about me. Generally, I'm a little long-winded and a lot indecisive. One goes with the other, in my opinion.'

'What about unhappy,' Cal said, 'since we're taking shortcuts?'

'Let's just say I've been happier. A long time ago I was happy. I don't think I've ever been happy since, not really.'

'I've been watching you,' Cal said, 'from over there.' He indicated his pickup parked on the far bank. 'You've been standing for a while. It's late. Are you thinking about jumping? I'm asking because sometimes I have to look for the bodies of people who've jumped and I'd rather I didn't have to search for you.'

Harry watched the water which glinted orange in the bridge lights. 'No. I don't think so.' He looked in Cal's direction. His expression was avuncular and kind. 'That's the trouble, you see. I've never been impetuous; I've never just jumped into anything. Can't have wanted anything enough, can I?'

'Do you wish you'd jumped, had been impetuous?'

'Yes, I think I do.'

Harry sounded so weighted down by sadness and regret that Cal said, 'Well, if it's all right with you, I think I'll stay here in case this is the first time you decide to jump.'

Neither spoke for a while, until a clock chimed in the distance.

Harry said, 'You know I said I was happy once. Then I was with Angela. But that all ended when she heard that bell. She took off her shoes and climbed up here.' He placed his hands on the iron railings, gripped tight. 'And let go. It was a few seconds after nine thirty when she jumped.'

'She jumped into the river?'

'Yes.'

'What happened?'

'She was killed. Two days later, a letter marked "personal"

arrived in my office. She wrote, "I felt you pulling away and I couldn't bear to live without you."'

'I'm sorry,' Cal said.

Harry sighed, a gust of remorse. 'She used to say love was reckless and if I really loved her I'd be reckless too, that I'd do anything to be with her. But I was married. So was she, unhappily. Also, I had a daughter.' Harry glanced at Cal. 'Maybe she was right.' His smile became uncertain. 'Maybe I wasn't ever wholehearted about her.'

The moment was revealing, bitter-sweet, tantalizing and short-lived, interrupted by a shout from a passing lorry. 'Jump if you're going to, you mad old bastard. Otherwise shift your motor before it causes an accident.'

Harry's car was parked on the bridge, its lights on, blocking one lane.

Cal said, 'Come with me.'

He drove Harry's car to a café on the far side of the river. Cal ordered an Americano for himself and tea for Harry.

'When did Angela die?' Cal asked.

'Thirty-one years and forty-three days ago.' Harry stared into his tea with the same fixed expression as he did the river. 'I've told no one apart from you.'

'Not your wife?'

'I couldn't hurt her. I didn't have the courage.' He shook his head. 'She's dead now, so I can't tell her.'

'Your daughter?'

'No.' Harry glanced at Cal. 'Since you know everything else of importance about me, I should probably tell you that I'm ill. I'll die soon. Other people in my position put their financial affairs in order. I've done that. The thing left for me to do is to acknowledge Angela. I should tell Kirsty – she's my daughter – shouldn't I? Before I die, I have to be reckless, for Angela, to prove I loved her, love her.' He paused then tipped his head a little towards Cal. 'Thank you.'

'For what?'

'For stopping, for talking, for letting me talk.'

'Are you going to be all right?'

'I won't jump if that's what you mean.'

'Promise?'

'I do, I promise.' He smiled at Cal. 'Do you think it would be silly of me if I went to Wales, to a nice out-of-the-way hotel where I promised I would take Angela?'

'Not silly, no.'

Harry stared into his tea. 'I've always wondered what it would have been like even to have spent a few days with her. I didn't ever do that. If I had, then perhaps I would have been reckless.'

'If you want to talk . . .' Cal wrote his phone number on a menu. 'Any time.'

Cal had returned to Edinburgh. Sometimes he wondered – as he did now – what had happened to Harry. Did he go to Wales? Or – Cal dreaded the thought – did Harry, finally, become impetuous? Did he jump?

Leaving the natural cantilever of rock at daylight, Cal was stiff and sore. The feeling of elation which accompanied his arrival at Sandwood Bay, at being alone, had dissipated in the night, gone.

Cal walked the clifftops. His demons walked with him.

In such a mood, he picked at familiar sores. One was

the ending of his marriage to Rachel – why he'd taken off to the coast with such frequency they'd become strangers. Another was the fracturing of his family – why his father had abandoned him and gone to work abroad after the death of his mother. In both cases, he was sure, the fault was his: he drove people away by his solitary behaviour.

Was that why he'd been such an elusive friend when Alex was alive? Had he tried to drive him away too?

He wished it were late autumn and the wind so fierce and sharp-edged he'd only be able to catch a breath by cupping his hands over his nose and turning away from the blast. Apart from the thrill of being out in such violence, nothing harried him then or nagged at him. The wind invaded his head, through his nose, ears and mouth, and emptied everything out.

He tried running instead but his demons ran with him.

On such a soft spring day, the breeze light and south-westerly, Cal found his head filling up with the idea that Harry Fowler had been found dead. From an anxiety, it turned into certainty. He *had* been found dead. He *had* jumped.

At dusk, Cal returned to the dunes. A sixth sense whispered that another night would be dangerous for him. Instead of sleeping out, he returned to his pickup and turned the radio up loud, filling his head with sound, a substitute for the wind.

Sometime after ten, on a news bulletin, he heard a name he recognized. Harry Fowler. 'I heard a knock,' his daughter Kirsty said excitedly, 'and when I opened the door he was standing there, as if he hadn't ever been away. I touched him just to be certain my imagination wasn't playing tricks. It was him, definitely him. He said he was sorry for causing so much trouble. He doesn't really remember where he's been or what he's done. None of that matters any more. He's going to live with me now and I won't let him out of my sight ever again. I'm crying I'm so happy.'

Cal was surprised to find he was as aggrieved for Angela, Harry's dead lover, as for himself. By the sound of Kirsty, her father hadn't confessed to having fallen long ago for another woman. Nor, it seemed, was Harry going to exonerate Cal. The frightened-away clients of the Sea Detective Agency wouldn't be rushing back. 'Is that it?' Cal demanded angrily of the radio. 'Harry, did you go all the way to Wales and return as half-hearted as you were before?' Cal drove off, going south.

9

The phone call lasted less than two minutes. In that brief time Kate Tolmie experienced a transformation. Before Rosemary Lauder answered angrily – 'Who the hell thinks it's all right to ring at ten thirty at night?' – Kate had been falling into an abyss of recrimination, guilt and depression.

More than a week had passed without any contact with Flora, and Kate had eaten little, drunk too much, hadn't been able to sleep at night for worry, was exhausted. After Mrs Lauder hung up without saying goodbye, Kate had been energized, as if a bolt of electricity had gone right through her, recharging her.

Zap.

Energized, alarmed and frightened: where was Flora? What had happened to her?

In reply to Mrs Lauder's snarled question, Kate apologized for calling so late and explained in half-completed sentences and ones that rambled about a 'spat between sisters, nothing serious . . . didn't want to let it fester any longer . . . well, actually it's quite serious' because Flora had been 'blanking her', not returning Kate's calls or emails and 'to be honest, Mrs Lauder, this has been going on for long enough and I couldn't endure another night without speaking to her and apologizing to her. Since she's staying with you . . . I thought if I rang at ten thirty, when she was likely to be in . . . If you or your husband answered, perhaps you might be able to persuade her to talk to me or at least come to the phone, because she wouldn't treat either of you like messengers to tell me to get lost.'

Mrs Lauder's response was as curt and to the point as Kate's had been long-winded. 'Your sister isn't here.'

'Do you know where she is? Have she and Alex gone away somewhere?'

Mrs Lauder made a noise like a laugh except it wasn't. 'She hasn't told you?'

'As I said, we haven't spoken for a while. Told me what?'

'Oh, it's not important. Obviously your sister didn't think so.'

'It sounds quite important, Mrs Lauder. Please tell me.'

'Well, if you're sure,' Mrs Lauder carried on in a cold, sneery voice. 'Alex is dead. We buried him three days ago.'

'Alex! Alex is dead? Is that what you said? Oh my God. Alex? I knew he was ill, but I thought he was expected to live for ages, like, months. Mrs Lauder, I don't know what to say –'

Mrs Lauder cut in. 'It doesn't really matter what you say, does it? Anyway, the death of a young man like Alex isn't very interesting, is it? I suppose that's why your sister didn't bother to tell you.'

'Mrs Lauder, I'm . . . I'm so sorry for your loss, you and your husband –'

'I don't imagine you care.' Again she interrupted. 'Your sister didn't.'

'Mrs Lauder, Flora loved Alex.'

'Really? You think so? Perhaps that explains why she

69

walked out on him.' Mrs Lauder sounded offhand when she wasn't. 'Though who can blame her? After all, what young woman nowadays wants to waste precious time on a dying boyfriend when she could be off having fun, doing something interesting?'

'She's not like that,' Kate said, caught between defending her sister, being sympathetic to a hurting, bereaved mother and being shocked by the news about Alex and Flora – why had she walked out on Alex? When? Had everything got too much for her – Alex's illness, launching the charity, the emotional strain, that horrible stalker writing those cards and, of course, the rift with Kate about their mother? Where *was* she? Despite her panic, Kate managed to say, 'Mrs Lauder, something's terribly wrong. That's not Flora.'

'That's *exactly* who she is. When you find her, tell her we won't ever hate anyone as much as we hate her.'

The line went dead.

Zap. The shock was both galvanizing and terrifying. Flora was missing. Flora was in trouble. Flora needed her big sister.

Straight away Kate was more like her old self, busy and purposeful, ringing round Flora's friends and work colleagues. She hadn't felt as capable since, well, when? Between calls, she tried to pinpoint the moment. Was it around her break-up with Pete when her survival instinct, the little that was left, finally did its job? *No*, she thought, *longer ago. Oh my God, since before we started going out. Since before I went to work in the gallery. Four years. It was four years ago.*

In her pepped-up state, Kate made two resolutions. First, if she found Flora – her stomach lurched at that:

70

if – she'd tell her, 'Talk about Alex as much as you want, day and night, as long as you need, I'll always listen.' Second, when some equilibrium between them was restored – *if* it was; *if* she found her – she'd say to Flora, 'About Pete, I was wrong and you were right. He wasn't good for me.' Then she'd address the emotional trigger behind every misunderstanding or flare-up: not Flora's dislike of Pete or her criticisms of Kate for sacrificing her personality to his, for allowing herself to be controlled by him, but the elephant which was always in the room: 'Our mother and why you and I have such a different attitude towards her.'

Kate prayed those conversations would be soon. But every phone call ended with Flora still worryingly out of reach. That time of frank exchanges, of the sisters being reconciled and reunited, remained as distant a prospect as it had been for more than a week.

Where's Flora?

After each phone call Kate asked that question with ever greater urgency.

No one seemed to know the answer.

After complaining about being rung so late at night or, in some cases, early in the morning, her friends said: *She's fine; she's with Alex, isn't she?*

When Kate said no, she had been, but not any more, they reminded her impatiently of Flora's practice of making unscheduled visits to charity projects on the foundation's list of potential partners. That's where she'd be, they assured Kate, scouting.

Kate shouldn't worry because *they* weren't.

Kate bit her tongue. *They* weren't worried because *they*

71

were unaware of Alex's death. Kate kept that to herself, partly because breaking such news on the phone and late at night was difficult, also because she resented their attitude – the assumption they knew Flora better than she did.

Well, they didn't. Flora's boyfriend was dead and buried. None of them knew that.

After two a.m., Kate noticed the number for Maria, the cleaner, on the fridge. She left a message, asking Maria to ring back as soon as possible.

Then, for the third time since talking to Mrs Lauder, she rang Flora's mobile, texted and sent an email – saying in each how awful the news was about Alex, how shocked she was, how sorry and how desperately sad Flora must be, how much Kate hoped she would make contact because if she, Kate, was 'put on this earth for anything, it's to be a big sister to you'.

By now, it was two thirty-four.

With no one else to contact, Kate went to the kitchen, made coffee. The quietness and stillness – Kate's separateness from Flora – made her wonder about people's tolerance to loss and bereavement. Their mother, Flora's first love, now Alex, her second – had Flora reached her limit? Had she suffered a breakdown?

'Where have you gone, Flora?' Kate said to the empty kitchen. 'Please tell me. Please speak to me. Please be all right. I'm so sorry. I won't fight with you ever again.'

For the next hour she wandered the flat, going from room to room, as if searching for Flora, until settling in Flora's bedroom. She searched the bureau again, taking out each of the drawers, reading Flora's papers and correspondence, looking for clues, examining the post-cards which offered the 'truth about your mother', becoming so angry with the writer she scattered them with a sweep of her forearm. As they settled on the floor, Kate noticed writing on the back of one of the accompanying envelopes. Flora had written a name, *Caladh McGill*, and underneath, circled a number of times, was *Speak to Alex about him???*, as though Flora had been wondering whether she should or not.

Kate used her phone to google 'Caladh McGill' and found a large number of references to someone called Cal McGill. He'd been in the news recently about the disappearance of a man called Harry Fowler. But Kate was more interested in the description of Cal McGill's work. He was an oceanographer who found lost bodies and his company, the Sea Detective Agency, was based in an industrial estate in east Edinburgh, only a couple of miles away.

Was he *Caladh* McGill?

10

In the half-light of early dawn, Sarah noticed an indistinct barrel-shaped object at the sea's edge. She assumed it had been newly deposited by the high tide. *Something interesting for Olaf to investigate*, she'd thought. Having already passed Olaf's parked trike at the end of the beach road, she'd anticipated an encounter with the man himself as she continued her pre-breakfast walk. But, disappointingly, there'd been no sign of him by the time Sarah reached Beach Post 23, a distance of four kilometres, her usual marker for turning round. Striding quickly back on wet, recently exposed sand, it wasn't long before, in clearer light, the barrel-shaped object was visible again. By then, it was high and dry. And the closer to it Sarah came, the less barrel-like it seemed. Soon she was near enough to see it had a head and silver curly hair. The barrel, she realized with a shock, was Olaf sitting on the sand with his legs pulled up. Why hadn't he moved since dawn? Was something wrong?

Her instinct was to ask him but she didn't, not straight away, because his motionlessness discouraged her. Instead Sarah went to the beach hut from where she could watch him while sweeping out sand. She hoped, by the time she finished, Olaf would have resumed searching the tideline for flotsam or might have looked round and seen her. Then, if he wanted company, he could approach her. But, ten minutes later, with nothing more to do in the hut, Sarah was hungry – she hadn't had breakfast – and Olaf still hadn't moved. She decided she couldn't delay any longer; she had to approach him because something wasn't right. Walking across the beach, she was nervous. Ever since she'd known Olaf, he'd always been the one who'd sought her out, never the other way round. She preferred it that way because Olaf was particular about company. Generally, he didn't want any and, long ago, when she'd understood that about him, she'd made a decision always to respect his space, to be welcoming when he approached her but not to inflict herself upon him without invitation.

Consequently, she wasn't at all confident about how she would be greeted, whether Olaf would be pleased to see her or not at all. To provide warning of her imminent arrival, at about ten metres' distance, she said, 'Oh, it *is* you, Olaf,' as though she hadn't been sure. Then, hurriedly: 'Am I disturbing you?'

His head shook. 'No, no you're not,' he answered without looking at her.

'Because,' Sarah carried on, as though she hadn't heard him or didn't believe him, 'because I could leave . . .'

A pause while she screwed up her courage; she had to take the risk.

'It's just that when I've got things on my mind and need someone to talk to, you always seem to appear, and I thought perhaps, this time, you might be troubled and need someone to talk to and, if you did, then it's my turn to listen.' She took a breath. 'Anyway, I thought the least I could do was to offer since you've been so helpful to me.

But if you'd rather I left you alone, that's all right. I won't be offended, really I won't.'

By the end Olaf was looking up at her. She hadn't ever seen sadder eyes.

'Someone . . .' Olaf said, his voice thinner and weaker than normal. 'Someone I know . . . has died.'

'Oh, Olaf, I'm sorry.' His expression and the weakness of his voice moved Sarah. She carried on without thinking. 'A woman you knew?'

'No,' Olaf replied with a shake of his head, 'a young man, someone I met a long time ago.'

'It's always worse when they're young,' Sarah said, regaining her composure. 'Would you like to talk about him? Because if you would, I'd like to hear about him.'

Olaf didn't answer straight away. He turned back towards the sea. Like him, she said nothing and watched the black hulk of a tanker slowly going north on the horizon.

Eventually, Olaf sighed. 'His name was Alex Lauder. Cancer got him. He was an oceanographer.' Olaf nodded towards the sea. 'We had that in common. He came to a conference here once.'

'Will you,' Sarah asked, 'be going to the funeral?'

'It's already been.'

Though Sarah wondered why Olaf hadn't attended, she didn't inquire. His answer closed off that possibility, she thought. It was typical Olaf, answering one question but leaving many more unanswered. Why hadn't he gone? Had he known about the funeral in advance? Why was he quite so upset? It also discouraged her from asking anything else. So, after saying nothing for long enough to allow him to volunteer more if he wished, Sarah said, 'I think I should let you be alone with your thoughts.'

Olaf said, 'Thank you.'

His tone was appreciative, Sarah was relieved to hear, not at all resentful. Walking back to De Koog, Sarah felt elated but she wasn't quite sure why. What exactly had Olaf told her about his dead friend? A name, a qualification, a missed funeral, but nothing more – nothing heartfelt, nothing else apart from that pained expression. Yet even being allowed to witness that was a breakthrough of sorts. More emotion was revealed in that look than in any number of Olaf's words. For those few seconds Olaf had let her in; he'd given her a glimpse, albeit a brief one, of his inner man. And by not asking any other questions, by not pressing him, she'd signalled to him that he could confide in her, reveal as little or as much as he wanted, and she wouldn't pry for more. She was as glad at having been able to demonstrate that to Olaf as she was sad for him.

And she dared to hope that Olaf found her as reassuring as she found him.

The overhead light dazzled Cal. He gazed around his windowless office as though for the first time. His eyes stopped briefly on particular objects: his camp bed, an open rucksack spilling clothes, the gantry of metal shelves where he kept his collection of flotsam – driftwood, sea beans, lobster-pot tags which crossed the Atlantic from Maine and a green turtle shell recovered from a beach on South Uist.

Next he glanced at the walls, at three large charts of the North Atlantic, the west coast of Scotland and the North Sea. The last two were stuck with different-coloured pins from which matching strands of wool stretched to a double row of newspaper cuttings. Among the headlines were 'Trawler skipper lost overboard', 'Body parts washed up on Cornish coast', 'Mother's beach vigil for child lost in storm': a yellowing, curling record of disaster and death. Other pieces of wool extended below the charts to a gallery of photographs: stark images of bloated, broken-jointed bodies on various Atlantic or North Sea coasts. Some of the prints were crooked, about to fall. Others had dropped to the grey-coloured vinyl-covered floor and been left to gather dust.

Cal wondered at the kind of person who would choose to work with suffering and tragedy as wallpaper, also as a haphazard, dog-eared floor covering; how strange not to have had that thought before.

Any other time he'd walked into his office he had a sense of achievement at all of his possessions being contained in this twenty-by-twenty brick box with adjoining garage/store. Everything he owned could be loaded on the back of his pickup, which had 124,000 miles on the clock and a rusting dent in the front passenger door. Before, that had been his ambition: not to be tied down by things, objects, people or commitments as others were; for everything to be uproot-able, portable; for his footprint to be slight and shallow.

He made an attempt at rekindling his former enthusiasm for that way of life – 'sustainability' and 'self-reliance' had been his ambitions then – but found he couldn't. Something had changed, and he thought that something was Alex's death or, to be precise, not knowing that Alex had been ill and was dying. Surely friendship was more important than living like this.

He recalled the letter his ex-wife Rachel had written as their marriage was disintegrating, bitterly describing him as just another geek with a hobby. Women knew what to expect when they got involved with a trainspotter or some dimwit who boosted his testosterone by watching repeats of *Top Gear*, but Cal's oceanography, his solitariness and his habit of sleeping under the stars on some faraway beach, made him out to be a romantic when he wasn't. As soon as he was in a relationship he tried to escape. A distant, deserted coast was where he ran to. It wasn't deliberate on his part, she'd conceded, but still, breaking up with him had left her with a nasty aftertaste of deceit. 'Whoever wrote "no man is an island" clearly hadn't met you.'

Cal didn't want to be that person any more. Could he be anybody else?

He sat heavily in the second-hand swivel chair at his worktable which he'd constructed from driftwood, adding later extensions, so that now it was five metres long, reaching almost from one wall to another. He studied the room once again, perhaps in the hope a different perspective might lead to a different opinion.

Not only was it unchanged but it begged an unsettling question: what kind of person would have placed greater value on *this*, this *horror show*, than on Alex's friendship? Cal gazed around the room again, his expression one of distaste. He'd blanked Alex, omitted to return his calls, was unaware of Alex dying, and for what? *This*: a business so fragile it was undone by one woman's tearful appearance on television; an environment so grotesque that Detective Sergeant Helen Jamieson, another long-suffering friend, now his only friend, said she'd attended murder scenes less disturbing.

An exasperated sigh escaped from him. He hadn't returned Helen's call from a few days ago, hadn't even checked whether she'd left a message.

In frustration, he kicked out at a leg of his worktable. The impact set off a slow-motion landslide of books, charts and files. Some fell to the floor with a succession of bangs. Others toppled sideways. Before, it had resembled a miniature shanty town, every available space occupied and each ramshackle edifice defying logic and gravity. Now it was a shanty town after an earthquake had struck. And, just as in real life when a baby is brought screaming from the rubble – a survivor, life carrying on – so Cal witnessed his own unexpected, if minor, miracle. Where once a towering pillar of reference books had stood, there was wreckage – and poking from it a twenty-pound note.

The money acted as a distraction. He peered into the new landscape of his table, pushing his fingers into dark hollows below collapsed paper masonry, finding another £14.03 in coins which he put with his other money, the residue of his survival fund, in a cleared space. He counted twice, arriving at the same total, £280.15.

He turned on his desktop computer, the only object on his worktable which had remained upright. A quick scroll through the first two pages of emails – there were 3,327 unread in his inbox – was sufficient for a conclusion about his business being unlikely to make a recovery despite Harry Fowler's reappearance. His uninvited correspondents were attacking from a different direction. Having previously accused him of assisting an old man to kill himself, now their unanimous opinion was that Cal had had a lucky escape, not just because Harry Fowler had turned up alive but because the old man's loss of memory also meant he had no recollection of anything that had passed between him and Cal, apparently even of having ever met him.

Cal thought about looking for a phone number or address for Harry's daughter Kirsty. Should he ring Harry or write? Should he urge Harry to tell the truth about their night-time encounter on the bridge, also about his lost love, Angela? Cal decided not to. If the old man's memory loss was genuine, that was that. If it wasn't, Harry was just being Harry, once again choosing not to be reckless or wholehearted. After all, Harry had warned Cal.

Also, Cal thought there was justice in Harry's behaviour, a punishment for Cal being similarly self-centred for the last years of Alex's life.

Cal crossed his office to the kitchenette, took everything out of the cupboards which was edible or drinkable, as if taking stock in preparation for a siege. On the counter were:

A litre of milk (less than half full).
A loaf of stale supermarket bread (unopened).
A jar of instant coffee (new).
A pot of Marmite (almost full).
A small tin of baked beans.
A large tin of plum tomatoes.
A packet of rice, another of dried pasta.
A pack of oatcakes (three left).
A box of decaffeinated green teabags (eight
    remaining).

He had enough food for two or three days, possibly enough money for two or three weeks. In the past he might have regarded that as evidence of success, his ability to survive without over-taxing the planet's resources. Now he thought how little he had, how precarious and tenuous his hold on ordinary life.

He put water into the kettle, switched it on and, while he waited for it to boil, he turned on his phone. While he'd been away, he'd had six texts and seven missed calls, all from Helen Jamieson.

Cal rang her.

'Where are you?' she demanded as soon as she answered.

'In my office.'

'Why didn't you get in touch, let me know you were all right?' She sounded exasperated. 'I've sent text, emails. I've left voice messages. God's sake, Cal, you've got a phone.'

'It's been turned off,' he said. 'I didn't have it with me.'

'God, Cal, what's wrong with you? When anyone else is in trouble, they rely on friends. Not you, no, not Cal McGill. When you're in trouble you cut yourself off, disappear. Where did you go this time?'

Cal said, 'Sandwood Bay.'

Helen made a sighing sound, exasperation.

Cal said, 'By the way, I didn't advise Harry Fowler about killing himself.'

'No, Cal, I know. Of course you didn't. But your disappearing act makes it look as though you did.'

The lid of the kettle was rattling so much that Cal said, 'Hold on.' After switching off the plug at the wall, he turned back to find a young woman standing inside the door: five ten, as tall as Cal, with red hair breaking free from a loose ponytail that was hanging over her right shoulder. She wore a blue mac, jeans and silver trainers, and was looking around Cal's office, appearing disorientated. 'I didn't mean to barge in. Sorry. The door was open.' She glanced at Cal. 'Are you Caladh McGill?'

The use of his unabbreviated name by a stranger surprised him. 'Who wants to know?'

'Hi, I'm Kate Tolmie.' She lifted her right hand uncertainly in greeting. 'I'm looking for my sister, Flora.'

Cal said, 'Helen, call you back?'

Helen stared at her phone, experiencing a conflict of emotions: relief at Cal having turned up, hurt at being cut off and dissatisfaction at *things* – Helen's shorthand for the undefined nature of their relationship.

Helen threw the phone on to the bed and gave herself the usual talking-to. How hard was it to say she hoped to be more than his friend? But did she? Did she really? If she did, surely she would have found an opportunity to tell Cal. Since she hadn't, the reason might be because, for her, romance was safer as occasional fantasy. Being friends with Cal, their relationship being no better defined, stopped her from minding there was no one else. She sighed. Sooner or later someone would walk into Cal's life. Maybe someone just had, this Kate Tolmie. Then she would mind. Or would she? Perhaps she wouldn't.

Could anyone live with Cal McGill?

Helen looked at herself in the full-length bedroom mirror. She tried to see the person others saw or *said* they saw: a Helen Jamieson who was handsome in an old-fashioned way rather than modern pretty, with natural curls and a peachy complexion. Instead, as her eyes flicked here and there, finding fault, she saw a woman who was too large, with unruly, thin hair; and skin which was only smooth and unblemished from being stretched tight.

Unhappy, she padded to the shower while muttering about her bad habit of concentrating on negatives, imagined or real, when she should be celebrating her advantages: an IQ of 173, plus her achievements, a law degree followed by a Masters in criminology. *Stop acting as if you're stupid, Helen.* The hot water flowing over her face, back and shoulders was soothing, calming. She imagined Kate

Tolmie walking unsuspecting into Cal's office and stumbling into a nightmare – all that mess and gore and rotting flesh, those photographs of bodies and newspaper reports about violent death, his macabre wallpaper. Most likely by now Kate Tolmie would be running and thinking she'd had a close call with a psycho and was lucky to have escaped with her life.

As Helen dressed in a work skirt and shirt, something else nagged at her. Those names, Kate Tolmie and her sister Flora: they rang faint bells. In fact, the more she thought about them, the louder the bells were. Something about a mother?

The memory was vague, distant, out of reach.

An object in the far corner caught Kate's attention. It appeared to be a half-sized man – a *creature* – made of driftwood and bits of tin and blue fishing net for hair, a mouth made from a circular piece of pink-coloured plastic and smoothed sea glass for eyes, eyes that seemed to stare back. Its presence, its *malignancy*, surprised Kate so that when she asked Cal whether or not her sister had been in contact she was momentarily off balance.

'No, no she hasn't,' Cal replied. 'I'm sorry. I don't know where she is.'

'But . . .' Kate said, 'she'd written down your name and "Speak to Alex about him" with a question mark. Alex, that's her boyfriend, was her boyfriend. Why would Flora have wanted to speak to Alex about you?'

'Possibly –' Cal shrugged, pulling a face to let Kate know he was guessing – 'because Alex was seriously ill, dying, and Flora didn't know if I'd been told.'

'What, you know Alex, knew Alex? You know Alex is dead?'

'Yes, he was a friend.'

'And Flora? Do you know her?'

'I met her once, briefly.'

Having experienced a rush of optimism driving to Cal's office, Kate now felt a plunging sensation, of hope draining away, as though a plug had been pulled inside her. In her pent-up state about Flora, it seemed to her that Cal, for some reason, was being unnecessarily taciturn. Surely the natural thing would have been to admit to having met Flora as soon as Kate mentioned her name? Something was off, wrong, and Kate wasn't sure what. Was it her or him?

'Did you,' she asked, 'attend the funeral?'

'Alex's?'

There it was again, Kate thought, Cal being guarded, as though his intention was to tell her as little as possible.

'No,' Cal continued, 'as I mentioned, I didn't even know he was dying.'

To conceal her confusion at what she now regarded as Cal's obstruction, she found herself being caught by the stare of the driftwood man, *creature*. 'What's that horrible thing?'

'That was given to me by a Norwegian called Olaf. He's a beachcomber. He makes them.'

Hurriedly looking away, Kate's attention was caught by a wall display of photographs. One, in particular, was transfixing, a large colour image of a beached torso minus its head, hands and feet.

'Would you like coffee?' Cal asked, apparently oblivious to Kate's growing alarm. 'The kettle boiled as you came in.'

His voice sounded muffled to her. She managed a nod. 'Milk?'

Kate didn't respond. By now her gaze had shifted to other similar photographs: beached bodies, bloated, grotesquely misshapen and with missing limbs, bones protruding. She looked quickly at Cal as he was pouring water into a mug. She attempted to reconcile this man – who was probably two or three years older than her, whose nose skewed to the right, whose hair was dark brown, cut short and who wore jeans and a T-shirt – with the horror story unfolding around her.

Suddenly he seemed capable of anything, including encouraging an old man, Harry Fowler, to jump into a river as well as holding back information about the disappearance of her sister. Was he also the sender of those anonymous postcards?

Cal, sensing her alarm and thinking he knew the reason why, said, 'I have a friend who's in the police and she says this place is only fit for a serial killer. If you're not familiar with these sorts of photographs, they're a shock . . . I'm sorry. I'm afraid, to me, they're work. I'm used to them.'

Kate barely heard the explanation. Everything in the room, this box of grotesque surprises, frightened her. Clearly, Cal didn't mind living among pictures of bodies, *sleeping* among bodies. She noticed his camp bed. *Would he lie about Flora being in contact, about knowing where Flora was?*

'Kate,' she heard him saying, 'as I mentioned, I've only spoken to your sister once. That was a year ago. She was with Alex. Then all I said was "Hi" and she said "Hello" to me. We were in each other's company for about five minutes. I understand why you're worried about her. I would be too. I know how much Alex loved her. I imagine she loved him as much. But you've got to believe me. I don't know where she is. If I did, I would tell you.'

Then: 'Here, here's your coffee. I've put some milk in.'

She stared at his outstretched hand and the mug. Tiredness, gnawing worry about Flora, the unnerving effect of McGill's office, his belated openness and apparent sincerity, unravelled her. 'You're the last person,' she said. 'Where else am I going to look? My God, I've lost her.'

She turned and ran for the door.

12

Helen gave in to curiosity as soon as she was in the office. Googling 'Kate Tolmie' produced 84,100 results. Helen scrolled down the first page and read about a Kate Tolmie who had won a beauty contest in Arizona, another who had won a lottery while on holiday in Spain and half a dozen stories about a Kate Tolmie who had once been Ken Tolmie, a wrestler. Helen let out a peal of laughter. *Please, please, let that be the Kate Tolmie who was Cal's visitor.*

Her attention was caught by another Kate Tolmie. The name was highlighted in an article about a mother of three, a British army helicopter pilot called Iris Russell who had been injured in Afghanistan. The woman described painful years of rehabilitation – she'd lost a leg and a hand – and her struggle to forgive those who accused her of being a bad mother because she'd chosen a war zone rather than to stay at home with her three children. The woman protested, 'Haven't we moved on at all? What century is this? Men who join the forces never have to deal with crap like this. Their wives or girlfriends look after their children. My husband looked after mine – it wasn't as if they were neglected. So why am I regarded as some sort of monster?'

The article went on to mention other women similarly criticized over the years – under Christina Tolmie were the names of her daughters Kate and Flora.

That Kate Tolmie. Her? Could it be?

Helen remembered the photograph: two red-headed girls, both wearing apple-green summer dresses, their grandfather in close attendance handing them rose petals to scatter while walking through the French town where their mother had last been seen. The picture was on every front page, running on every TV news bulletin. For a time, Kate and Flora Tolmie, then aged six and four, were famous. Everyone had an opinion about Christina, a single mother, who left her daughters behind to distribute clothes in Romania's orphanages and disappeared without trace on the return journey. Some said she was an inspiration, a modern heroine; others that her behaviour was reckless. Around the bereaved girls swirled a passionate debate about what it meant to be a mother in an age of gender and job equality.

Helen, aged ten at the time, had been fascinated by the story. She devoured newspapers for information and watched TV news bulletins, because her parents had been killed in a car crash when she was six, the same age as Kate. Her interest in other children who became orphans was all-consuming, if complicated. Apart from being distressed at another child having to suffer her fate, there was also the conflicting emotion of feeling less alone, of there being someone else like her, of Helen not being such an anomaly, a freak. Helen included girls like Kate and Flora Tolmie in an imaginary world where they all lived together in one big orphan family. Only girls were allowed entry into Helen's make-believe community. They would look out for each other, the older girls being guardians to the younger, taking on the role of parents.

Gosh, Helen thought, *Kate Tolmie*.

*

Cal wrote:

> You are, of course, entitled to your opinion about my motives in stopping to talk to Harry Fowler and my alleged role in his subsequent and temporary disappearance, but some facts might help. My work in recovering lost bodies at sea possibly makes me more aware than others of suicide risk. In Mr Fowler's case, I saw a man, alone and late at night, standing on a bridge over a river and thought I should check if he was all right. After a pleasant conversation, mostly conducted in a nearby café, it became clear my concern was misplaced. Contrary to speculation, I was not asked for advice, nor did I give any, nor would I, on where or when he should jump into the river so that his body might not be recovered.

Rather than Cal's response to the scores of emails in his inbox having a moderating effect, the opposite happened. The replies were instant (did these people sit at their computers all day in a frenzy?), accusing and abusive. All he had done, he realized, was further stir up the metaphorical mob which was howling and screaming outside his door. The more he protested his good intentions, the worse the clamour for his ruin or slow death by disease or violence, even his public execution by being hurled from the same bridge.

Since none of his frightened-off clients had been in further contact following Harry Fowler's reappearance, Cal experienced a feeling of powerlessness and of defeat. The mob had killed off his business, if not him yet.

He swore as his phone vibrated beside his keyboard. The screen lit up with Helen's name.

Cal answered. 'It's not a good time, Helen.'

She persevered. 'Is Kate Tolmie still with you?'

'No.'

'Is she about twenty-nine with red hair?'

Cal said, 'Probably, yes, why?'

'That name, Kate Tolmie, rang a distant bell. So I googled her and discovered why. When she was a child she was involved in a famous missing-person's case. Her mother, Christina, was due to take a cross-Channel ferry from Calais to Dover but vanished. Her van was found abandoned in a nearby town. Foul play was suspected, abduction, a sexual attack, even murder, but there wasn't any evidence. A few suspects were questioned, though no one was charged. There wasn't a body. There wasn't any blood . . . Cal?'

'Yes.'

'Do you know this already?'

'No.'

'Kate Tolmie didn't tell you?'

'No. She didn't stay long. She was anxious about Flora, her sister. She wanted to know if I'd been in contact with her or knew where she was.'

'Why you?'

'Flora's boyfriend died recently. He was a friend of mine.'

'I'm sorry. You didn't tell me.'

'No.'

'Do you?'

'What?'

'Know where Flora is?'

'No.'

Helen told herself to stop. She wasn't sure if Cal was

being deliberately obtuse, but she didn't like the role she had slipped into: a detective sergeant carrying out an interrogation.

'Cal,' she said, 'are you interested in hearing about Christina Tolmie?'

'Yeah.'

'Well, at the time, it was a huge story. It had everything: a good-looking woman – Christina was a single mother, then thirty-one – and two abandoned daughters who were as photogenic as she was. There were pictures of her girls in every newspaper, scattering roses where their mother had last been seen. What made it different from any other missing-person story was the storm that blew up about Christina. She'd taken a van-load of clothes to orphans in Romania, driving solo across Europe, leaving her daughters in the care of her widowed father. She'd stayed two weeks before driving back. But when the ferry left Calais, she hadn't checked in. Her van was found not far away in a town called Gravelines. It was in a side street, unlocked and empty apart from some clothes in the back. The police never found out what happened to her. A witness said a woman answering Christina's description – she was striking, with red hair, like her daughters – had gone into a café and asked for a local man by the name of Jacques Picoult. Apparently, he'd taken off in his boat two days before. While police hunted for him, the rumour was of smuggling and of Jacques Picoult being involved – a concealed hatch was found in the back of Christina's van. However, Christina's father dismissed that possibility. He said the hatch was where Christina kept her money, passport, camera and medicines when she was travelling.

There wasn't anything else to connect Picoult's disappearance to Christina's. The French police eventually tracked Picoult to Portugal. He was living on his boat and claimed to be unaware of the hunt for Christina. Under interrogation, he said he left Gravelines in a hurry because a young woman – apparently she was eighteen – claimed to be pregnant by him. The day he abandoned her, she hanged herself from the streetlight outside his front door. That was why he hadn't returned. Picoult also admitted to knowing Christina. They'd both worked in Somalia for an international relief agency. But he hadn't seen her or spoken to her for some years. His alibi checked out. So it could just be that Christina drove to Gravelines instead of going to the ferry at Calais because en route she'd heard Picoult's relationship was in trouble and wanted to commiserate.' Helen paused. 'Cal, are you listening?'

'Yes, go on.'

'Anyway, there was a moral panic about the case – people said Christina was wrong to have left her children to provide clothes for orphans in Romania, as if she'd brought disaster on herself. The father of Christina Tolmie's daughters was considered to be a possible culprit in the absence of any other obvious suspects or explanation about her disappearance. No one knew who he was. His name wasn't on Kate's and Flora's birth certificates. Apparently, Christina never told anyone his identity. Some newspapers played "hunt the father" and published names of men who'd known Christina. Jacques Picoult was one of them. The effect was to make Christina appear promiscuous, even though her friends said she was not. They described her as fiercely independent and uninterested in having a relationship or being tied down by a man or marriage. All that did was feed a narrative about Christina Tolmie being an immoral woman who slept around to become pregnant and then abandoned her children to go and care for orphaned Romanians. There were lots of theories about what happened to her – from violent to salacious. Every line of inquiry fizzled out. It's as much a mystery today as it was twenty-three years ago. If that's your Kate Tolmie, she has quite a story.'

13

They hadn't spoken for two days, which was unusual for Sarah and Lotte. Often they'd bump into each other outside their houses or shopping in Lidl. Or one or other would drop round for coffee. Or they'd text or chat. But since Lotte's warning to Sarah about Olaf, there'd been nothing, not a word. A few times Sarah had picked up her phone intending to make contact but, on further reflection, hadn't rung or messaged. The reason for her hesitancy? She was loath to give Lotte another opportunity to theorize about the 'mystery of Olaf'. A hiatus, Sarah hoped, would lead to the subject being forgotten, especially as Olaf was particularly vulnerable at the moment.

Why, though, had Lotte not been in touch with her?

This was the question which interested Sarah. In fact, it had evolved into a different question: was Lotte trying to replace her? The possibility first occurred to Sarah two mornings before when, going downstairs, she'd listened in to Lotte talking to Olaf and was astonished to hear her confess to having had murderous, vengeful thoughts about her husband and his mistresses: 'If he hadn't died when he did, I don't know what I would have done – I'd have killed him and his girlfriend, his latest girlfriend. Actually, I'd have killed her first and ripped out her heart to give to him.' The revelation was as startling as it was new to Sarah. If it was true, why was Lotte confiding in Olaf, having warned Sarah to be careful about trusting a man who wouldn't talk about his past? If it was a fabrication, what was Lotte doing? Was she setting some sort of trap for Olaf?

Then, this morning, when Sarah was again listening in, Lotte told Olaf about her weekly trips to Amsterdam to visit an elderly aunt, who was her only living relative. After explaining how she shopped, cooked and read her stories, Lotte made a loud sighing sound and demanded of 'God above' to be saved from 'a miserable old age like that', a supplication Sarah had heard many times before. 'Promise me, Olaf,' Lotte went on to say, 'if I ever become doddery and confused, you'll force a bottleful of sleeping pills down my throat.'

The same promise had been asked of Sarah. She'd agreed. Wisely, Olaf merely grunted.

Sarah was put out, swithering about what to do. She missed Lotte. At the same time, she was angry with her. Was Lotte playing games with Olaf or was she not? If not, was she, Sarah, no longer Lotte's confidante?

Either way, she was restless to know and also anxious to protect Olaf from Lotte.

Sarah sent a text:

Lunch today? One p.m.? I'll book.

Lovely, see you there,

Lotte replied, as though nothing was any different.

Sarah apologized for being late. 'You're not,' Lotte replied, smiling. 'You know I'm always early.' Lotte's other habit, being simply dressed and elegant, also caused a comment from Sarah. 'I'm always so wild-looking by comparison to you,' she said, after sitting down, running her fingers through her corkscrew hair, pinning it at the back.

They ordered without looking at the beach restaurant's menu; both chose seared tuna and salad. The waiter brought their usual drinks: water and a glass of Chardonnay for Sarah, another of Sauvignon Blanc for Lotte.

Sarah found herself relaxing. This was the old Lotte. This was how they were with each other, comfortable.

Instead of mentioning Olaf, a subject to be avoided until the end, Sarah said, 'Oh, I can't remember whether I've told you or not. I'm off to London tomorrow evening, flying from Schiphol, just for a couple of days, seeing suppliers.'

'You did mention it,' Lotte replied. 'Anyone interesting?'

An easy discussion followed. They talked about clothes, designers, trends and Sarah's on-off dilemma about her shop being so niche, so summer-and-beach-focused, and in such a seasonal location as De Koog. 'I should expand, open in another, bigger seaside destination but –' Sarah made a face – 'it's a risk and a lot of extra work.'

'Well,' Lotte replied, 'your shop pays your bills and a little bit more. And you have the winter off. You enjoy your life as it is, don't you? Sometimes it's better not to be too ambitious.'

Lunch continued in the same supportive, friendly vein. By coffee they'd discussed the house at the end of their street being for sale, the chilly weather, how late the tourist season was going to be. Sarah told Lotte about having delayed the opening of Sarah's Beach Fashions. After

Lotte paid – it was her turn – they walked back together. As was their habit, they didn't speak much apart from making observations about the village or the people they saw or recognized. Sarah volunteered little and replied briefly because she was becoming tense. The subject of Olaf still had not come up. Sarah would have to raise it soon before they reached Wintergroen, the street where they lived. Having mulled things over since early that morning, Sarah thought she should begin by saying how kind Lotte had been to Olaf, by taking him in, treating him as a friend; and then, more circumspectly, she would broach the 'surprising change' in Olaf because, in Sarah's experience, he was a man who liked to choose when, if, he had company. Without actually saying so, Sarah hoped to imply that Olaf might be feeling trapped by Lotte's attention, but was unable to object because he was worried about losing the roof over his head.

On arrival at Wintergroen, Sarah became flustered. In her confusion about how to raise the subject of Olaf, she said something else to Lotte. 'Obviously not tomorrow, but one of these times when I'm going to London, why don't I book a flight for the day you're visiting your aunt? Then we can travel together. I'll go to the airport and you can carry on into Amsterdam.'

Although Sarah hadn't intended to ask that question, she was curious to hear the answer. She expected Lotte to be dismissive, to say travelling together was impractical because Sarah would have to make appointments in advance, whereas Lotte never knew from one day to the next when or if her aunt would be well enough for a visit, sometimes from one hour to the next.

And Lotte said exactly that.

Sarah found herself trying again. 'I know, what about next week? There are some designers in Amsterdam I'd like to see, and I'll have the time since I've postponed the opening. I could do that while you're with your aunt. We could travel back together too. Let's pencil in a day.'

'No, Sarah,' Lotte snapped. 'I've told you. I can't plan ahead.'

Taken aback by Lotte's firmness, Sarah stopped walking, but Lotte carried on.

Sarah observed her friend's back, how upright it was, how unbending, no give in her posture as there had been none in her response. Sarah waited for her to stop. But Lotte carried on even though, by now, she must have realized Sarah was lagging behind. When Sarah followed, she made no effort to catch up. The two friends walked twenty paces apart, one behind the other, until Lotte stopped by the gate to her house and waited for Sarah. 'You're being silly,' she said in an amused way as Sarah carried on past her without speaking. 'It's not like you to be silly,' she threw after her.

Sarah stopped at her gate and looked back. Their eyes met and Sarah wondered whether Lotte's spikiness about Amsterdam had been about something else, *someone* else. Even though he hadn't been mentioned, were they fighting over Olaf? Were they now rivals?

14

Rather than attempt to outlast the virtual siege – his instinct was to defy bullies – Cal surrendered to practical, short-term considerations. His lack of clients, dearth of income and meagre savings of £280.15 combined into a clamouring mob of a different kind. The idea occurred to him of submitting notice on his office/storeroom. If he did, he would be liable for four more weekly rental payments, altogether £1,000, approximately equivalent, after deductions for repairs, to his deposit on the property. The neatness of that transaction appealed to him, especially as his remaining cash was sufficient for little more than one week's rent. He glanced at his inbox, noticed half a dozen new messages wishing him harm, then let out an exasperated shout before writing an email to his landlord ending his tenancy.

Afterwards, he stacked books and files into manageable piles, tore charts, maps and photographs from his walls and swept litter and accumulated dust – as thick as sediment – from the floor. Everything was either put in bin bags or removed to the storeroom apart from his worktable, a lamp, a desktop computer, two chairs, his camp bed, his rucksack of clothes and the shelves on which he displayed his beachcombing finds.

Then, exhausted, he closed his eyes and slept restlessly before sitting up in a sweat. He'd dreamed he was ill and dying like Harry Fowler. He was worried: who would organize his funeral? Who would break the law for him as he had for Alex? Who would arrange for his coffin to be dropped into the North Atlantic to be transported by currents into the Arctic?

Soon after waking, one person's name came to mind: Helen.

'Huh,' he said to the ceiling of his office.

He sent Helen a text:

You're a good friend.

He lay back and watched encroaching shadows of darkness – like curtains being slowly closed – until a look of consternation crept across his face. He texted again:

To explain, for some reason I was thinking about funerals and it occurred to me no one would organize mine apart from you.

Helen replied immediately.

Fuck, Cal. Is that it? I'm your good friend because I'll organize your bloody funeral? Nothing else?

Cal's expression changed to puzzlement. His intention had been to let Helen know how much he appreciated her, but he appeared to have done the opposite.

His phone rang. Without the deadening effect of books and papers, the noise sounded insistent, even angry. He looked at it with resignation – expecting it to be Helen – but the displayed mobile number was unfamiliar. Should he take the call? Had one of the clamouring, encircling mob found his phone number?

'Hello,' he answered.

'Is that a Dr Caladh McGill I'm talking to?' A woman's voice, English, querulous.

He was surprised at her knowing the long version of his first name and at her correct pronunciation, fleeting considerations as he braced himself for abuse. Another surprise followed when the woman said, 'I'm ringing about Flora Tolmie. Is she a patient of yours?'

He was temporarily wrong-footed, caught between curiosity – where was Flora? Was she all right? – and whether he should correct the woman's misapprehension about his medical qualifications. Because the woman sounded matter-of-fact, demanding and authoritative, it occurred to him she might be a police officer. Was Flora dead? Was this woman about to ask for Flora's medical records?

'Do you know where she is?' Cal asked. 'Is she all right? Is she alive?'

15

The duvet trailed behind Kate Tolmie like a coat being dragged after a drunken party. At the front door of the flat, she came to an abrupt stop, swayed one way and another as she drifted between sleep and not. The buzzing noise which had startled her awake reverberated inside her head.

Instead of saying 'Who's there?' when she picked up the entry phone, Kate pushed on the release button, which steadied her. She listened for the bang of the door downstairs and for the sound of ascending footsteps. They were heavier and slower than Maria's. Anyway, Maria always let herself in with her own keys. Kate gasped: could it be the police? Dread juddered her into the present. Had Flora been found? Was she dead? The thud of the footsteps and their reluctant pace suggested bad news.

During the night, Kate had decided she couldn't wait any longer. What was more important, her sister being angry with her – she was anyway – or finding her? After looking out some recent photographs, Kate drove to a police station to report Flora missing. Afterwards, she wished she hadn't, or hadn't been so honest. The officer at the reception desk looked bored as soon as Kate told him Flora was twenty-seven and 'no, she doesn't have mental health issues'. To impress on the policeman there were good reasons for worry, Kate added, 'We had a terrible argument, then her boyfriend died.'

'So –' the policeman yawned – 'it could be she's upset and just isn't speaking to you.'

Kate said, 'Her friends don't know where she is either.'

'Or she's told them not to tell you where she is?'

Which, Kate conceded, was possible.

The policeman sighed before putting down his pen.

Looking through the peephole, waiting for the figure to appear, Kate thought perhaps a missing-person's report had been entered on the police computer and a match had been made. To what? A body? Kate's imagination was racing when a man wearing a yellow jacket appeared. He was small, dark-haired and in his mid-thirties, Italian-looking: a courier. Kate was relieved and not relieved at the same time. Were the police even looking for Flora?

'It'd better not be for someone else in the building,' she grumbled to the man after opening the door.

'Flora Tolmie?' He held up a brown A4 envelope.

Kate nodded, said 'OK', then tucked the envelope under her right arm, which allowed her to clutch the duvet around her as well as to provide a scribbled signature. 'Hands and sleep, I don't have sufficient of either right now,' she muttered, before pushing the door shut with a foot.

In the kitchen, she placed the envelope on the table and recognized the rectangular address label. It was illustrated with a logo of a baby's hand clutching at a miniature rainbow and, in small print, also in rainbow colours, was written 'Help the Christina Tolmie Foundation care for vulnerable children'.

Having worried herself sick about Flora, she was suddenly optimistic. Her sister must have been in contact with her office yesterday or that morning, probably with Luke, her supercilious assistant, otherwise why would a courier have been dispatched to the flat? Her sister must have said she would be returning today. She must be all right.

Hope, Kate was aware at that moment, thrived without much nourishing, unlike the vulnerable children that her sister wanted to help. Kate cautioned herself against jumping to big conclusions on such flimsy evidence.

For a while, she stared at the envelope, as if trying to discern its contents. The only thing preventing her from tearing it open was the thought that Flora might be on her way. What if she returned and found the envelope opened? She'd be cross, but she'd be cross anyway when Kate owned up to breaking into the bottom drawer of her desk, splintering the wood, and rifling through her confidential papers, also at having reported her missing to the police.

Kate resolved to open the envelope. What older sister wouldn't after so many days of worrying? Alex was dead, Flora disappeared, gone off radar but apparently, wonderfully, had been in contact with Luke in her office.

Kate worked out her excuse – *I was scared, terrified; you'd have done the same if it was me* – as she slid open the envelope's flap and pulled out another, smaller, white envelope, attached to which were three green Post-it notes written by Luke. Kate resented him because, whenever she rang, he would always say Flora was busy and would promise to pass on a message, though never did and always ended the call by eliding 'Got it thanks bye' into one word.

Gotitthanksbye.

As if he couldn't get off the phone fast enough.

Hi Flors . . . Luke's message began.

Calling Flora 'Flors' was another of Kate's dislikes about Luke. 'Flors', in Kate's opinion, made her sister sound girly, lightweight, not to say part of some privately educated, entitled, posh in-crowd, which she wasn't.

Luke's note continued:

. . . I wasn't sure whether you were due back in the office today or not. By the way, your sister rang two nights ago (at two thirty-seven a.m.!!). She left a message wondering where you were, sounding hyper – one drink too many, I think! She said you weren't at Alex's house any more. I didn't return her call because I thought you might be hiding from her (I remember you telling me about a bust-up!). Concerning the attached card, I spoke to Maria by phone yesterday and gave her the gist of it in case you were in touch with her – it's similar to the others but, still, I thought you'd want to know. Maria's guess was you'd be back today. Just in case you're having a slow start or are en route I thought I'd send this to your flat. I rang your mobile yesterday and this morning and texted, but I know the signal's intermittent at Alex's.

When will we see you? Remember I'm off two days next week, Tues and Wed?

Hope you're rested after your holiday.

Luke

Hope, Kate then realized, died suddenly. It didn't linger, expire slowly or shrivel like a malnourished infant. One moment it was there, the next gone. Kate read the message again in case she'd been mistaken, but no, it was as unambiguous as Luke's contempt for her was hurtful. Flora had not recently spoken to Luke. Luke did not know about Alex being dead. Nor, it seemed, had Flora been in contact with Maria. Where was Flora? What had happened to her? The questions sounded shrill in Kate's head, like loud alarms going off.

Kate pulled off the Post-it notes. Underneath, in a hand she'd seen before, in the same black ink, was written *For the urgent attention of Flora Tolmie, chief executive of the Christina Tolmie Foundation.* Inside the envelope was a plain white card inscribed with a familiar message: *Wait outside Haymarket Station, Edinburgh, at twelve p.m. on Thursday if you're interested in discovering the truth about your mother.*

Kate wanted to shout, yell, scream at the top of her voice, at whoever was manipulating Flora, playing on her emotions. This on top of everything else. *No wonder things had got too much for her,* Kate thought, with a stab of guilt about her own unsupportive behaviour.

Kate glanced at her phone, which was on the kitchen counter. Since her break-up with Pete and the final argument with Flora she'd become disconnected, unaware of dates and time. Today, she saw, was Thursday. Twelve p.m. was in fifty-three minutes. 'All right, let's play this game,' she muttered.

She went to the bathroom, turned on the shower, then turned it off again because there wasn't time to wash. She cleaned her teeth before going to her bedroom. As she had the day before, she put on Flora's clothes – to feel closer to her – and brushed her hair. She looked in the mirror and thought she could be mistaken for her younger sister, which was good – the anonymous writer of the cards wouldn't be frightened away. Flora preferred a casual, quiet look – jeans, trainers or flats, jersey and shirts in pastel colours – whereas Kate usually liked to make statements in bolder colours, nipped-in skirts or trousers, tailored jackets, high heels.

If in clothes and temperament they were different, in looks they were similar.

Both had red hair, Flora's shorter and silkier than Kate's. Otherwise, the most noticeable physical difference was height – Kate was the taller by two inches and, wearing heels, sometimes as much as five or six inches, though not today. She wore Flora's silver trainers.

As Kate slammed shut the front door, she resolved to display another difference between the two sisters. Kate wouldn't stand and wait for someone to approach her. She'd know if anyone looked at her with any more than a passing interest. She'd trust her instincts. If she noticed a man staring at her and she felt threatened, she'd photograph him with her phone, challenge him, warn him off, tell him to stop writing anonymous letters to her sister or she'd make sure his picture was all over social media.

Her phone! It was in the flat. She ran back upstairs, left the flat door open as she hurried to the kitchen. There it was, by the kettle. After picking it up, she found herself staring at the jar of kitchen knives. A spasm passed through her, of fear: what if the man was a predator? Should she protect herself in case he attacked her? Going back downstairs Kate felt emboldened at feeling a knife in her pocket, an echo of a sensation she'd experienced once before and in comparable circumstances.

That first time, she imagined herself as a warrior going into battle for her sister.

This time was similar.

However, standing outside the station, the effect soon dissipated. Things weren't as Kate envisaged. There were more people – apart from commuters going in and out of the ticket area, a large group of tourists was milling about having alighted from two coaches. Others, like Kate, were waiting, single men as well as women. Kate's eyes would meet theirs and, once or twice, they'd look for a moment too long, as though letting Kate know their interest or attempting to gauge hers. Kate was surprised by the attention. She'd thought dressing in Flora's softer, casual style would make her less noticeable, but the opposite was turning out to be the case. Where was the mystery card-writer? Who was he? Was he one of the well-dressed office workers, passing by on their way to lunch, or was he hiding among the tourists? Kate was sure he was a man.

After ten minutes, Kate changed tactics. She stood with her eyes cast down before looking up quickly in the hope of catching someone staring at her. The first and second times, the trap caught no one. Before the third time, she became convinced she was being watched. She felt a change of atmosphere. Even though the weather hadn't altered – it was bright and pleasantly breezy – her skin became clammy and cold. She experienced an involuntary spasm of alarm followed by another of rebellion – why should a man do that to her or her sister, make her feel frightened? Her hand gripped the knife in the right-hand pocket of her coat. Once again she felt empowered, the sensation an echo from her past. Her eyes flicked up, now angry: where was he? She glanced left, right and straight ahead in succession but didn't notice anyone looking away or anyone paying attention to her at all apart from passing sideways glances, mostly from men but from women too.

She set the trap again, before jerking her head up.

But no, still she couldn't spot who it was and now she was beginning to think her mind was playing tricks on her. Another coach arrived, disgorging more tourists who assembled outside the station for a roll call by their guide before catching a train to Glasgow. A gap appeared in the thicket of bodies just as she lowered her eyes once more. She noticed a man who was sitting on the ground, a cap in front of him, begging, with a cardboard sign against his legs. *HOMELESS*, it said in large, faltering capital letters in black, and then, underneath, *Help me and you will be caring for a vulnerable person.*

It wasn't just the writing or the black ink that was familiar, it was also the message, an adaptation of 'Help the Christina Tolmie Foundation care for vulnerable children', and there was the man's stare, not sliding, lascivious, predatory or threatening, as Kate expected, but – and this she found as unnerving – admiring as a kind old uncle might be: fond and protective. Kate was thrown, not only by the fact that this man had probably been there all the time – she hadn't been looking on the ground – but by his features. Despite the grizzle of stubble, there was something about him she recognized. She cast back to the last time she had given money to a beggar, or the time before. Her habit was to drop a coin and to keep walking. She didn't engage or look into their faces. So she doubted it was a fragment of that sort of memory. She glanced quickly once more at the wording of the placard. It was a signal, she decided. This was the man.

Instead of rushing over and shouting at him, shaming him in public, taking his photograph, as she thought she would, she stayed where she was, glanced down again to try to regain her composure. She was off balance because she felt an unmistakable affinity to the man. The sensation had come out of nowhere, which she found baffling as well as peculiar – this man of all men, a beggar, who had sent alarming messages to Flora and who, by his appearance, hadn't washed or shaved for days and was dressed in several layers of old clothes, each one dirtier than the next. If she looked at him again, she told herself, she'd experience a different feeling, see a different man, see evil. But when she raised her eyes, the shifting forest of legs momentarily obscured him. Kate was impatient, nervy. She wished the tourists would go. Out of the corner of her eyes she noticed a flash of colour, movement, and glanced in that direction. Kate's attention was caught by a woman whose expression was reminiscent of Maria's, though her face was different, her skin paler and cheekbones having better definition. The woman was probably a similar age to Maria, late forties, but stylish-looking with well-cut hair and expensive clothes, a mulberry-coloured coat and cream shirt, whereas Maria only wore tracksuit bottoms and cheap tops from TK Maxx. After that rush of impressions – a fraction of time having passed – the woman glanced at her watch, displayed frustration at a missed rendezvous and turned away.

Kate turned back, disconcerted at having allowed herself

to be distracted and at her confused state: who was the beggar? Why was he familiar?

By now the milling tourists were filing into the station, the number of obscuring legs decreasing. Kate looked for the man but was dismayed to discover him gone. Still, there were his upturned cap, the 'homeless' placard and a crumpled grey blanket, so she doubted he'd gone far. Perhaps, with the money he'd collected, he was buying a drink or some food in a café along the street. Kate walked in that direction – the peculiar and puzzling sensation of affinity muddled up with anger pulling her along. She braced herself for a confrontation. She'd demand to know why he was writing letters to Flora. She'd photograph him, warn him off. She'd keep enough distance so that if he turned nasty she'd be able to make her escape. Wearing Flora's trainers instead of her more familiar high heels gave her confidence of being able to out-run him. Once again, for courage, her hand went into her mac pocket, to hold on to the knife.

16

North Parade, Southwold, on the Suffolk coast: a fine terrace of Victorian houses overlooking a beach and, jutting out, a 190-metre-long pier; seaside England at its most traditional and recognizable. Cal parked outside Sandcastle Guest House at twelve twenty-five p.m. and, having driven for seven hours, paid cursory attention to the view as he picked over his phone conversation with Gwen Hawes, the guest house owner, from the night before. Then he'd feared for Flora. He'd wondered if she was dead because Mrs Hawes sounded official, like a police officer. But, as soon as Cal asked if she knew where Flora was (was she alive?), Mrs Hawes surprised Cal by unleashing a torrent of complaint against Flora.

'Know where she is! Alive! She hasn't been out of my best room for twelve days. I've had to cancel two, no, three bookings all at short notice because she won't tell me when she's leaving, *if* she's leaving. She won't even open the door to me. Every day I put food outside her door and I say, "Tell me who I can ring, your family, your boyfriend, someone, anyone because this can't go on." Then, tonight, she gave me your name and phone number and I thought hallelujah, finally! I'm trying to run a guest house, Dr McGill, not a care home for an unhappy woman. Can you come and fetch her or send someone who will? Because this can't go on. If she's still here after tomorrow, I'll have her thrown out. I'll call the police. I've warned her.'

After taking down the guest house address, Cal said, 'Just to be clear, Mrs Hawes, I'm not that kind of doctor, a medical doctor.'

'Then what sort are you?' She was snappish, as though Cal was responsible for Flora.

'I have a PhD in marine science.'

'What use is that? The girl's ill. It's a proper doctor she needs.' A loud sigh followed.

'Mrs Hawes,' Cal asked, 'why's Flora in Southwold?'

'No, no, Dr McGill, I'm not going to waste any more time on her. All I want to know from you is whether you're going to remove her.'

'Flora has a sister. Haven't you contacted her?'

'It's you she wants, Dr McGill, heaven knows why. You or nobody, she said.'

The call ended abruptly and Cal's eyes had travelled around the bare walls of his office as if snatching a last look at the diminishing prospect of a simpler life without commitments.

Caladh.

Had Alex told Flora that Caladh was a friend she could rely upon? Was that why she'd asked for him?

He texted Mrs Hawes:

I'll come.

When?

As soon as I can. I'm in Edinburgh. It's a long way.

Now, in North Parade, Cal thought he knew why Flora wanted to see him and no one else, also why she'd abandoned her boyfriend on his deathbed. Alex must have told her about his wish to be buried in the sea loch and of Cal's long-ago promise. Had he asked Flora to contact Cal to confirm the arrangements? Had she been horrified at the idea? Had she wanted a grave she could visit? Had they fought, causing an unhappy Flora to leave? That was the most likely explanation, though it didn't explain why Flora had left Scotland and travelled to a seaside guest house in Suffolk.

Cal prepared himself for an uncomfortable confrontation with Flora. What would he say if she asked about Alex's funeral? Would he admit to burying him at sea, confess to breaking the law? If she exposed him, he'd never escape baying mobs.

He was disturbed from his preoccupation by raised voices.

Outside the guest house, a young man in dark trousers and check shirt was complaining to a middle-aged woman. She had spiky-purplish hair and large crimson-rimmed glasses. After answering him briefly, she paid the young man little further attention. Instead she inspected the boot scrape by the front door, plucked at a lavender bush and gathered up some loose gravel with the side of her foot. The young man continued his remonstrations until he was interrupted by a blonde in tight white jeans, a tan-coloured leather jacket and red and white trainers who called from the pavement, 'Victor, come on, there's no point arguing with the deaf cow.'

He answered back, 'No, Jen. We booked. It's not right.'

The flare-up ended as suddenly as it started when the blonde went to link her boyfriend's arm. She pulled him away. After an impotent roar of frustration, he accompanied her in the direction of the pier. Once they were at a safe distance the woman stared after them before looking across the road only to find her sea view blocked by a dirty old pickup. Irritation showed in her expression as she caught sight of Cal: *what now?*

Cal opened his door. 'Mrs Hawes?'

She tipped her head as though she couldn't quite hear.

'Are you Mrs Hawes?' Cal raised his voice.

She stared back.

'Gwen Hawes?' He crossed the road.

'If it's a bed you're after,' she said, 'I'm sorry. One of my rooms is out of service.' She glanced after the retreating couple as though calling them in evidence. 'I sent those two a cancellation yesterday. Said they didn't get it. What am I supposed to do? I can't let a room I haven't got. I'm not a magician.'

Cal said, 'It's not a room I'm after. I'm Cal McGill. You rang me last night. *Dr* McGill.'

Mrs Hawes's mouth moved as if she was sucking a bitter sweet. Her owlish spectacle frames gave a benign impression, her darting eyes the opposite. 'So it's you, is it?' She looked Cal up and down, then from Cal to his pickup, finding little of reassurance in either.

Her eyes narrowed while she chewed at the inside of her right cheek. After subjecting Cal to further silent scrutiny, she glanced in the direction of her open front door. 'Well, since you're here, you might as well go in. First floor, straight across the landing, the room's called Sea View. Name's on the door.'

She stepped aside. As Cal passed, she said, 'Today, not tomorrow, not next week, today. Flora Tolmie leaves my guest house today. All right?'

Cal nodded.

'Dr McGill?'

Cal glanced back.

'Don't take me for a pushover.' Mrs Hawes's hands were on her hips. 'Because I'm not one and I don't mind if you tell that to your friend.'

Cal said nothing. As he climbed the stairs, he was accompanied by a sense of foreboding, of that long-ago promise to Alex being the ruin of him.

17

'Let go of the knife. Move away. Do as I say. Now. Please.'

Kate looked at the policeman, a bulging-eyed, ruddy-cheeked young man with an anxious expression who talked in too loud a voice. He was crouching, his right arm extended. 'Miss, let go of the knife. Move away from him.'

'He's been stabbed.' Kate's head shook, confused by the policeman's misdirected concern, confused by the blood which welled and oozed from the man's stomach, around the knife's hilt. 'Is an ambulance on the way? Is a doctor coming? He needs help.'

'Miss, you've got to let go of the knife.' The policeman stretched out his arm further as if to reach her, still keeping some distance. The fingers of his open hand beckoned. 'Please.'

A siren whooped before becoming silent. Kate saw the ambulance stop by the lane's entrance. 'Thank goodness. Tell them to hurry, can't you?'

'Miss. Look at me. *Miss.*'

Instead Kate looked at the knife, at the stain which seeped across the man's clothes, at the blood on the lane, at grey cobbles spattered with dark scarlet.

'Oh, hurry,' Kate said. 'Please hurry.'

'Miss, no one will attend to him until you've released the knife. Please, miss, move away. Look at me. Here.' The fingers beckoned again.

Kate glanced at the policeman, then behind him. A man and a woman wearing green overalls and carrying bags were walking quickly along the lane.

'Here!' Kate shouted out. 'Hurry! Can you help him?' She looked at the policeman again. 'Why aren't they coming? What's wrong with them?'

'They'll attend to him the moment you let go of the knife. Please. Let go of the knife. Move away. Now.'

Kate stared at him. 'His hands are on top of mine.'

'If you remove yours his will come too. Do it. Now. Please.'

Kate glanced back at the injured man. She moved her fingers, tried to lift her hands. His hands held hers tighter. Hers were warm and sticky with blood, his were colder. 'Don't die,' she said. 'Please don't die.' She was startled to find his eyes were open. He was watching her.

His expression was soft and rheumy, that look of fondness, of affinity she had seen earlier. 'My perfect girl,' he whispered. His eyes filled with what Kate thought were tears.

'No, not perfect,' she managed to reply, and he smiled, wheezed, winced, the pain creasing across his face.

Kate felt the knife shift. 'Oh God, please help him!' she shouted behind her. 'Please, one of you, help him.'

When she turned back, he was still watching her. His head nodded slightly as if in approval.

Kate said, 'Who are you? Why do I know you?'

A smile creased his face. 'Flora . . .' he said. 'I'm your father and you're . . .' His expression became indulgent before he winced with pain. 'My girl, my perfect girl.'

*

Kate inspected her spread-out fingers with a puzzled, far-away expression as though wondering whose they were, how they had become so sticky, messy, why her wrists were cuffed. 'Is that blood?' she asked the curly-haired woman beside her. 'Real blood?' Kate's attention shifted to the scene across the lane. Two paramedics were at each side of the stabbed man, two more at his head. All Kate could see were his boots and blood. 'Is any of this real?'

Like her hands, her voice appeared separate, strange, part of her, yet not part of her.

'I'm afraid so,' the woman replied. 'What's your name?'

'Kate.'

'Your other name?'

'Tolmie.'

'Hello, Kate. I'm Helen Jamieson. I'm a detective sergeant. You've had a shock, Kate, haven't you?' Helen watched for a reaction. 'Do you know who that man is, Kate?'

Kate shook her head.

'Are you certain?' It was a question but not a question, more an expression of curiosity. 'Don't you know him?'

Kate looked into Helen's face with the same bemused expression with which she had been regarding her bloodied hands. 'Do I? I don't think so.'

'He says he's your father. He says your name is Flora. But Flora's your sister, isn't she?'

'Yes. Flora . . .' Kate blinked, as though trying to remember something. She wiped her face with her left hand, leaving a crimson smear on her cheek.

'Is that man your father?'

Kate said, 'I don't have a father. I've never had a father. He can't be my father.'

'No?' The same soft expression of curiosity.

'No.'

'What happened to him, Kate?'

Kate shuddered. 'There's a knife in his stomach. It's horrible.'

'Who put it there, Kate? Did he do it or did someone else?'

'I think he did.'

'Did you see him?'

Kate shook her head. 'No.'

'Did he tell you he'd stabbed himself?'

'No.'

'Was there anyone else in the lane?'

'I didn't see anyone.'

'So you found him like this. It was just you and him, no one else?'

'I think so, yes.'

'What was he doing?'

'He was holding on to the knife and the blood was coming out through his clothes.' Kate stared at her hands. 'Blood everywhere.'

'So he'd already been stabbed when you found him?'

'Yes.'

'And slumped down like that?'

'He was standing when I first saw him. Then he fell.'

'Did he say anything?'

'He said I was perfect.'

'I think he said something more.'

Silence.

'Didn't he call you his perfect girl?'

'Yes.'

'That was an odd thing for him to say. Why would he say that?'

'I don't know. I think he thought I was Flora.'

'Why would he think that?'

'We look alike.' Kate stared at her hands before wiping them on Flora's jeans. 'I'm wearing Flora's clothes.'

'I see,' the policewoman said.

Silence.

'The thing is, Kate, the guys over there . . .' Helen nodded towards the paramedics but kept her eyes on Kate. 'They say he's been stabbed in the back as well as the front.' Helen widened her eyes, inviting Kate to draw a conclusion. 'Someone else must have done that, Kate, don't you think?'

'There wasn't anyone else,' Kate said.

'Because,' Helen carried on, 'I don't see how that poor man could have stabbed himself in the back and then removed the knife and stabbed himself in the stomach.'

Kate listened. Helen watched her reaction. 'Can you explain that, Kate?'

'No.'

'It's a hard one . . .' Helen paused. 'The thing is . . . the thing I need to find out, and quickly, is whether someone dangerous is out there or whether –' Helen watched Kate's eyes – 'you stabbed him.'

'No.' Kate shook her head. 'No.'

Kate saw a paramedic stand up and speak to a uniformed policeman close by. The policeman looked in Helen's direction. There was a brief shake of his head followed by a nod of hers.

'I'm sorry, Kate.'

'Why?'

'Your father's dead.'

'I don't have a father. I've never had a father.'

A wicker tray with leftover breakfast was on the carpet outside Flora Tolmie's door. Cal poured coffee into her used cup, gulped a cold mouthful, then another. He heard Mrs Hawes moving about downstairs, followed by the sound of a radio, two men having a heated discussion about the state of the economy. After returning the cup, Cal wiped his mouth with the back of his hand. 'Flora, hi . . . it's Cal McGill.' His knuckles rapped on the door. 'Flora . . .' A floorboard creaked followed by the snap of metal. Cal wasn't sure whether she was letting him in or locking him out. He tried the handle and opened the door on to a room which was high-ceilinged, simply furnished with a sand-coloured rug, framed prints of beach scenes on the wall, a bedside table and lamp, an armchair covered with chintz print of sailing ships and a large iron bedstead. Flora was walking away, towards the window. She was five feet six or seven, barefoot, dressed in black jeans and a lime-green jersey. Her hair was lighter in colour than Kate's – pale ginger compared to rust-red – shorter, shoulder-length rather than down her back, finertextured. She stopped by a round table on which was an old-fashioned and battered small brown suitcase held together by two frayed leather straps. She spoke without looking at Cal. 'I know Alex is dead.' Her voice sounded dead too.

'I wasn't sure if you did or not,' Cal said. 'I'm sorry.'

Her head shook, a succession of tiny tremors, and Cal wondered if she'd spoken those words out loud before: *I know Alex is dead.*

The quiet in the room was in contrast to the noise of the radio downstairs. It provided a jarring and contentious intrusion, the argument about the economy gaining passion. Cal reduced the volume by closing the door. 'Alex loved you, you know,' he found himself saying when he turned back to Flora. 'When I met you last year . . . do you remember? . . . I asked him whether you two were serious, forever serious, and he replied, yes, he thought so, he hoped so.'

She looked at Cal, her face smaller, rounder and softer-edged than Kate's. Her eyes were dulled and lifeless like her voice. There was no anger in them, nor any animosity against him. Perhaps, Cal thought, she was unaware of his role in digging up Alex's grave and burying him at sea.

She asked, 'Have you spoken to Alex's family?'

'Yes,' Cal replied, 'to Mrs Lauder.'

'She blames me for Alex's death? Did she tell you that?'

'She talked about a lot of things,' Cal replied. 'I don't think she knew what she was saying. Her son had just died. She was upset, flailing about for an explanation, to make sense of it all, for someone to blame.'

'What did she say about me?'

'Really, she wasn't herself.' Cal tried to deflect her again.

'Tell me,' Flora insisted. 'Please.'

Cal sighed. 'She said Alex lost the will to live after you'd gone. She said you abandoned him because he was dying.

She said your interest was the future, having fun, not Alex, not what might have been.'

Flora's head jerked as if he had hit her. 'That's not true.'

For a while neither spoke. Apart from her right forefinger stroking the edge of the suitcase on the table, she didn't move. Cal wondered if that was all she wanted to know. Had he left Edinburgh early in the morning and driven 400 miles for an exchange lasting less than a minute? In that brief time, he realized Mrs Lauder's assessment of Flora was wrong. Rather than a young woman who was cut and dried about leaving her dying boyfriend, this flesh-and-blood, living and breathing version of Flora Tolmie appeared not to have moved on at all.

Which begged the question: why did she leave Alex? If not about his burial arrangements, then what?

Flora's finger stopped. 'I didn't know Alex was going to die the next day. I thought he would live for weeks, months even. The doctors said . . . I thought I would see him again.' Her finger started moving, faster than before, in agitation. 'Afterwards . . . Alex's father rang me to tell me I'd killed his son by running out on him. He said I wouldn't be welcome at the funeral.'

'I know,' Cal said. 'Mrs Lauder told me.'

'Can I . . .' She hesitated. 'Can I ask . . . about . . . ?'

Cal noticed how her head shook, more little tremors. These, it occurred to Cal, were not caused by shock or emotion as before but by the question she was about to ask. His answer appeared to matter.

'About the funeral?' he suggested.

She shook her head, then took a deep breath, steeling herself before carrying on. 'Before I left . . . Alex gave me a ring. He asked me to be his wife. Everything had been planned. His father would marry us in church the next day.' Another breath. 'I felt uncomfortable. It was all so sudden.'

Cal said, 'You felt you should have been consulted?'

Flora looked towards the window. Her finger continued to stroke the suitcase. 'Alex hadn't mentioned marriage before. We talked about everything, *everything*. We loved each other. I thought we were happy as we were. But, without telling me, Alex had arranged a surprise wedding. There was no time for discussion. I had to say yes or no.'

'And he was dying,' Cal said. 'Difficult for you.'

'I didn't want to hurt him. I loved him.'

'What did you say?' Cal noticed the fingers of her left hand were clenched tight and pressed against her thigh, hiding where a ring might have been.

'I tried to sound happy, to *be* happy.'

Cal nodded, sympathizing.

'As soon as I put on the ring, Alex said I might grow to hate him after he was dead, also I'd question whether he ever loved me. He said the ring, the wedding, would be proof of his love and if I found myself hating him, I should look at the ring. I should read the marriage certificate. I should take out the photographs of the wedding.' A little cry, despair, escaped from her. 'He'd even arranged a photographer.'

'Why did he think you would hate him?'

'I don't know. He wouldn't tell me. It was to do with his past.' She frowned. 'He said it was the reason we met, why he arranged to meet me.'

'Where was that?'

'In a supermarket, pushing trolleys. I thought by accident. He always told me it was love at first sight for him. But it wasn't, was it? He knew I was going to be there. He planned it. He must have followed me. What reason would he have had? A bet? Did he pick up girls in supermarkets? He said I would hate him if I found out. What could it be? Why wouldn't he tell me?'

Cal was still puzzling over Flora's revelation – Alex wasn't that kind of person; he didn't have secrets – when she sighed.

'I took off the ring. I said I couldn't wear it, not until I knew why I'd hate him. I told him I'd go away for two or three days. Then I'd speak to him again. I'd only return if he was prepared to be honest, open with me. I thought I'd see him again.' She watched Cal. 'You were his friend. Why would I have hated him?'

'I've no idea,' Cal said. 'None. Are you sure he wasn't confused? He was ill, taking medication. At that stage, he might have been muddled, frightened. He might have imagined you hating him. The drugs . . . He was desperate, clinging on to life. The ring and the wedding were his responses. He was trying to hold on to you as well.'

A long exhalation followed: sadness as well as exhaustion. 'Why did he die?' she asked. 'He was expected to live for weeks, months.' The speed of events appeared to daze her, also the feeling she could have done something, said something different, to change how things ended between them. 'You know my mother went missing a long time ago?'

'Yes, I gather you've been trying to find out what happened to her.' Not for the first time Cal was surprised at the direction of the conversation. He played along. 'You've launched a charity in her memory, haven't you?'

'The timing –' a shadow darkened Flora's face – 'was awful. I had so much to do, dates in the diary, clothes to collect and distribute, and then Alex found out he was dying. We sat down and talked about everything. At the time, during the week he was living in a small flat in Oban because he was involved in a sea loch research project at SAMS. At weekends he would either stay with me in Edinburgh or I would go with him to his parents' house. For his treatment we thought he should be with his parents because he could walk in the hills every day, visit the sea loch nearby, continue his research. I thought that would help to keep his strength up, his spirits up. He thought so too. I said I would drive north to be with him every Friday afternoon, after lunch, and leave again on Monday morning. I made him promise to tell me if the arrangement wasn't working for him, and if it wasn't, I'd drop everything and come to live with him because nothing was more important than him.'

A pause, a silent punctuation that Cal recognized as regret: if she had the conversation again she would have chosen differently.

'So,' she continued, 'during the week, we'd speak every day, twice a day, and I'd tell him about work, about the people I'd met, you know, just chat. I thought he'd want to be distracted . . . a respite from having to think about hospitals and doctors. At weekends, we'd go for walks when he felt well enough.' She looked out of the window, then back at Cal. 'Perhaps that's why he bought a ring, arranged a wedding without telling me. He thought I wasn't in love with him any more because of the time I spent away from him, trying to set up the charity. Do you think he thought that?'

Cal said, 'I don't know. Even if he did, it wouldn't explain why he talked about you growing to hate him.'

Flora's eyes suddenly opened wide. She looked shocked, startled. 'I shouldn't have taken the ring off, should I? I shouldn't have given it back to him. I should have said, "I don't know what all this is about, Alex, but I'm going to leave you for a day or two to give you time to explain your past, this thing that you think will make me hate you, and I'll continue to wear your ring until you do, because I can't imagine anything you've done, anything in your past, could ever make me hate you." If I'd done that, if I'd kept his ring on, he'd still be alive.'

Not just dazed, Cal thought, but a young woman who had been in this guest house bedroom too long and had begun to invent a narrative of blame about Alex in the absence of any other explanation about the suddenness of his death.

Cal glanced around the room. 'Why are you here?'

'I didn't know where else to go,' Flora replied, misunderstanding him. 'I didn't know what to do. I needed time to think.'

Instead of repeating the question, he said, 'Your sister's been looking for you.'

'You've spoken to Kate?' Flora sounded surprised.

'She came to my office, asking if I knew where you were. She'd heard about Alex. She told me you'd written down my name, also "Speak to Alex about him". She thought you might have been in touch with me. I said you hadn't. She was upset.'

Flora turned away, upset too.

Cal tried again. 'I meant why here, in Southwold? Why did you come here?'

'Because —' Flora looked at the small brown suitcase — 'Mrs Hawes heard me on the radio talking about a suitcase that was with my mother when she vanished. The description was familiar to Mrs Hawes and she contacted me to say it had washed up near here on the beach, and had spent the last twenty-three years hidden under some newspapers in her garage.'

She glanced at Cal. 'I've spent most of my life trying to find my mother and this is the first clue to turn up since she disappeared.' A shrug, then her eyes widened: her answer to Cal's question about Southwold: why here? 'I didn't know where else to go,' she repeated.

Cal nodded.

'Cal, please . . .' She was nervous. What she was about to ask mattered. 'Will you help me find my mother?'

18

Flora unbuckled the straps, snapped open twin metal fasteners and flipped back the suitcase lid. Inside were two identical holdalls, plastic, both water-stained and unevenly discoloured. The shades varied between pale pink, orange and brown. The original red colour only remained in stripes at the corners. Flora unzipped one and removed clothes – a blue jersey, followed by two shirts, white and pale blue, grey trousers, socks, pants and black lace-up shoes – by the size, for a child. Apart from the shoes being old-fashioned, Cal noticed the leather soles were without scratches or visible wear.

After laying out the clothes, Flora said, 'I was four years old when my mother disappeared. Her van was found abandoned in Gravelines, not far from Calais. Apart from this suitcase, nothing has turned up since, no witness or sighting, no sign of her.' Flora's hands gripped the suitcase's edge. Cal had the impression she had little else left to hold on to. 'I didn't tell Alex about it being found straight away.'

A pause.

'When I did, he was angry, which wasn't like him. He was concerned about me going to Southwold, spending more time away. He said I'd be chasing ghosts. I told him I hadn't seen the suitcase for twenty-three years and a little longer wouldn't matter. Being with him was more important to me.' She glanced at Cal, shook her head. 'He didn't believe me. He continued to behave oddly, as though the suitcase was somehow a threat to him. Two days later he produced the ring and asked me to marry him.'

Another pause.

'I asked Alex about you – he was always talking about you and your work. But he was insistent I shouldn't contact you. He said you wouldn't be interested. When he was asleep I found your number in his phone.'

Cal said, 'Interested in what?'

'I need to know –' she glanced at the suitcase – 'whether it's possible, after all this time, to work out where this came from.'

'That depends.'

'On what?'

'Whether you have dates, when and where it was found, when it was lost, the more exact the better.'

'My mother was last seen on the sixteenth of August . . .'

'Twenty-three years ago?'

'Yes,' Flora said. Her mouth flinched. 'I don't know the exact date the suitcase was found, except it was later that month. Mrs Hawes recalls her husband bringing it home after an early-morning walk on the beach. The next day he lost his job with a local estate agent. She remembers the sequence because his redundancy money, twenty-five thousand pounds, paid for the alterations to convert this property into a guest house – they added a kitchen and new bathrooms. In all the upheaval, furniture being moved in and out, the suitcase was left in the garage. Mrs Hawes discovered it a few weeks ago when she was having a clear-out after her husband's death.'

Flora ran her fingers along the front of the suitcase. 'This was mine when I was young. I used it for dolls and dressing-up clothes. Whenever my mother went away . . . She was always going away . . . I made her take it with her. I thought it would keep her safe.'

She angled the lid towards Cal. 'Please look after my mummy' was painted inside in big, uneven letters, each letter a different size and colour. The paint was faint, faded by time and water but legible. 'And when she came home,' Flora continued, 'there'd always be a present for me inside. Recently, I talked about that on the radio. I said I'd painted, "Please look after my mummy" inside the lid and Mrs Hawes heard the interview. She got in touch.'

Flora held up the trousers from the holdall and unfolded them. Like the shoes, they looked unworn and for someone small, a boy. 'My mother used to fill up her van with second-hand clothes and take them to orphanages in Romania and other countries. When she came back she told us about the children she met, how unhappy they were. Before her last trip, she asked me what present I would like and I said, "Can I have a big brother, one of those unhappy orphanage boys?" because I was always fighting with Kate and she was bigger and stronger than me.' Flora put down the trousers and picked up a white shirt which had gone greyish, followed by a pair of grey socks. She shot an anxious glance at Cal. 'My mother wouldn't have done that for me, would she? She wouldn't have tried to bring me that present, an orphanage boy? That wouldn't be why she never came back, would it?'

Not just a narrative of blame about Alex's death, Cal

thought. Flora also regarded herself as responsible for the fate of her mother.

'Will you help me?' Once again she stared at the suitcase. 'I have to find out where this came from.'

'I'll do what I can,' Cal replied guardedly. What he meant was, *It's difficult, an inexact science, time has passed, I can't promise a result.*

'Oh,' Flora said, misunderstanding, 'not for nothing. I'll pay, of course I will.'

From the table, behind the suitcase, she grabbed at a shoulder bag, removed her purse and opened it. 'Oh God, I haven't got enough, have I?' She counted some notes. 'Two hundred pounds . . .?' she inquired doubtfully. From another flap she took other money. She counted again. 'And about seventy euros? Sorry. I'll transfer more.' She reddened. 'Stupid, my phone's in the car.'

Cal said, 'Really, you don't need to pay me,' as Flora returned to her bag and brought out a pen. 'No, I do,' she insisted, writing on one of the notes which she'd put on the table. 'There, that's my phone number and email address. Send me your bank details.'

Cal changed the subject. 'The other holdall. What's in it?'

'Nothing, it's empty.'

Going closer, he opened and closed the zips, checked inside both bags. 'That's helpful.'

'What is?'

'They're waterproof. The air inside would have given buoyancy. The suitcase would have floated higher in the water. That's important . . .'

A knocking interrupted them.

Mrs Hawes's head pushed round the opening door. 'Time's up. I want you out!'

'Please, Mrs Hawes,' Flora said, 'not now.'

The two women argued but Cal paid little attention because his phone had vibrated in his pocket and he was reading a text from Helen Jamieson.

I need to talk to you. NOW. A man's been murdered by Haymarket Station. Kate Tolmie's in custody. She was arrested at the scene holding a knife, the murder weapon. Before he died, the victim mistook Kate for her sister Flora, said he was her father. Cal, where is Flora? Where are you? Ring me.

19

The assembled detectives talked quietly while glancing at a slight, vulpine-looking individual at the front of the room. He was crouched in a chair, wore old jeans, a black T-shirt under a faded, cracked leather jacket. He was nervy-looking, as though in urgent need of drugs or whisky. At either side of him, seated on the edge of desks, were two detective inspectors, hemming him in, as if preventing an escape. They were burly, overweight, wore shirts and ties, apparently a different species of humanity to the crouching man who looked half starved. That and his pallor suggested poverty, one of society's cast-offs, a criminal. The impression changed as soon as he pushed back his chair and lifted up his thin, sharp face. The room became hushed, still.

'Do any of you know how many murders there were in this city last year?' Detective Chief Inspector Richard Beacom spoke softly. The detectives leaned forward to hear him. 'There were four. Just four, that's one every three months. Today, we've had three.' He glanced at the clock on the wall. 'It's only mid-afternoon, so there's time for more. Three in one day: you know how stretched we're going to be.' His mouth pulled to one side. 'Your partners, spouses, children, dogs, cats, favourite bars, mothers, cocaine suppliers . . .'

Nervous laughter which died.

'You're going to become strangers to the lot of them until these killers are caught. This is going to be a test. Don't fail it. That's why I'm here, why I've been brought in, to make sure you don't screw up any more, OK?'

Beacom's eyes darted from detective to detective. 'OK.' This time he wasn't asking a question; he was telling them. 'Here's what we've got.

'At seven twenty-three, the body of a man thought to be in his twenties or thirties was found on wasteland in north-east Edinburgh. A dog walker made the discovery. The victim was naked, without hands and a face – all three apparently blasted off by a shotgun. Which would have been noisy. And messy. None of the missing body parts have been recovered. The victim has not been identified. Motive? It could be territorial – drugs – sex, jealousy or betrayal, perhaps two or more in combination.

'The second murder happened at seven minutes past eleven. Two youths pursued by six or seven others, reports vary, ran through the Grassmarket in central Edinburgh, turning over open-air restaurant tables, scattering tourists. After the youths had departed the scene, a waiter was discovered to be dead. His throat had been cut. We don't know whether the killing was planned – the stampede to distract the intended victim – or was done on the spur of the moment. Did the waiter get in the way of the pursuing gang? Was he in the wrong place at the wrong time? The victim was aged nineteen, unmarried, Somali by origin. Was his killing opportunistic prejudice or premeditated? None of the youths has been identified or arrested. They wore hoodies.

'The third murder . . .' Beacom's face tipped upward, as if to God. 'Even an atheist like me can be excused a prayer today.' His cheeks expanded. He blew out air. 'Lord, don't let there be a fourth. Lord, are you listening?'

Laughter, which died.

'The third murder was reported by a member of the public at twelve seventeen. Louis Dufour, mid-fifties, was found bleeding to death close to Haymarket Station. A female suspect, Kate Tolmie, twenty-nine, was arrested at the scene. Dufour, a serial offender, was well known to the Metropolitan Police. He had convictions for fraud, petty theft, some violence. Before he died, he claimed to be the female suspect's father, which might explain his presence in Edinburgh. When police arrived on the scene at twelve twenty-six, Kate Tolmie was holding the knife in Dufour's stomach. She was covered in his blood. Motive? In this case, it's probably clear-cut. If Dufour was her father, she had every reason to be aggrieved against him: he abandoned her before birth, played no part in her life. It's possible she hadn't ever met him before. Although Tolmie denies sticking the knife into Dufour – he was also stabbed in the back – it's unlikely anyone else was involved. CCTV shows Dufour departing Haymarket Station at twelve thirteen. Four minutes later, the alarm was raised by a member of the public who saw the suspect kneeling by Dufour's collapsed body, holding the knife. Who else would have had opportunity in those four minutes? Also, another similar knife was found on the suspect in her coat pocket.

'So . . .' Beacom studied the assembled detectives. 'Are we agreed about the third case, the Dufour murder? There isn't a killer still on the loose?'

A murmur of agreement.

'So, we concentrate our resources on the other two inquiries. Thank you, everyone. By this time tomorrow I want the killers found. This is your opportunity to show you're not as bad a team of detectives as recent results appear to show.'

One of the inspectors leaned down and spoke into Beacom's ear. 'Thank you, DI Ronaldsay.' Beacom raised his hand. The departing detectives stopped. Beacom said, 'As you know, DI Ronaldsay is running the headless corpse inquiry and DI Welby the Grassmarket murder. DS Jamieson will take on the Dufour case.' He nodded at Helen who was still standing at the back of the room.

The other detectives scowled in Jamieson's direction.

'No doubt you're wondering why Helen's been given the Dufour murder. I expect you think it's because I've brought her with me and I'm giving her the easy job. Well? Do you?'

No one replied.

'Tell them, Helen,' Beacom said.

'Tell them why I'm on the Dufour murder, boss?'

'Yes.'

'I suppose because I spoke to Kate Tolmie, the suspect, at the scene.'

'That, yes, but not only that.'

'What else, sir?'

'You didn't agree with me just now when I said, about the Dufour case, that there wasn't a killer on the loose.'

'Didn't I, sir?'

'No,' Beacom replied. 'Explain why not.'

Helen glanced around her new colleagues, appearing uneasy, reddening. 'Well, sir, because I don't think Kate Tolmie would have killed Dufour, at least not when she did.'

'Why not?'

'She didn't have time to talk to him, not if only four minutes passed between Dufour leaving the station and the eyewitness seeing Kate Tolmie holding the knife and kneeling by Dufour's body.'

A murmur, disagreement, rippled around the other detectives.

Beacom held up his hand. The murmur stopped. 'And why would she have wanted to talk to him before sticking a knife into him?'

'Well,' Helen said, 'Kate Tolmie's mother, Christina, disappeared twenty-three years ago. She wasn't married but she had two children, both daughters, by an unknown father. Kate was six when Christina went missing in the French town of Gravelines, near Calais. Whether Dufour was the father or not, he was the reason Kate Tolmie went to Haymarket Station. She was there instead of her sister, Flora, who'd received an anonymous card instructing her to be there at noon to discover the truth about her mother. Since that was Kate's reason for going, I think she would have asked some questions before killing Dufour. Four minutes didn't give her any time. It doesn't make any sense that Kate didn't take the opportunity to talk to him, because she knows that, with Dufour dead, the truth about her mother's disappearance almost certainly died with him.'

Beacom smiled. 'You see.' He glanced around the other detectives. 'That's why I've brought Helen with me. She can be a pain in the arse sometimes, but she's thorough.

I like that.' He squinted at the other detectives as if trying to find a similar quality in them. Apparently disappointed, he said, 'You lot could learn from her,' and stood up.

At the door, he glanced back over his shoulder. 'Helen.'

'Yes, sir.'

'Let me know when you're ready to interview Kate Tolmie. I'll sit in.'

'Yes, sir.' *Thank you, sir, for making my colleagues resent me even more than they do already.*

Cal found a breaking news report on the *Scotsman* newspaper website. He read from his phone: '"The dead man is believed to be Louis Dufour, in his mid-fifties, an alcoholic, sometime drug abuser of French origin with an extensive criminal record."' Cal looked up. 'Shall I go on?'

Flora mouthed yes.

Mrs Hawes stood by the door, her lips pressed tight, the colour from her face draining away, an alarmed expression forming.

'"According to police sources",' Cal continued, '"Mr Dufour told paramedics before his death that he was the father of a twenty-nine-year-old woman who was found at the scene of the stabbing. She was arrested and is helping police with their inquiries."'

He refreshed the page. '"Detectives also want to interview the suspect's twenty-seven-year-old sister, Flora. The two women are said to be co-owners of a flat in the Bruntsfield area of Edinburgh."'

Cal looked up and asked Flora, 'What do you want to do?'

'What? What?' Flora appeared to be waking from a stupor.

Before Cal could repeat his question, Mrs Hawes began to move around the room, speaking loudly as she went. 'No, I'm not having the police here, not being dragged into this. Do you hear?' She was collecting Flora's possessions – a washbag from the en-suite bathroom, two books on the bedside table, pyjamas from under a pillow, a shirt and jeans from the end of the bed. In between, she stopped and complained – how she, Mrs Hawes, had been taken advantage of, how she wished she'd never contacted Flora. 'Now this, *this*.'

She threw Flora's things on to the landing and stood by the open door. 'You're leaving, both of you, and if you tell the police or anyone else you were here . . . if you men-tion the Sandcastle Guest House, ever, my lawyer will be on to you. Go. Get out. This second. Now.'

Outside, on the pavement, Flora stood by her car, a white Mini. She seemed disorientated, as if she'd taken a blow to the head and, in a manner of speaking, Cal thought, she had. Her reactions were slow motion, delayed. 'I should go to Edinburgh, to Kate,' she said as though she was not sure if she should or not, as if she was asking Cal.

She opened her car door and Cal said, 'Are you all right to drive?'

'I'm fine, really.' She glanced towards the sea, before sitting in the car. Her hands gripped the steering wheel as previously they'd clutched the suitcase. Her eyes met his. 'It's my fault, isn't it . . . ? All this . . . this nightmare . . . what's happened to Kate?' Before Cal could answer, she cried out, 'Oh, the suitcase, it's still in the room!'

'Don't worry,' Cal reassured her. 'I'll look after it.'

Flora nodded and watched Cal — at first she appeared to be wondering whether she could trust him, then her expression became puzzled. 'Alex was wrong about me. I won't ever hate him.'

'I know,' Cal said.

As Flora drove away, Cal almost shouted after her, *The suitcase doesn't matter, only Kate matters.* But the suitcase *did* matter. It was the beginning of a story, a silent witness to Christina Tolmie's disappearance. And it mattered because the mystery gave Cal a chance, or so it seemed to him at that moment, to counter the narrative which usually played in his head: he let people down, was an unreliable friend.

There and then he made a promise, just as he had to Alex on the sea loch. 'Will you help me?' Flora had asked him. In reply, he'd said, 'I'll do what I can.' Now he nodded: *Yes.* He nodded again as though fixing his resolve. *Yes*: he'd work out the suitcase's journey — how it washed up at Southwold. Also, if luck was with him, he'd discover what happened to Flora's mother. This investigation, he decided, would be his finale.

In memory of Alex, he'd be Caladh.

He turned back towards the guest house to collect the suitcase and found Mrs Hawes standing guard on her front path. She scuffed at some loose gravel, plucked at a lavender bush and kicked against the boot scrape as if trying to dislodge dirt from her shoe. The performance was similar to that which Cal had witnessed earlier when Victor, the angry young man in the check shirt, had been remonstrating about his cancelled booking. Then, Mrs Hawes had put on a show of being oblivious to anything apart from her front path. Now, she was unable to keep up a similar pretence. While going through her repertoire, she glanced slyly at Cal.

Cal approached. 'That wasn't necessary.'

Mrs Hawes stopped plucking at the lavender bush, looked along the street one way, then the other, avoiding catching Cal's eye, as if she had heard her name being called and wasn't sure from which direction.

Cal said to her, 'Was it?'

Instead of answering, she put her hand in her overall pocket and took out an envelope. 'That's some money she left. If it was meant for me, tell her I don't want it, I don't want anything to do with her or anything of hers to be connected with my guest house.'

Cal took the envelope. 'What about the suitcase?'

'What about it?'

'It was Flora's.'

'Was it?' Mrs Hawes turned and walked towards her front door.

Cal said, 'You told Flora your husband found it the day before he was made redundant. What was the date?'

Mrs Hawes didn't look round, didn't reply.

Cal tried again. 'Mrs Hawes, that suitcase might lead to Christina Tolmie, Flora's mother. The date's important.'

In the doorway she stopped, turned her head a little, not far enough to see Cal. 'The suitcase was my husband's property for longer than it was that young woman's or her mother's. I don't think we have anything else to say to each other, do you, *Mr* McGill?'

The door banged shut.

Cal stayed where he was for a few moments, then

muttered, 'Bitch' before crossing North Parade. He looked at the beach below. All those years ago a suitcase had washed up there. Where had it been? What caused it to become separated from Christina Tolmie?

He went to his pickup, folding Flora's money into his pocket. Just as he was about to open the driver's door, he noticed wisps of black smoke rising from the rear of the guest house. A fire seemed to have started in the back garden. As Cal watched, the smoke became thicker, blacker. He suspected he knew what was being burnt. He crossed the road to a B & B two doors away which advertised 'Vacancies' and 'Pets welcome'. After ringing the bell, Cal was met by a woman who was attached to a large, stragglyhaired, thin-faced dog. Cal looked from one to the other and the woman laughed.

'Don't say it.' She put on a child's voice. 'Say, missus, did you always look like that or did you take after your dog?' She smiled at Cal. 'I'm always getting that from kids.' She looked at her dog. 'Isn't she gorgeous, though? I don't mind if I look like her at all, do I, Saffron?' She ruffled the dog's head. 'If it's a room you're after, the owner's out, I'm afraid.'

'Pity,' Cal said, 'because I'm scouting for my aunt. She likes seaside holidays but prefers a room without a sea view.' He shrugged. 'She says it's because the noise of the waves keeps her awake but really it's because rooms at the back are cheaper. She's always been careful with money.' Cal smiled, glanced along the road. 'You don't know how long the owner will be?'

Cal resolved never again to pretend to have a helpless grandmother or aunt or to act the dutiful grandson or nephew.

The woman seemed not to notice his awkwardness. 'Tell you what,' she replied. 'I could show you a room at the back. I come here so often I'm almost resident. Aren't I, Saffron?' The dog stretched its neck to meet her hand. 'Maggie – she's the owner – won't mind a bit.'

'Could you?' Cal said. 'That would be kind.'

'Now, gorgeous, you just stay here for a minute . . .' She patted the dog and looped the lead handle over a coat hook.

Cal followed the woman along a black-and-white-tiled hall and up polished wood stairs.

'First floor all right?' she asked when she stopped outside a door. 'This one's unoccupied. I'd show you mine but I look out over the sea.'

'It's just to . . . Well, you know how it is. My aunt doesn't often get away. I don't want her to be disappointed.'

The room was gloomy with thin curtains covering the windows. There was an armchair, two single beds, a bedside table between them and a lamp. 'Simple but clean,' the straggly-haired woman said.

'Yes, I can see.' Cal sounded encouraged. He went to the window and peered out through a gap in the curtains. He glanced right. In a small courtyard garden, Mrs Hawes was standing beside an incinerator, a galvanized bin, into which she was lowering the suitcase suspended at the end of a garden fork, holding it in the flames. Black smoke was drifting around her. Cal took out his phone. 'So I can show my aunt the view from the back window,' he explained. 'Of course, she'll have the final say.'

Afterwards, Cal gave the room another inspection. 'You know,' he smiled at the woman, 'I think she'll be happy here.'

Going downstairs, the woman announced her impending arrival to her dog, which was letting out excited yelps – 'Yes, yes, my darling, you just love your walk on the beach, don't you? Love to run into the sea and get wet, don't you?'

Cal's thoughts were on Mrs Hawes. In Flora's room, and afterwards, she had given the impression of being worried about the reputation of her business being damaged by any association with Flora. Watching her in her back garden, Cal witnessed a different Mrs Hawes. This version – the rictus expression on her face, the frequency with which she glanced about her – revealed a woman in fright at approaching and imminent danger. What, Cal wondered, was she so afraid of?

20

Sarah checked the time after putting down her suitcase inside the front door. The bus would arrive in fourteen minutes. She'd better go and see Lotte, say goodbye before departing for London. One of them had better behave normally. She glanced along her hall at her driftwood man, remembering the awkward walk home from lunch the previous day, remembering Lotte being so high-handed and dismissive. *You are being silly.*

Following their fight yesterday – *Was it a fight? What was it, exactly?* – Sarah wondered if Lotte's warning about Olaf (*Sarah, be careful*) was proprietorial. The suspicion hardened when Sarah knocked at Lotte's door and no one answered. At Lotte's gate, she ran into Jan De Vries, the neighbour on the other side, a retired lawyer from The Hague, who said he'd seen Lotte leaving early, about seven in the morning: 'One of her Amsterdam days.'

'Why didn't she say she was visiting her aunt?' Sarah blurted with more force than she intended.

Mr De Vries shook his head, apologized, said he didn't know and looked a little worried at having got Lotte into trouble.

Sarah thanked him and hurried to the bus stop, trying to work out Lotte's motive for keeping her trip to Amsterdam a secret. Was it because she thought Sarah might offer to travel with her? No: she knew Sarah's flight to London wasn't until evening. Also, when Sarah had suggested travelling together in the future, she'd added, 'Obviously not tomorrow,' and Lotte hadn't said anything about Amsterdam.

'Of course,' Sarah said under her breath, the truth dawning as she waited by the bus shelter. 'Lotte arranged to visit her aunt after our lunch! When I reminded her I was going to London she made sure she went to Amsterdam today. That way, she'll have Olaf to herself tomorrow and the next day while I'm away.' Sarah's expression was puzzled. 'Why does she want him to herself?'

Later, on the bus to the ferry, Sarah stared out of the window. The fields passed by without her noticing. She was anxious. A few days ago, she was unaware of tension between Lotte and her. Sarah was also concerned about Olaf. 'Please don't,' she said out loud to the window. 'Please, Lotte, don't say anything stupid to him, like why his driftwood men don't have mouths.'

For the remainder of the journey to the south of the island, she reflected on her driftwood man, what it meant to her. It was made of wood, tin and plastic which had washed up on Texel. Like the others, it didn't have a mouth. It couldn't tell a story. Not Olaf's – as Lotte thought – but Sarah's, a story of guilt which she'd only ever confessed to her driftwood man: how one night twenty-three years ago she lost her virginity to a good-looking, funny boy called Danny Allison. One night, one mistake, and Ruth Jones, her school friend, her best friend, was dead; one night which changed everything.

Like the flotsam collected by Olaf for his driftwood men, Ruth's body had washed up on the beach by De Koog, a long way from home, but half a mile from where Sarah now lived.

21

The nervous smile, frightened eyes, white-white skin framed by cascades of red hair: Helen recalled two girls in summery dresses scattering roses in a French town. Then, Kate Tolmie had held her younger sister's hand while walking with their grandfather in Gravelines, following in their missing mother's footsteps. Twenty-three years later, here she was, all grown up, the promise of beauty realized, with that same bewildered expression. Once again terrible events swirled around her, once more her life was out of control, the future uncertain. When, for the record, Helen introduced Detective Chief Inspector Richard Beacom, Kate replied, 'You think I killed him, don't you? You do, otherwise why would you be here, a detective chief inspector?' Her eyes flashed with alarm, the same but different from the frightened little girl lost in the photograph. 'I didn't kill him. I didn't. You've got to believe me.'

'A man's been murdered,' Helen replied quietly. 'You were at the scene. We want to find out what happened. That's all. OK?'

Kate looked at her hands, as if blood stained them still. She breathed in, settling herself. 'I suppose so. Yes, OK.'

In the same muted manner, Helen asked, 'Why don't you start at the beginning?' After glancing at the file on the table, she asked, 'Kate, why did you go to Haymarket Station?'

'You know why.'

'Tell me again.'

Kate sighed. 'A courier delivered an envelope to our flat. It had been forwarded by Flora's office, by her assistant. Inside the envelope was a postcard which said, "Wait outside Haymarket Station, Edinburgh, at twelve p.m. on Thursday if you're interested in discovering the truth about your mother." I didn't know where Flora was, so I went instead.'

'Is this the card?' Helen held up a see-through bag. The card was inside.

'Yes.'

'It isn't signed?'

'No.'

'Did you know who wrote it? At that time, did you have any idea?'

'No.'

'You were aware Flora had received other, similar cards?'

'Yes.'

'She told you about them?'

'No, I found them in Flora's desk.'

'Someone broke into the bottom drawer. Was that you?'

'Yes.'

'Are these the cards?' Helen pushed them one by one across the table. They, too, were sealed in see-through bags.

Kate nodded at each. 'Yes.'

'When another card arrived this morning, you decided to go to Haymarket Station?'

'Yes.'

'Why?'

'To stop him.'

'Stop him doing what?'

'Doing that to my sister, sending her cards, frightening her.'

'Where is your sister?'

'I don't know.'

'Don't know or won't say?'

'Don't know.' Her eyes closed briefly as though praying Flora was safe.

'You said "stop *him*". A man?'

Kate nodded. 'I thought so, yes.'

'You didn't know who?'

'No.'

'So you went to Haymarket Station to meet this . . . this man. Why didn't you ring the police? Weren't you frightened?'

'I didn't think the police would be interested. Anyway, I'm the big sister.'

'Aren't big sisters allowed to be frightened?'

'No.'

'How did you plan to stop him?'

'Talk to him, warn him off, take his photograph on my phone and tell him I'd expose him if he didn't stop writing to Flora.'

'That's it? That's all you intended to do?'

Kate nodded. 'I thought he'd be a creep, a pervert.'

'You weren't curious about him? You didn't want to know –' Helen turned one of the postcards towards her – 'the truth about your mother, how he knew the truth about your mother?'

'Not then, no.'

'Why not?'

'I didn't think he knew anything about my mother other than what he'd heard or read following Flora's appeal for information about her disappearance.'

'You thought it was a trap, some pervert, that's the word you used, playing games with a young woman?'

'Something like that, yes.'

'You said, "Not then, no" when I asked if you were curious about him. So, you were curious about him later? When?'

Kate nodded. 'When I saw him.'

'Why?'

'I thought I knew him. He was . . . familiar.'

Helen noticed how carefully she chose that description, how puzzled she was at using it.

'Familiar how?'

'The way he looked, his expression . . . I thought I must have met him before. I couldn't remember when.'

'A family resemblance?'

Kate shook her head. 'I don't know.'

'Describe his expression.'

'Kind.'

'Is that it?' Beacom growled. Then, mocking Kate's voice: 'Kind, *kind*, what does kind look like, exactly?'

Kate appeared flustered. 'And sad,' she said hurriedly to Helen.

'Then what happened?'

'When?' She glanced nervously at Beacom, who moved in his seat.

'After you saw him, this man,' Helen said.

'The station was busy. There were tourists, people coming and going. I lost sight of him. When the crowds cleared, his cap was still there, also his placard saying, "Help me and you will be caring for a vulnerable person", and his blanket, but he'd gone. I went to look for him.'

'At this stage you hadn't spoken to him?'

'No.'

'He knew you'd seen him?'

'Yes.'

'And he seemed familiar to you, kind?'

'Yes.' She invested the word with emotion and directed it at Beacom.

'But,' Helen continued, 'there hadn't been any communication between you, a gesture, a sign or a message of any kind?'

'No.'

'You'd just looked at each other?'

'Yes.'

'What did you do next, when you saw he wasn't there any more?'

'He hadn't passed me, so I thought he must have gone in the other direction. I went along the road, looked for him in a café and a pub, but he wasn't in either, so I went round the corner. There was an opening to a backstreet. That's where I saw him again, about fifty metres along it, leaning his head against a wall. A pool of liquid was round his boots – I thought it was urine.'

'Was there anyone else in the lane?'

'No.'

'You're sure about that?'

'I didn't see anyone. Whoever stabbed him must have gone the other way.'

'What did you do?'

'I went closer.'

Another disbelieving growl from Beacom: 'Even though you thought he was urinating?'

'Yes.'

Helen glanced at Beacom. He was leaning back, studying the ceiling.

'Why,' Helen asked, turning back to Kate, 'why didn't you wait until he'd finished? Wouldn't that have been more normal?'

'I don't know.'

'You just wanted to stop him bothering your sister?'

'I suppose I did, yes. I wasn't thinking about anything else.'

'And,' Helen continued, 'this was your chance, and you weren't frightened because, as you pointed out, big sisters aren't allowed to be frightened?'

'Yes, I think so. I don't remember.'

Helen registered the flustered look in her eyes when Beacom said, 'There's another way of looking at this.' His voice was as sharp-edged, as unsympathetic as his vulpine looks.

Kate gave Helen a pleading look: *Believe me.*

Beacom continued, still looking at the ceiling: 'You thought he was urinating and wouldn't see you coming because his back was turned. So you went along the lane and stabbed him. You said you wanted to stop him and that's exactly what you did. You stopped him by killing him. Job done.'

'No,' Kate replied. 'No.'

'Kate,' Helen said hurriedly. 'Kate. Look at me, Kate. You had a knife with you, didn't you? We found one in your coat pocket.'

Kate nodded, lowered her eyes.

'Why?'

'I don't know.'

Beacom laughed, a single explosion. 'Oh, come on, you had it with you because you took it with you.'

Kate whispered, 'Yes.'

Beacom said, 'Louder.'

'Yes. But I wouldn't have used it. I wouldn't ever have used it.'

Helen said, 'Was the knife the reason you weren't frightened, not because you're the big sister? Did taking a knife give you confidence?'

Kate looked at her hands.

Beacom leaned forward and jabbed his right arm at Kate. 'I think you took two similar knives with you, one with a black handle and one with a green handle, one for each pocket, as an insurance policy. If the man grabbed one of your hands you'd be able to stab him with the other. That's what you did, isn't it?' Beacom jabbed again. 'You stabbed him with the black-handled knife.'

'No. I took one knife. It had a green handle.'

'What happened next?' Helen asked. 'You thought the man was urinating. You were going towards him.'

'He fell down. I saw blood. It wasn't urine. When I reached him, I rolled him on to his front and saw the knife sticking into him.'

'Why did you put your hands on the knife?' Helen was giving Kate less time to think now; the questions were quick-fire.

'He was grabbing at the knife, trying to pull it out.'

'You wanted to stop him?'

'I thought he might bleed more. There was blood every-where.' Kate's eyes flicked up to Helen, then Beacom, trying to make them understand. 'Everywhere, everywhere.'

Helen pressed again: 'Did you say anything to him?'

'I said, "Please don't die".'

'What did he do?'

'He looked at me. He seemed to know me. And –' she looked puzzled – 'I thought I knew him.'

'He spoke to you, didn't he?'

'He said I was his perfect girl.'

'Why?'

'I don't know, except my mother used to say to me, "Why can't you be perfect like Flora?"'

'Did he think you were Flora?'

'He would have been expecting Flora. The card was for her.'

'After he said you were his perfect girl, what did you say?'

'I said, "Who are you?"'

'What was his answer?'

Kate's eyes closed. 'He said he was my father. He repeated I was his perfect girl.'

'Was he your father?' Helen asked. 'Was that why he was familiar?'

'I don't have a father. I've never had a father.'

Helen opened a file and picked out an evidence bag, inside which was a scrap of paper. 'You said you didn't communicate with him before he went into the lane?'

'I didn't.'

'This was found in your father's cap, the one he had out for coins, after the stabbing. It's a typed note: "There's a backstreet round the corner. I'll meet you there. Flora.'' Helen watched Kate. 'Did you write that?'

Kate shook her head. 'No.'

Beacom snarled. 'Oh, come on, you did communicate with him. You know you did. You planned it. You told him where to go and that's where you killed him.'

'No.' Now she was pleading again, staring at Helen. 'No, no.'

Helen was at her desk, doodling. Beacom sat opposite. 'I know that look of yours,' he said. 'Spit it out.'

The pen in Helen's hand stopped. 'Sir,' she said, 'why would she have taken two knives, the same make, with the same length of blade, both three inches? It doesn't make sense.'

Beacom: 'As I said, a knife in each pocket, a knife for each hand.'

Helen: 'She's right-handed. The knife we found in her coat was in her right-hand pocket. But let's say she had two knives, a knife in each pocket. Why did she stab him with the other knife, the one in her left-hand pocket?'

Beacom: 'Both knives could have been in the same pocket, the right-hand one.'

Helen started another doodle when her phone rang. 'Hello . . . Speaking . . . Yes . . . Yes . . . Go on.'

After putting down the phone, she scored her pen through her doodle. 'Oh, Kate Tolmie!'

'What?' Beacom asked.

Helen sighed. 'When Kate was sixteen she was expelled from school because she attacked some other girls for bullying her little sister. She stabbed one of them with a knife, stuck it into the girl's hand. There were no charges because everyone wanted it to be kept quiet. After that, Kate and Flora were schooled at home, by their grandfather.'

'So there's a pattern,' Beacom said. 'Big sister Kate knifes anyone who makes life uncomfortable for Flora.'

'It looks that way, sir. Except . . .'

'Go on, Helen.'

'Well, sir, Kate was expecting a creep, but instead she discovered a man who was familiar, with whom she had some kind of emotional connection. That threw her. She felt an affinity with him. Even though she still can't say it, every cell in her body suspected he was her father. She wouldn't have stuck a knife into him without asking.'

Beacom frowned. 'There are two other murder investigations, two other killers roaming the streets out there, Helen.'

'Sir?'

'No, Helen.'

'Please, sir, let me have forty-eight hours. I'll find the sister, Flora. I'll look into Louis Dufour's background. I'll cover all the bases, sir. Just to be sure . . .'

Beacom stood up. 'Forty-eight hours,' he said, then walked off.

Helen rang Cal. He answered quickly. Helen thought that a good sign.

'Where are you?' she asked.

'Why?'

Helen sighed. She'd been wrong. She recognized that wary tone of voice. Cal was going to be difficult. 'Perhaps,' she replied coolly, 'because I'm investigating a murder and I'm trying to work out why a young woman with Kate Tolmie's history would stab a man who might be her father without even saying hello, without asking him: "Where have you been all this time, Dad?" or "What happened to my mother?"'

Cal answered as though shrugging. 'I don't know. Kate didn't mention her father when she came to my office.'

Helen persevered. 'Did Kate say anything about a man writing anonymous cards to Flora?'

'Nothing.'

'Do you know where Flora's gone, whether Flora knew that big sister Kate was planning to meet up with Louis Dufour at noon today outside Haymarket Station in Edinburgh armed with a knife?'

'No,' Cal said after a delay. 'Flora didn't know about the meeting or about a knife.'

Helen waited.

She waited some more.

'Cal?'

'Yes.'

'Answer the first question. Where's Flora? You've been speaking to her, haven't you?'

No reply.

'Cal, where is she?'

'Somewhere between here and Edinburgh, in a car.'

'Where's here, Cal?'

'Southwold, Suffolk.'

'Suffolk! What are you doing there?'

'I've been watching a woman burn a suitcase.'

'Why?'

'Because Flora's my client now and the suitcase was with Christina Tolmie when she disappeared.'

'Cal?'

'What?'

'Tell me what's going on. A man's dead after writing anonymous postcards to Flora Tolmie. Flora's been missing for a week but, lo, suddenly, she appears to have been found by you and you're working for her and that work possibly has something to do with a woman burning a suitcase which belongs to Christina Tolmie – sorry, belonged to her twenty-three years ago – which makes me wonder why anyone has suddenly decided to burn it now. Cal, I have forty-eight hours – no, that's wrong, I have forty-seven hours and fourteen minutes – to work out what's going on and whether Kate Tolmie is a murderer. I'm your good friend, remember.'

No reply.

'Cal, help me.'

'It wasn't Christina Tolmie's suitcase,' Cal answered.

'You said it was.'

'No, I said it was with her. It didn't belong to Christina. It was Flora's.'

'And?'

'No.'

'No what?

'That's all. I can't say anything else without Flora's permission.'

Cal ended the call.

'Huh,' Helen said to her phone. Then she texted:

Some friend! You can organize your own bloody funeral, Cal McGill.

22

Gwen Hawes turned the pages of her old diary until she was at the last day of July. *The baby kicks so strongly and with such frequency my ribs hurt.* Her eyes drifted to the facing page, the first day of August. It was blank.

That was the start, she recalled as she dabbed her finger against her tongue, tasting smoke from the fire as well as the bitterness of the memory. She flicked to the next page, the next and the next. Soon twenty-five similarly blank days had been skipped as she hurried past that painful period which, because of her pregnancy, should have been happy. She stopped at 26 August where she'd written in large letters: *We're going to be all right! Stephen has explained everything!!!* Those last three exclamation marks, in red ink, had smudged because she'd been crying, for a change, joyfully. She glanced at the left-hand page – the last which was blank – and experienced again the sensation of catastrophe looming. The foreboding which went unrecorded in her diary stabbed into her with its old ferocity.

Had Stephen been unfaithful and, if so, with whom and for how long?

The past had been haunting Gwen Hawes ever since she'd cleared out the garage and found the old suitcase hidden behind a tool cupboard and wrapped in newspaper. Other newspapers had been placed on top in deliberate concealment, an unwelcome discovery which spoke to Gwen across almost a quarter of a century. The message it had to deliver was a shock: evidence that all those years ago, on 25 and 26 August – she glanced from one diary page to the next – Stephen had lied to her.

Why? To hide what?

Sometimes she took the view that Stephen's lies had been small lies, ancient lies, which mustn't be allowed to undermine the latter years of their partnership, which were contented and companionable. But mostly worry ate away at her because, in her heart, she knew lies, however small or distant, were significant in a marriage. They were the screens behind which men like Stephen hid larger deceits, which made her wonder if, after all, her marriage had been a lie too, a construction founded upon dishonesty.

Her agitation about the lies – after all this time, did they matter or not? – was agony. It led her into a course of action which now she regretted. If only she hadn't listened to Flora on the radio! If only she hadn't recognized her description of the suitcase! If only her desire for an explanation hadn't got the better of her! By contacting Flora, Gwen had drawn attention to herself, to Stephen, to the guest house. A murder investigation was underway. If the victim, Louis Dufour, was Flora Tolmie's father, as he claimed, the police might look again into the disappearance of Christina Tolmie. If so, would Flora reveal the discovery of the suitcase? Would Cal McGill? Would detectives come calling to inquire how it came into Stephen's possession and why it had been hidden for so long?

Gwen closed the diary.

Through the kitchen window, smoke was still rising from the incinerator. Her sight blurred as her mind returned to that late August, between six and seven o'clock in the morning, when she saw Stephen on the beach, carrying something. By then she'd been awake for three, perhaps four hours, watching for him from the front bedroom. As he drew closer she saw a small suitcase in his right hand. Her first thought was: *That looks heavy; it must be full.*

The next: *Oh, Stephen's been seeing another woman and now he's moving her in.*

She hadn't been startled by that conclusion. Mentally, she'd been preparing for another woman since Stephen had moved out of their bedroom. After that his habits became irregular. Sometimes he slept downstairs; at others he didn't appear to sleep at all. She'd be woken by the softened thud of the front door and she would rise from bed, stand by the window and stay on watch for him. Sometimes she'd be awake half the night, imagining him with someone else, imagining with whom. When, after dawn, he'd return, she'd make herself invisible by stepping back into the shadows of the room.

She never told him about her vigils, nor did she confront him. As with those empty pages in her diary, she thought that writing down her suspicions or voicing them would give them substance. Also, she was uncertain of her judgement, the pregnancy, as much as Stephen's habits, causing her to have such disturbed nights she spent the days exhausted and irritable. No wonder he went for long walks. In his place, she might have done the same.

The morning he brought the suitcase back, she put on a show of being similarly oblivious and incurious. She bathed, dressed and went downstairs after eight, as usual.

Stephen was at the kitchen table, having breakfast and reading the newspaper. He was in his suit and tie, ready for work – he was residential sales manager for a local estate agency. She'd said, 'Good morning, Stephen. Did you sleep well?' and he'd replied, 'Yes, all right, I suppose.'

Gwen didn't ask, 'Why "I suppose"?' Nor did she inquire about the suitcase, though she could think of nothing else. It wasn't in the hall or the kitchen. Where was it? *Whose* was it? Had he put it in his room downstairs? Was he moving another woman in? Were *her* nightclothes already under *his* pillow? Would she be sleeping there tonight?

Then, unprompted, as a by the way, Stephen said he'd found something on the beach that morning. 'I thought I saw you standing at the window, watching. Aren't you curious to know what it was?'

'Did you find something?' she'd replied, reddening, feigning indifference at having been seen. 'I wasn't really looking. I'd got up to go to the toilet.'

'Well, I found a suitcase,' he'd said.

Gwen's heart beat fast at him telling her. Had she jumped to the wrong conclusion? Perhaps it didn't belong to another woman. Perhaps her pregnancy *was* making her insecure, irrational. Perhaps that was also why Stephen was behaving oddly. Hadn't she read that fathers-to-be reacted to their wives being pregnant, especially first-time fathers, and the impending arrival of another person in the marriage?

She'd drunk tea while Stephen speculated about the suitcase. Probably, he said, it had washed up during the night, though it could have been left on the beach by a family holidaying in Southwold – it was August, after all, peak season. A clue was in the suitcase's contents, boys' shorts, shirts, underwear – possibly spares for a child who had been playing on the beach all day. By luck, the clothes had been packed into a watertight holdall and were unaffected by sea water leaking into the suitcase. Also, luck again, there was an address inside the lid, a street in Worcester, and two initials. RT.

They played a game guessing what or who RT might stand for. Stephen suggested Richard, Robert or Ricky for the 'R' and Turnbull for the 'T'. Gwen thought Roderick Tuffnell. No, she was certain that was his name, though she wasn't sure why. Five pounds to whoever's guess was closest, she'd said, and stuck her hand out.

Their handshake sealed the bet, the first time they'd touched each other for a while. Stephen went off to work, saying he would put the suitcase outside his office window to dry before asking his secretary to wrap and post it. He'd enclose a letter so that 'RT' could reply to confirm receipt. Then they would discover his real name.

That evening Gwen noticed a change in Stephen. He talked more. He was comfortable in her company. Though his half of their bed was still cold and empty that night, he didn't pace downstairs nor walk on the beach until dawn: good signs, she hoped.

At breakfast the next morning, he suggested dinner. They hadn't been out together for ages. He had something to tell her.

She'd been alarmed all day: what was Stephen going to say? Was he going to confess to an affair? Instead, that evening, Stephen apologized for being distant. Problems at work had been the cause. His company was merging with another, a consolidation which dispensed with his job. He'd been anxious about the future, about money, whether they could afford their mortgage, whether they'd have to move towns because there weren't any estate agency vacancies in Southwold. One thing on top of another, he'd said: a bloody great mess. He hadn't wanted to worry her. Being pregnant was stress enough. But, good news! That afternoon, he'd been called in to the boss's office and told his payoff would be £25,000, a lot more than expected, if he left right away. Apparently, the company would save on tax if it was all done quickly. He'd smiled at her then. How would Gwen like to be his partner in business? What would she think about turning their home into a guest house? The money would fit out two new bathrooms, both en suite, and a new kitchen. The income from guests would pay the mortgage with enough left over for them to live modestly. They wouldn't have to leave Southwold.

She remembered that moment. The elation: from having thought Stephen was having an affair to that. She'd dreamed of running a guest house, had chosen that terrace in North Parade and the house for that very reason.

Going home arm in arm with Stephen she hadn't ever been happier; she had her husband back. They'd be starting a family business as well as a family. On cue, the baby kicked its approval. That night they'd gone round the house working out what alterations to make. Afterwards, Stephen sat at the kitchen table writing down possible names.

'For the baby?' Gwen asked. 'Isn't that bad luck?'

'For the guest house,' Stephen replied.

Gwen said, 'Why don't we call it the Sandcastle Guest

House?' and Stephen had looked up and said, 'That's damn well it; that's what we'll call it.'

Before going to sleep Gwen wrote in her diary, the first time for twenty-five days.

During the night she'd woken and found Stephen in bed beside her.

As far as Gwen had been concerned, that was 'damn well it' for twenty-three happy years until Stephen died. Then, after his funeral, she'd found the suitcase hidden in the garage. Stephen hadn't posted it off to Worcester, despite telling her he had: one lie. Nor, she discovered when she opened the lid, was there an address inside or the initials R. T. Not Roderick Tuffnell's suitcase or his clothes after all.

Another lie.

There was just a faded message painted by a child: 'Please look after my mummy'.

Whose mummy? Why had Stephen lied?

After agonizing for three weeks, Gwen heard Flora Tolmie on the radio. She was talking about her mother's disappearance and described the suitcase in precise and familiar detail. Gwen googled 'Christina Tolmie', read about her and studied photographs. Her impression was of a hippy-ish, good-looking young woman more concerned about abandoned children in eastern Europe than being a mother. She had two daughters, Kate and Flora, whose father or fathers were unknown. The police had appealed for him/them to come forward to be eliminated from their inquiries. But he/they never had. Each report she read described Christina as free-spirited, which suggested promiscuity.

169

The coincidence of dates shocked Gwen. Stephen brought the suitcase home – the suitcase she now knew to have been in Christina Tolmie's possession – eight and a half days after her disappearance.

Stephen? Could he be implicated? Had he had an affair with her? Those small, ancient lies made anything seem possible in Gwen's leaping imagination. Was that what he had really been doing those nights, meeting her, having sex with her? Was that why he'd lied about the suitcase, why he'd hidden it away?

That other empty holdall in the suitcase was also concerning, even incriminating. Stephen hadn't mentioned it. Why not? Gwen recalled how the suitcase appeared to be heavier when she saw Stephen bringing it from the beach. Had there been something else in the suitcase apart from boys' clothes? If so, what?

Gwen started to lose perspective as well as judgement. The feeling reminded her of those days when she dared not write in her diary. Who was this man she'd been married to almost all her adult life? What had he done, what terrible thing? Having heard Flora on the radio, she'd been unable to think of anything else. After a few days of alternately being consumed by both suspicion and curiosity, she rang the Christina Tolmie Foundation and spoke to Flora. She told her about the suitcase.

What did she hope Flora would say or reveal when she saw her? Something, anything – in her fevered state all she wanted was an answer to the questions which were always on her mind: had Stephen had an affair with Christina Tolmie? If not, why had he lied?

'I'm sorry you've had to come all this way,' Gwen had

said as she took Flora into the kitchen. The suitcase was open on the table. 'Have you been to Southwold before?'

Flora had shaken her head and Gwen said, 'Well, this is what you've come to see.' Gwen stood to one side, expecting Flora to approach the table. But she stayed rooted to the spot, as if her mother's corpse had been laid out. 'It's the one your mother had with her?' Gwen asked, though the answer was already on Flora's face. 'Take your time, dear,' Gwen said. 'It'll be a shock, no doubt.'

'Who found it?' Flora asked. 'When? Where? How long have you had it?'

'My husband found it on the beach. His name was Stephen.' She studied Flora for a reaction in case one of her childhood memories was of her mother having had a friend called Stephen, but there was none. 'Well, I remember it was the day before Stephen lost his job working for an estate agent in Southwold and we spent his redundancy, £25,000, on converting this place into a guest house. What with one thing and another – I was pregnant at the time – Stephen and I forgot all about it. It must have been put in the garage when the conversion work was being done. Stephen probably put it there.' She watched again in case repetition of her husband's name jogged a recollection. 'He died recently,' Gwen continued, 'I cleared out the garage and found it. It was a surprise to come across it after all this time.' Gwen added, 'It must be difficult for you, seeing it again, all those memories.'

Flora nodded.

Gwen carried on. 'I wonder how it made its way here. I suppose it could have washed in on the tide. I don't know if your mother visited Southwold. Did she? Perhaps she had a friend who lived in the town or somewhere nearby? Perhaps something happened to her here and the suitcase – well, I'm not sure how it would have ended up on the beach – but perhaps someone put it there or perhaps she lost it.'

Flora looked nonplussed as though other possibilities apart from it being washed up hadn't occurred to her. 'I don't think she had a friend here. As far as I know she never visited Southwold.'

'She didn't have, oh, I don't know, a lover, someone she might not have wanted you to know about?'

'No, I don't think so.' Flora frowned. 'But I was only four.'

'No, no, I'm sure you're right,' Gwen said quickly. 'It'll have been the tide; of course it will have been. My memory's so foggy, but I'm almost certain that was Stephen's theory, the tide. I was just wondering out loud because, as I said, it wasn't me who found the suitcase; it was Stephen.'

Flora approached the table, unzipped both holdalls, looked inside, spent a few moments lifting out and putting back the clothes. She glanced at Gwen. There were tears in her eyes.

'What, dear?'

'I'm sorry,' she said, looking away. 'Would it . . . Could I stay here tonight? Is there a room I could have?'

'I do have an empty room, yes, tonight. It's at the front, upstairs, Sea View.'

'Would you mind? Could I take the suitcase with me? It's just . . .'

'There's no need to explain. Yes, dear, of course you can.'

After that it had all gone wrong. Flora had shut herself away in the room and Gwen thought she must have said something that rang a bell with Flora or that Flora had been offended by her mentioning a possible lover.

Every day Flora stayed on, locked in her room, Gwen had to turn guests away. Was that Flora's plan? Was it punishment for the past? Perhaps she'd recognized Stephen's name after all. Gwen was at her wits' end.

Then, when Flora asked her to contact Dr McGill, she'd been relieved. Maybe reacquaintance with the suitcase had caused Flora to have a breakdown. Perhaps she'd had one before – the reason why there was a doctor she could summon. Gwen's consolation had been temporary. After speaking to McGill on the phone, she entered his name into her computer and had been alarmed to discover he was an investigator of sorts. He'd omitted to inform her of that. Gwen thought a conspiracy possible. Was Flora summoning him for a purpose? What did she know? Was McGill going to team up with her? Were they in this together? Gwen was beside herself with worry.

When McGill, in Gwen's hearing, told Flora a man claiming to be her father had been stabbed and that Kate, her older sister, was in custody, she panicked. Would the murder cause detectives to reopen the investigation into Christina Tolmie's disappearance? If so, was the suitcase evidence as McGill said? Was Stephen implicated?

If not, why had Stephen lied?

Why had he hidden the suitcase?

What had been in that second empty holdall?

Gwen closed the diary, held it to her breast and left the kitchen. As she went outside, she felt as she did for those twenty-five blank days that August. She was lost, lonely and desperate. Gwen used the garden fork to stir the remains of the suitcase in the incinerator. The ashes glowed. A flame flared and Gwen fed it by tearing out pages before dropping in the diary.

Like the suitcase, it was evidence best destroyed. But evidence of what?

23

In a café on Southwold Pier, Cal ordered a large Americano, a panini filled with Cheddar, and googled 'property Southwold'. Scrolling through the first ten pages of search results, he found the names of four estate agents operating in the seaside town. Cal eliminated two because, according to their websites, they'd been in business less than a decade. The other two, both long established, traded as Donald & Fairbrother and Harwood Gee Property. Cal rang the first and asked 'an odd question': whether anyone had worked there for twenty-three years and, 'if so, could I speak to him or her?'

The female answering his call giggled. 'Sorry, sorry, it's just that we've had someone in who's been complaining about his property not selling for six months . . .' She broke off, snorted. 'Your property hasn't been with us for twenty-three years, has it?'

'No, no,' Cal answered. 'I'm trying to find out about someone who might have worked for your company back then, a Mr Stephen Hawes. I know he was an estate agent in Southwold.'

'Wait a sec, would you?' Cal heard another short giggle followed by a shout directed at the others in her office. 'How long has Martin worked here?' The answer was indistinct. She returned to Cal: 'Sorry, fourteen years. That's as far as any of us go back.'

'Do you know Harwood Gee Property?'

'I know . . .' She sounded uncertain about carrying on. She giggled once again. 'I know Harwood lost a leg in a war, Iraq or Ireland, can't remember which, and Gee lost an arm in a boating accident. They claim to be "The estate agent which makes you profit from property" but everyone here refers to them as "The estate agent which loses you an arm and a leg". Sorry, haven't been much help, have I?'

'Not really,' Cal said, 'but thanks.'

Harwood Gee's address was close to the lighthouse, south of the pier. Rather than walk along North Parade and past Sandcastle Guest House, Cal kept to the beach. When the lighthouse towered at his right, he climbed steps to street level. After one wrong turn he found Harwood Gee, which occupied a two-storey building. Property for sale was displayed in one of its two front windows; for rent in the other. Cal noticed the company's marketing slogan – 'The estate agent which makes you profit from property' – and smiled.

The office was bright, white walls, blue carpet, with a pale-wood reception desk at which sat a young man in a white shirt and butterfly-patterned tie, with slicked-back black hair and a scowl which became pronounced as Cal approached.

'Can I be of assistance?' he inquired in a doubtful manner, as though it was apparent, from Cal's dress or general demeanour, that he was unlikely to be in possession of a property to sell or a deposit to put towards a purchase or a rental lease.

'Probably not,' Cal replied. 'But I think he might.' Cal nodded towards the right-hand of two glass-fronted offices behind the reception desk. It was occupied by a man in his fifties or sixties. He wore red braces, which clashed with the purplish tones of his nose and cheeks. Cal noticed he had two arms, both of which were his own, and wondered if the desk concealed a missing leg. 'Is that Mr Harwood?'

'It is, but if it's about a property you can talk to me.' The assistant placed his hands palms down the desk. 'Now, are you buying, selling or renting?' Once again, he sounded doubtful.

'None of those.' Cal nodded in Harwood's direction. 'I'd prefer to deal with him.'

The young man said, 'Sorry, who did you say you were?'

'I didn't,' Cal replied. 'I'm Dr McGill.' Doctor sounded better, was more persuasive. 'Look,' he added, dropping his voice, 'it's private, a bit sensitive.'

'Oh, oh, of course.' The young man stood, opened the door into Harwood's office. After a brief exchange, Harwood waved his hand, a single gesture to invite Cal in as well as to dismiss the assistant. 'What can I do for you, Dr McGill?' Harwood leaned back in his chair.

'Would you mind if I closed the door?'

'Absolutely, please do.' Another gesture indicated one of two wooden armchairs in front of his desk. 'How can I help?'

Cal sat. 'Do you know if someone called Stephen Hawes worked here some time ago – he and his wife Gwen own the Sandcastle Guest House on North Parade? Well, she owns it now. He's dead.'

Harwood leaned forward. 'I'm aware of Stephen Hawes.'

Cal noticed his careful phraseology, his extra attention. 'This was where he worked?'

'You could say that – the company's changed its name since then. It was Gee & Croft back then. Hawes was the residential sales manager. Around the time he left, Croft retired and I bought in.'

'The reason I'm asking . . . it's to do with an inquiry . . . well, if I can explain. I'm trying to find out exactly when a suitcase washed ashore on the beach, below North Parade, I think it was. All I know is that Mrs Hawes, Gwen –' he used her first name to suggest intimacy as well as her cooperation – 'says her husband Stephen found it the day before he stopped working here, when he was made redundant. That stuck in Mrs Hawes's – Gwen's – memory because what with one thing and another going on back then – her pregnancy, Stephen losing his job – the suitcase was put away in the garage and forgotten. Mrs Hawes discovered it again recently when she was clearing out some of her husband's things.' Cal paused. 'You knew that Mr Hawes, Stephen, had died, did you?'

'I did, yes.' As with his earlier reply, Cal picked up circumspection, as though the name Stephen Hawes was one to be kept at a distance.

Cal carried on. 'The exact date of his redundancy is important because the suitcase is connected to a woman who went missing round about the same time. It's the lost piece in, well, a jigsaw. Yes, that's what it is, a jigsaw. I'm an oceanographer, by the way. My PhD – that's the Doctor in Dr McGill – involved ocean tracking, working out where things float, where they go, where they come from. That's what I'm hoping to do with the suitcase, track back to where it first went into the sea. Accuracy's difficult at the best of times, so having as much precise information as possible matters. Knowing which day it was recovered would be a good start.' His expression turned doubtful to acknowledge how long ago it had been. 'Anyway, I thought I would try, so that's why I'm here.'

'So,' Harwood said, 'you want to know when Stephen Hawes was booted out, is that it?'

'Yes,' Cal added uncertainly. 'Booted out? I was told made redundant, but –' his gesture conceded to the other's better knowledge – 'Mrs Hawes mentioned a payment for redundancy, but perhaps he had shares in the company, was bought out, or it was compensation of some kind. It doesn't matter. It's only the date I'm after.'

Harwood glanced away from Cal. His eyes slid back. 'Well, my memory is that I started the next day, new broom, what!' He reached down to his right, opened a drawer and pulled out a dog-eared blue file. After turning over some papers, he announced, 'Twenty-seventh of August. That's the date I started.'

'Twenty-seventh of August, twenty-three years ago?'

He checked the file. 'Yep, time flies, what?'

'Which means Stephen Hawes left on the twenty-sixth of August and the suitcase washed up on the twenty-fifth.' Cal sat up straight as if preparing to leave. 'Appreciate your help. Thanks.'

Mr Harwood said, 'No bother at all.' Then: 'So Hawes's wife told you he'd been made redundant?'

'Yes, paid off, apparently with twenty-five thousand pounds.'

'Well, just for the record, neither is correct. He was sacked by the senior partner at the time, Ronald Gee, the father of my current partner. Gross misconduct, if you want to know. Hawes had been entertaining women in properties the company managed or had for sale. Apparently, he, *they*, liked to have sex in different bedrooms, preferably someone else's. It was cheaper and in a small town like this I suppose more discreet than going to a hotel. He passed the women off as potential buyers or tenants, got away with it for ages until he was caught coitus interruptus, what! Hawes paid ten thousand quid to hush it all up. Otherwise the client would have gone to court claiming damages and alleging the property had been kept on the market purely to be available for Hawes's sexual convenience.'

'So Stephen Hawes didn't get twenty-five thousand pounds in redundancy or compensation?'

'Not a penny, not likely, what!' Harwood tapped his nose. 'Sounds like a story Hawes concocted for his wife. There wasn't any danger of anyone here contradicting him. If the truth got out, the company's reputation would have been trash, especially in a small town like this. We'd have gone out of business.'

'I see,' Cal said. 'Mrs Hawes, Gwen, says the twenty-five thousand pounds was invested in starting the guest house. If he also paid ten thousand pounds to an aggrieved client, that's thirty-five thousand pounds. Did he have that kind of money?'

'Never had any money at all, according to Ronald Gee. Hawes was always borrowing from the company, taking salary in advance. The surprise was he had enough money to settle with the client. Hawes wasn't the kind of man to have ten thousand pounds in his back pocket, or even a hundred, so God knows where he got hold of another twenty-five thousand quid for the guest house. I thought that must have been his wife's money.'

'No,' Cal said, 'but it doesn't matter. Well, it doesn't to me. Thanks.'

Cal was at the door of the office when Harwood said, 'Must have won the Lottery.'

Cal stopped and looked back. 'Was it running twenty-three years ago?'

Harwood's arm stretched towards the ceiling, his index finger pointing. When his arm descended, the finger settled on Cal. 'Or . . . or . . . or that suitcase was stuffed with money.' He smiled, pleased with himself. 'What, that's it!' A loud guffaw followed. 'What!'

Helen's desk was covered in files, scribbled reminders and Post-it notes with the names of journalists requesting briefings or answers – was the suspect's name Kate Tolmie, sister of Flora, who recently launched a charity in memory of her missing mother? Were Dufour's murder and Christina Tolmie's disappearance connected? Was Flora also a suspect? Information was leaking out. Helen blamed her detective colleagues who hoped she'd mess up in the glare of publicity. Rather than distract her, it made her focus; she was studying a three-page summary of the investigation into Christina Tolmie written by a detective inspector as an aid to any police officer coming to the case cold. It described in bare detail Christina's last journey, included maps and witness statements and concluded with two headings.

Under 'Suspects' was a single word: *None*.

Under 'Questions still to be answered' was a list.

Is Christina Tolmie alive or dead?

If alive, is she being kept against her will or was she the architect of her own disappearance? Either way, why hasn't she been found?

If dead, how did she die, why, in what circumstances? If murdered, who killed her? What motive?

Why did Christina Tolmie drive to Gravelines when she should have been checking in for a ferry from Calais to Dover?

Why did she inquire about Jacques Picoult, a resident of Gravelines, before she disappeared?

Below, at the bottom of the page, was a handwritten message: *No suspects and no answers. Good luck, whoever you are.*

Helen checked the date of the summary. It was written five years after Christina Tolmie went missing. Five years, Helen thought, and a police operation on both sides of the English Channel, thousands of hours of interviews, house-to-house searches in Gravelines, front-page media coverage for weeks and an investigation file so big it would take days to read, and not a single question of any significance had been answered, not one new lead of any interest had emerged.

Until now.

Until a petty criminal called Louis Dufour wrote some postcards promising the truth about Christina Tolmie and then, with his dying breath, claimed to be the father of a young woman he thought was Flora Tolmie and, in that same expiring breath, referred to her as being 'perfect'. After an age of nothing, a mother's description of her younger daughter had travelled across time and had been spoken by a beggar dying in a backstreet in Edinburgh. How? Why?

Who was Louis Dufour?

Helen called up Dufour's criminal record. His last

address was in Stoke Newington, London. He had convictions for multiple offences, including shoplifting, theft from cars, petty fraud and handling stolen property, his crimes turning more serious in time with his descent into alcoholism. When drunk, Dufour was unruly, aggressive. He picked fights. When sober, he was a danger to anyone in darkly lit streets who looked as though they might have money. His last offence, a late-night assault on a bank employee, was described by the judge as unprovoked and violent. The man's nose was broken. Dufour, who stole the man's wallet and mobile phone, was sentenced to three years in prison. He was released a month ago. Apart from prison, his previous haunts were all in London. Helen counted four different addresses in the city; also, on three occasions he was described, in reports, as homeless or a rough sleeper. Why had he turned up in Edinburgh?

Perhaps Edinburgh was new territory for him, where he was unknown. The postcards to Flora suggested deliberation, a plan, rather than Dufour's usual opportunism. Although Luke, Flora's assistant, couldn't remember the date the first card arrived in the charity's office, he said it would have been about three weeks earlier, so, soon after Dufour's release.

Something else nagged at Helen: Dufour's record stretched back eleven years. He was fifty-seven when he died. Did his criminal career start when he was forty-six? His offending was regular, a pattern of behaviour. Why did it start then? Did a marriage or relationship break up? Did he have money troubles? Had alcoholism been the trigger?

Did it start then?

Helen sent Dufour's details, his photograph, his

fingerprints, his previous known addresses, to Europol with a request for

any criminal records, in particular any convictions dating back eleven or more years ago.

She added,

While I'm asking, I'm also interested in a man called Jacques Picoult who, until twenty-three years ago, resided in Gravelines, France, before living off his boat at various different locations along the Portuguese coast.

While waiting for a response, Helen hunted through the papers on her desk for the printout of Kate Tolmie's phone contacts, among them Flora's mobile number. Helen's call went straight to voicemail. 'I'm Detective Sergeant Helen Jamieson,' she said in a message. 'I expect you know your sister Kate has been arrested on suspicion of murder. I'm sure you'd like to help her. Please ring me on this number. It's urgent.'

Next she watched a recording of Kate's interrogation. If she was lying, Helen concluded, she was a good liar, particularly when describing Dufour as being 'familiar'. Kate's expression exactly matched the puzzlement in her voice. Helen redirected her attention when an email, typically succinct, arrived from Europol.

Negative Louis Dufour. Jacques Picoult record attached.

Like Dufour's, Picoult's record was also extensive, a catalogue of petty theft and dishonesty. He stole cash, jewellery, cameras or gadgets from yachts – his speciality. After leaving Gravelines two days before Christina

Tolmie's arrival, he went south in his boat. Police investigating her disappearance found him a week later. His alibi stood up. When Christina Tolmie vanished, he was one hundred miles away in St-Valéry-en-Caux, Normandy. Afterwards, he appeared to have based himself in Portugal, travelling up and down the coast, trying though often failing to stay ahead of the police – he had further convictions for stealing from yachts; a one-man, sea-going crime wave.

Helen put Picoult's record alongside Dufour's. There was little difference apart from geography and, latterly, the violence. Also, Picoult's criminal record suddenly ended eleven years ago just as Dufour's began, which Helen thought was too coincidental not to be significant.

She compared the two men's photographs. Both were dark and similar looking – eerily so, Helen thought. Were they the same man? She wasn't sure because time, prison and drink had taken their toll on Dufour and Picoult's photograph had been taken thirteen years ago at the time of his last conviction. Then, he was clean-shaven, healthy-looking, tanned with white teeth, whereas Dufour was older, grizzled, his cheeks and eyes sunken, his teeth blackened, some missing: a retreating shadow of a man. Also, Dufour's photograph had been taken when he was dead. Despite the differences, however, the shape of face, the chin, the spacing between the eyes and the length of nose were similar. Could one have aged into the other?

Helen referred to the summary of the Christina Tolmie case. She found the name of the restaurant in Gravelines which Picoult used to frequent, and then, from Google, its email and phone details. Helen rang. 'Do you speak English?' she asked when a man answered.

'Of course.'

'Am I speaking to the owner?'

'You are.'

'How long have you been the owner?'

'For forty-six years.'

'I'm a detective based in Edinburgh, Scotland. My name is Helen Jamieson. I'm investigating a murder of a man of French origin. I know this is unorthodox but I'm in a hurry. If you look at your email, you'll see I've sent you a photograph. I'd like to know if you recognize the man.'

Helen heard two men talking, followed by an exclamation: *'C'est Jacques Picoult!'*

'Are you sure?'

'Oui. Sure. Certain.'

'So,' Helen said, ending the call, talking to Dufour's photograph, 'eleven years ago you stopped being Jacques Picoult and started being Louis Dufour and you moved from Portugal to London. Why?'

Why?

One question had been removed from her list. Another appeared.

Helen rang the lab about the delay in establishing paternity, whether Picoult/Dufour was Kate's father or not. After listening to the same excuses about staff illnesses and holidays, she said, 'How many people does it take to analyse a few drops of blood?'

Helen swore. What if Kate and Flora had different fathers? Picoult/Dufour might not be Kate's but could still be Flora's, as he claimed. She needed blood or a swab from Flora, from the perfect girl. *Where was Flora?*

Another question.

24

Cal found a map of the southern North Sea among the detritus of papers, charts, empty water bottles, boots and discarded clothing on the pickup's rear seat. Unfolding it across his steering wheel, his eye travelled from Gravelines, ten miles north-east of Calais, where Christina Tolmie had last been seen on 16 August twenty-three years ago, to Southwold on the Suffolk coast, where the suitcase had been discovered before breakfast eight and a half days later. Cal measured the distance at ninety-five miles.

On a notepad, he wrote: *Time – when did suitcase go into the sea; was it night of 16 August after last sighting of CT, the next morning, a day later, two days later?*

On another line, he wrote: *Where?*

Last-known position was an important detail.

Then: *What happened?*

As though looking for answers, he glanced through the pickup's side window towards the sea. Instead of an explanation he found further obscuring. Night was closing in as if a concealing veil was being deliberately drawn. He turned in the other direction, towards the Sandcastle Guest House, which was similarly unforthcoming. The front door was shut, as were the curtains, Mrs Hawes also hiding. The only lights were those which flickered and danced in the windows – reflections of streetlamps and occasional passing cars. Otherwise the property was in darkness, appearing to be shut up.

Cal's attention returned to his notebook.

He wrote: *Stephen Hawes/money/connection to CT?*

After propping his notebook against the windscreen, he switched on the other reading light and, from the rear seat, brought a chart of the UK continental shelf, a laptop and a file containing an Admiralty tidal stream atlas for 'North Sea Southern Part'. Having studied each, he reached for his notebook.

Was money in suitcase? If so, why?

Underneath he wrote: *Was the money motive for Christina's disappearance?*

Then: *Was a boy with her? If not, why were there boys' clothes in the suitcase?*

On another line: *Money/boy/connection? Was Christina paid to take a boy? Why? A present for Flora?*

Cal turned on his laptop. Soon the screen was displaying an ocean model of the English Channel and North Sea. It was colour-coded with dark and lighter blues, blue-greens, yellow-greens and yellow. Most of the North Sea was dark blue, which equated to flow of 0.5 metres a second or slower. By contrast, much of the English Channel, particularly along the English south coast, was lighter blue or blue washed with yellow – one metre a second or more. The Strait of Dover was a flare of bright yellow as the North Atlantic Current forced oceanic water through the constriction between France and Britain. With each flood tide, far greater volumes of water entered the North Sea than returned in the ebb. The flow was two, three or four times faster than elsewhere, at the quickest exceeding 2.5 metres per second.

Cal looked from the screen to the chart. Each confirmed the same provisional conclusion: for the suitcase to have arrived at Southwold in eight and a half days it was unlikely to have begun its journey at Gravelines where Jacques Picoult kept his boat at L'Anse des Espagnols in the tidal part of the River Aa, close to where Christina Tolmie had last been seen. If the suitcase had been thrown/dropped/lost in the River Aa, it might have been carried seawards on an ebb tide, past the resort of Petit-Fort-Philippe and its lighthouse. If that was how it reached the sea, the suitcase would initially have drifted in the wrong direction towards Calais until the ebb turned to flood. Then it would have retraced its journey, going back past the mouth of the River Aa. During the next few days, discounting tidal fluctuations, the suitcase's direction of travel would have been north-easterly, carried by huge volumes of water being forced through the Strait of Dover, the so-called net transport. With a prevailing wind, it would have gone towards the Belgian and Dutch coasts, not towards the English east coast and Southwold, which was north-north-west of Gravelines.

Next Cal checked his data file for wind direction and strength – he had records stretching back fifty years. On that 16 August and for subsequent days, there was a light to moderate south-westerly. Only later, around 23 August, did the direction change, blowing from the east. For the suitcase to have drifted from Gravelines to Southwold, it would have had to travel across the flow of the sea and, for a week, the wind direction. Neither was likely.

The relative speed of its journey provided other evidence to back up Cal's conclusion. The suitcase covered about ninety-five miles in eight and a half days, an average speed of 0.465 miles per hour. Although possible, that made little allowance for diversions. In Cal's experience, flotsam of any shape or size seldom travelled in straight lines. A meandering pattern was more usual. Flotsam wasn't like a train or taxi that went directly from A to B. If it started its sea journey at A and arrived at B, it was likely to have visited F or G and possibly other letters of the alphabet too. No. Cal's gut told him, and so now did his preliminary calculations, that the suitcase, probably, went into the sea at least halfway between France and Britain, somewhere off the east or north Kent coast, perhaps the eastern reaches of the Thames Estuary. With a helping and light south-westerly breeze, it could have drifted off the east coast of Britain past Harwich, being close enough to shore for the wind's change in direction around 23 August, a stiff easterly of 15mph, to have delivered it to Southwold about the time Stephen Hawes was pacing the beach and agonizing about having to confess to his wife about his lost job and womanizing.

Was he also praying for a financial windfall? If so, were his prayers answered when he came across the washed-up suitcase? Did the empty holdall once contain £35,000?

This was the part of his work Cal enjoyed, the guess-work, the speculation, the intrigue, being the detective.

'Yes, that could work . . .' He spoke to the chart as though it had provided the answer. 'But if its journey started halfway across the Strait of Dover or somewhere to the north, off the Thames Estuary, how did it get there? Did someone throw it from a boat? Was there an accident of some kind? Was Christina Tolmie on the boat?'

Cal swore. There were always unknowns, information just out of reach.

He glanced at his phone. The time was almost eight thirty. He was tired, having woken before five that morning to drive from Edinburgh. His eyes closed but his mind kept churning. He had a net to cast. How far? How wide? Who or what was he trying to catch?

His imagination took him close to the north Kent coast or into the Thames Estuary. He thought up scenarios: an accident or something premeditated, perhaps bloody and criminal, in the course of which Christina Tolmie was thrown or dumped into the sea with her belongings. Perhaps she had other possessions apart from the suitcase.

He recalled the boys' clothes in the suitcase. Was a boy also on the boat? Had he shared Christina's fate?

Cal paused: was he right to assume such a catastrophic scenario? After some thought, he decided he was. Even if catastrophe hadn't happened, there was no point in him working on any other assumption. He needed something to track, preferably bodies, luggage or wreckage. The police would have followed up any obvious leads. They were expert at finding connections onshore. Cal's expertise in backtracking allowed him to do the same offshore. The motion of the sea, the variability of winds, the various sizes, shapes and buoyancy of different objects combined to make things appear disconnected. For Cal, they were the oceanographic equivalent of a criminal conspiracy. They concealed evidence.

Sometimes, when he was asked for an example of the sea's ability to confuse and cover up, he told the story of a fellow scientist who released simultaneously two buoys in the Southern Ocean from either side of a ship, separated by fifteen metres of sea. A month later, after drifting, the distance between them had expanded to two hundred kilometres. Instead of buoys, he would tell his questioner, imagine wreckage and a dead body being found as far apart. If there was no convenient floating timber with the boat's name and if the corpse had no wallet, passport or other proof of identity (the sea often stripped bodies of their clothes), which police force would make a link between the wreckage and the corpse?

For someone like Cal, making that connection was possible by tracking back, hindcasting. The degree of accuracy was contingent on the quantity and reliability of data, also on the duration of the sea journey. The longer it lasted, the greater the interplay of natural forces – wind, current and tide – with the object and the greater the risk of error. The object's size, buoyancy and windage all made a difference to the outcome. Cal told clients one week at sea allowed for greater accuracy of calculation than two. For every additional week, the probability of errors and their margin increased exponentially, an already inexact science became more inexact, possibly too inexact. For this particular puzzle, Cal thought the balance to strike was between casting his net far enough and too far, a balance between minimizing error and maximizing time and distance so that he was able to include in his search for connections a body or wreckage that might have started its journey at the same time as the suitcase but which travelled some distance before being sighted or recovered.

He leaned over the chart, his finger tracing a course from east of the Strait of Dover to the Dutch and

German coasts, then from the same starting point to Denmark's northern tip, then to the south coast of Norway and along the Norwegian Deep towards the country's west coast.

Cal sighed: that was the problem. Flotsam, wreckage, a body setting off in the southern North Sea could end up almost anywhere to the north. Anywhere included the Suffolk coast, north-west Europe, southern Norway or, eventually, being transported into the Arctic.

First he must draw some boundaries, which meant making some assumptions about how fast a body from any such catastrophe might have travelled.

Cal opened a file on his laptop titled 'North Sea: washed-up bodies'. It was a record of reports of bodies, some still unidentified, which had been found on British, continental European or Scandinavian North Sea coasts or in the sea in between. He scrolled through the entries, taking an interest only in those which detailed location, date and precise time of a body going into the sea – usually an observed suicide, a swimming or fishing boat accident – and exactly where and when it was recovered. He selected those entering the sea between the Strait of Dover, Felixstowe on the Suffolk coast and the Dutch port of Rotterdam.

There were eight.

At eight thirty-seven p.m., on 17 October 2003, a suicidal waiter on a cross-Channel ferry between Calais and Dover jumped overboard. His name was Mohammed Khalily, aged twenty-two. Three minutes later, Fraser Simpson, a thirty-nine-year-old water sports coach from Lancashire, attempted a rescue by diving in. In the darkness and the conditions – the sea was choppy – both men died. Khalily's body turned up forty-eight days later on Sylt, an island belonging to Germany close to the Danish border. He was found by a dog walker who threw a ball into the shallows where his corpse was floating. It hadn't been there when the dog walker passed by half an hour earlier. The discovery was made at ten forty-five a.m. on 4 December. The distance of 340 miles was travelled in thirteen hours short of forty-eight days. His average speed was 0.298 mph.

Fraser Simpson's remains were found sooner, after twenty-one days, by the crew of an offshore supply boat fifty-six miles east-north-east of Great Yarmouth. The distance travelled was 148 miles. The average speed was 0.294 mph.

Another six fatalities at different times and different seasons produced similar results. The general direction of drift was north-easterly, the average speed between 0.278 and 0.321 mph, depending on buoyancy. A wetsuit was worn by the body which travelled quickest; the slowest was a boxer murdered after betraying some gamblers who paid him to throw a fight. One of his killers took a photograph of him being dropped from a yacht. The murderer's seized phone provided the position and exact time. Cal wasn't surprised at his slow speed. The boxer was young, muscle-bound and fit. Muscles weighed more than fat. After death, his body might have hung under water. It might also have sunk until decomposition returned it to the surface.

Cal worked out the average speed of the eight bodies: 0.292 mph.

The next calculation was more of a hunch, a trade-off between casting his net wide enough and accuracy. The greater the time and distance, the more variables and unknowns there would be and the greater the margin of error. Cal decided on twenty-six days, twelve longer than his preferred limit of two weeks, but a necessary stretch to increase the prospects of including any recovered wreckage or bodies connected to the suitcase.

He multiplied the average speed of 0.292 mph by twenty-four hours to calculate how many miles would be travelled each day – a fraction over seven. Multiplying that by twenty-six days provided the outer limit of his search area: 182.2 miles.

Using a pencil, he drew an arc across his map of the North Sea.

Next he called up his contacts file and sent emails to coastguards, harbour authorities and fishermen's associations and beachcombers – his extensive network of informants and enthusiasts all around North Sea coasts. He outlined his area of search and inquired about any bodies, identified or otherwise, which had washed up or been recovered at sea between 16 August and 11 September twenty-three years ago:

a long time, I admit, but I know how meticulous many of you are about record-keeping.

He was interested in cases

where the circumstances/causes of death were subjects of continuing speculation

and where

origins of the body's sea journey were either unknown or thought to have started in the southern North Sea.

He asked for dates, coordinates and, if possible, the time of day or night, along with a brief commentary about conditions of discovery – had the body washed ashore on an area of coastline frequented by people or not? If not, was there any indication if it had recently arrived from the sea or if it had been there for some time? He was also interested in unidentified boat wreckage, the same search area and same dates. In conclusion, he reiterated to his contacts that:

I'm hoping for anything that fits with an unreported accident having taken place, one that involved a person or persons going into the sea north or east of the Strait of Dover. Please send anything and everything. In anticipation, thank you.

The time was past midnight. Cal closed the laptop, reclined his seat and slept.

25

Flora Tolmie crossed the road, hurrying. Her movement was awkward, her legs and neck stiff from driving for seven hours, her arms folded tightly around her as if only they were holding her together. As she turned the corner into her street, a terrace of Victorian tenements in Bruntsfield, Edinburgh, a blustery, cold wind buffeted her. She faltered, put her head down and pressed on. As she approached her building, her progress was accompanied by the slamming of car doors and her name being shouted by strangers.

'Flora, did Kate kill him?'

'Flora, will you stand by Kate if it turns out she stabbed your father?'

'Flora, what's it like to be the sister of a murderer?'

Flora this, Kate that: familiarity and hostility in every question.

'Flora, what would your mother think?'

At that Flora halted mid-step. Reporters and photographers crowded round her. There was nowhere for her to go: the pavement blocked; a privet hedge to her left; cars parked at her right. She stood still, her chin pressed to her collarbone. 'Think of what?' she said to her feet.

Another voice: '. . . of Kate, you, this situation?'

Flora remembered Kate saying, *She left us, remember. She decided that looking after other children in another country was more important than being at home with you and me. So why are you rewarding her by dedicating your charity to her and looking for her? If she's alive, she hasn't made any effort to contact us. If she's dead, why put us through this? Why stir everything up? What gives you the right without asking whether I mind or not? By the way, I do mind, I mind a lot.*

Another voice cut in, as sharp-edged and as chill as the wind: 'Flora, what if your mother was here now? What would you say to her?'

Flora lifted her face to the questioner.

The jostling of bodies, the questions, stopped. The stillness was expectancy.

She blinked at a sudden glare of lights and again in confusion. 'I don't . . .' She hesitated. 'I don't know what I'd say to her.' Then, looking at her feet: 'Please, let me go inside. I've driven a long way. I'm tired.'

The reporters shuffled backwards.

At the gate to her building, she stopped. 'Actually, there is something.' She turned round and waited for the reporters and photographers to settle. 'This . . . this situation . . . this tragedy, is my fault. A man's been killed, a man claiming to be my father, my sister's been falsely accused of his murder, and none of this would have happened if I hadn't appealed for information about my mother's disappearance. I'm sorry for what has happened. But my sister isn't a murderer. She isn't capable of killing anyone. She's generous and caring. I wouldn't have wanted any other sister. I love her. That's what I would tell my mother.'

Going up the stone stairs to her flat, she found she was shaking. At her front door, she had to use both hands to hold the key steady. As the door swung open, the light in the stairwell penetrated her hall and Flora gasped at a human-shaped shadow seated outside her kitchen.

26

Cal woke with an unsettled, claustrophobic feeling. The pickup's windows were misted, nothing visible outside. After pushing open the driver's door, he emerged blearily on to the pavement and stretched his arms, back and neck. Squinting into the early-morning light, he noted the tide was ebbing, the sea silvery in contrast to the gun-metal of the night. A glance left caused Cal to start. Mrs Hawes was standing in her doorway, watching him. Her motionlessness, also how her hands were tucked into the gaps between her coat buttons, suggested she'd been there a while. Without acknowledging her, Cal returned to his pickup, banged shut the door, wiped a window on the other side from the Sandcastle Guest House so he could see out but Mrs Hawes couldn't see in. Then he tapped the space bar on his laptop.

The time was six twenty-seven. Cal entered his pass-word. Overnight, dozens of emails had arrived in his inbox, the remnants of the baying mob, as well as responses to his request for information about bodies or wreckage. After a quick scroll through, he realized most of the latter were apologies for incomplete records, records not going that far back or records which *did* go that far back but contained no report of any relevant incident. Cal selected an email headed 'Unidentified corpse'.

It had been sent by a German lifeguard whose father, a

retired detective, had been involved in investigating the 'suspicious' death of a body recovered at sea by a fishing boat around midday on 5 September, twenty-three years before.

> He was male, mid-twenties, never identified, being without a life jacket, clothes, papers or individual identifying marks. His face and body were lacerated and his left hand missing – severed. His injuries were consistent with being struck by a propeller, though the post-mortem concluded he died from asphyxiation before his body entered the sea. His DNA profile was circulated but no match found.

The lifeguard provided coordinates for the body's discovery.

Cal calculated the distance from the North Sea side of the Strait of Dover, roughly where he thought the suitcase might have started its journey. The body had been recovered almost 165 miles away. If it had travelled at the average speed of the bodies with which Cal had worked out the parameters of his search, its sea journey would have started around 13 August. But Christina Tolmie – still in possession of the suitcase, Cal assumed – was last seen in Gravelines on 16 August. Either the man was already dead and drifting before Christina reached the French coast or he'd gone into the sea somewhere else altogether. Which suggested to Cal the body was unlikely to be connected to her disappearance. Even so, he inputted the details into his laptop and selected 'PIW, deceased, without survival suit or buoyancy aid' from a drop-down menu of different 'targets'. PIW stood for 'person in the water'. A 'target' could be anything adrift – a ship, a body, a life raft, kayak, even a bait box. All had determining characteristics, including buoyancy, shape, orientation to the wind, ballast, the depth at which the 'target' floated, each one influencing speed of travel, also direction. The likely divergence of a 'target' from wind direction was built into each menu entry – Cal had compiled the menu from published work by the US Coast Guard Research and Development Center as well as from research conducted for European-based marine search and rescue services. For the rest, Cal relied on sophisticated ocean modelling, which included meteorological and other relevant data from drifters – floating oceanographic information gatherers. To trace the dead man's possible journey, Cal began to run the model backwards, from where his body had been found.

Then he worked through other emails containing reports of bodies. There were four: three men and a teenage girl. A theory was attached to each death: criminal in one case (sent by the German lifeguard), and three suicides, one of which might have been an accidental drowning after drinking too much (the girl). Cal also inputted eight reports of floating wreckage. Finally, he added the suitcase. Its backtrack started from Southwold. Now all he could do was hope that one or more of the bodies or wreckage were in close proximity to the suitcase on or soon after 16 August. If that happened, Cal would have the point at which the suitcase and perhaps a body went into the sea and began to drift before, in time, diverging.

At nine thirty a.m. he took a break, ate stale bread and drank water from a bottle. He got out of the pickup, walked about, stretched and glanced in the direction of the Sandcastle Guest House. Mrs Hawes had gone; her front door closed; the curtains still drawn; the guest house again giving the appearance of being shut up. Cal returned to the pickup, took the precaution of locking the doors – he thought there was something unhinged about Mrs Hawes's manner – before closing his eyes once more. He dozed, waking after ten. He checked his searches.

A quick scan through fourteen thumbnail icons resulted in Cal enlarging six and selecting four – the suitcase and three others: two were bodies, one was wreckage. On 16/17 August all were in the southern North Sea in the vicinity of the Strait of Dover.

Cal checked the identity of the body closest to the suitcase. It belonged to Ruth Jones, sixteen, who had last been seen in Margate, Kent, on 16 August, the same day as the last recorded sighting of Christina Tolmie on the other side of the Channel. Twenty-one days later, on 6 September, her body washed up on Texel, the most southerly and biggest of the West Frisian Islands, lying off the Dutch mainland between the North and Wadden seas, the latter an extraordinary and rare marine ecosystem which extended north towards Germany and Denmark. Cal was familiar with Texel. He'd done research there. It was famous for its long history of beachcombing: shipwrecks, lost cargoes, dead whales, flotsam of all kinds, including human bodies, washed up there.

Could there be a connection between Ruth Jones and the suitcase, also with Christina Tolmie?

After googling the teenager, it seemed unlikely.

Not only did Ruth and Christina disappear on different

sides of the Channel, they occupied different worlds: Ruth was Margate born and bred, a schoolgirl with a troubled family and past; Christina was a free spirit, a traveller, aid worker and mother. As far as Cal could discover from searching old newspaper reports, no link had ever been made between the two cases.

Ruth's photographs showed her to be happy-looking, with long dark brown hair, big eyes and a wide smile: a pretty girl. The facts about her life presented a less engaging picture. She was an only child. Her parents had separated when she was three. For the next nine years, she lived with her mother, Rita, until her death from heart failure. Then Ruth slipped through cracks in the system. The authorities only had fleeting sightings of her – when she was arrested for shoplifting; when she cut her wrists while having a bath in the house where her drunken father lived. Her school attendance was poor. She flitted between her father's house – departing when a new girl-friend was moved in – and bunking with friends.

The night before she was reported missing, Ruth should have attended a gig in Margate. She didn't show up, according to her best friend, Sarah Pauling. Nor, later, did she appear at Sarah's house, having arranged to spend the night there. In the morning Sarah wasn't 'especially alarmed, because it wasn't unusual for Ruth to meet some-one, stay out all night, because she liked dancing and having fun'.

By midday, having again searched for Ruth around town, Sarah became worried. 'It wasn't like Ruth not to be in touch in the morning, to tell me what happened, what boys she'd met, who'd tried to kiss her, who'd she kissed, you know.'

Sarah went looking for Ruth at the father's house. She wasn't there so Sarah went home and told her mother about Ruth being missing. Mrs Pauling contacted the police.

Cal understood why the search for Ruth Jones was muted in contrast to the enduring fuss about Christina Tolmie. From the tenor of the newspaper reports, as well as unattributed comments from police, the suspicion from the start was that Ruth's disappearance was deliberate. Either she'd run away, probably with a boy she'd picked up, or, given her previous suicide attempt, she'd killed herself. A press conference was held; an appeal for information made; some posters put up. When her body was discovered on Texel, in the absence of any other evidence, suicide by drowning was considered a possibility. A firmer speculation was misadventure – had she gone into the sea after having drunk too much?

Ruth's father, Mikey, was a dissenting voice. He insisted his 'darling daughter' had been taken advantage of and murdered. An unnamed police source responded: 'Of course he would say that because if she killed herself he's to blame. Now that she's dead he's making out he's a loving father when he never was when she was alive. He didn't ever know where she was or what she was doing, whether she was safe or not.'

Cal wondered: was a connection with Ruth Jones too far-fetched? Why, in real life, would her path ever have crossed Christina Tolmie's even if, in death, according to his backtracking, she had been in the approximate vicinity of the suitcase?

Experience had taught him never to rule anything out

because of improbability. That was his advantage over the police, being able to connect seemingly disconnected objects and events in the marine environment.

Anyway, Ruth Jones was the best prospect; none of the other bodies had been as close to the suitcase at the right time. By luck, he had a good contact on Texel: Olaf Haugen, the beachcomber, who lived in a farmstead built from recovered flotsam, driftwood planks, wire and corrugated sheeting. Cal knew Olaf through Alex – Alex first met Olaf while attending a conference at the Royal Netherlands Institute for Sea Research on Texel. Afterwards, Alex passed on his details because he kept meticulous records of flotsam washing up on the island, including ships' containers and other high-value cargoes, then a focus of Cal's research. Some weeks later, Cal stayed with Olaf. A memento of his visit was the driftwood man which resided in Cal's office ('a malign presence' according to Helen).

Cal now remembered Olaf's missed call during the Harry Fowler fiasco. He hadn't rung Olaf back. He wondered if Olaf knew about Alex's death. Cal checked his sent emails. Had he included Olaf in his round-robin about bodies? He had, but Olaf hadn't replied, which wasn't like him.

Cal wrote:

Hello Olaf (again),

I don't know if you read my previous email but I now have details of a specific case that interests me. It happened before your time on Texel but, given your knowledge of the island's tradition of beachcombing and of many of the more unusual finds, you might have heard about it. I'm inquiring about the discovery twenty-three years ago of a young woman's body which washed up on the beach by De Koog. The date she was found was 6 September. Her name was Ruth Jones. She was British, from Margate in Kent. Cause of death was never established. Suicide was thought possible. So was drowning after going into the sea, drunk. Do you know anything about the circumstances of her discovery? Have you heard anything? I'm trying to make a connection to a woman called Christina Tolmie who disappeared in France about the same time. All I have is a suitcase that Christina Tolmie had in her possession before she vanished. It contained boys' clothes and possibly (a guess, this) money.

Cal wondered about mentioning Alex's death. On reflection, he thought Mrs Lauder would have told him because she used Alex's phone to contact his friends. Olaf's number would have been among them. Probably, she'd spoken to Olaf before Cal – that night Cal had been out, walking the disused rail line. Perhaps Olaf had rung to check Cal knew.

Cal decided to mention Alex's death when Olaf replied: better not to include such news as a 'by the way, were you aware?' in an email about something else.

Cal clicked on send, then opened his door, inhaled, got out and stretched. Out of the corner of his eye he saw that Mrs Hawes was at her first-floor window, watching him. Instead of looking at her, he took the steps down to the beach. Cal went to where the sand was firm and wet, where Mrs Hawes could see him. Using the heel of his boot, he wrote: *WHERE DID STEPHEN GET THE*

MONEY? Closer to the sea, he wrote: *IT WAS £35K, NOT £25K.* When he turned round, Mrs Hawes was watching, her hands at her mouth.

Cal shouted in her direction, 'Well?'

Mrs Hawes lurched back from the window. Should Cal let the tide wash the message away or should he obscure it with his boot?

The tide could do it. He had to drive to Margate and find Ruth Jones's father.

27

They sat opposite each other at the kitchen table, facing in different directions: Helen towards the window, Flora watching the clock. Both were beyond sleep and as aware as the other of time running out and the case against Kate being as persuasive as it was when Flora opened her flat door, gasping, 'Who are you?' and Helen had replied, 'Detective Sergeant Jamieson – I let myself in with your sister's keys. You don't mind, do you?'

Neither had spoken since Flora had said, 'You've asked me that already. You've asked me every question more than once, and I wish I had other answers, better answers, answers that would help Kate, but I don't. I don't, all right. Stop, please, *please*. I've told you all I can, all I know. Kate wouldn't have killed that poor man. She wouldn't.'

In that ensuing interlude, Helen realized why she was trying so hard to prove Kate Tolmie's innocence despite the strength of evidence against her. Helen was being guided by hollowness, a feeling inside her which she felt first at the age of six when her parents were killed in a motoring accident. That emptiness was like a gnawing hunger. If she'd been sent a postcard offering 'the truth about your mother', she'd have been eager for information, whatever it was, good or bad: anything being better than the dull ache of nothingness. Not so, it seemed for Kate. Otherwise why would she have stabbed Picoult without talking to him? Even Flora had behaved in a way that Helen never would. After receiving that first card, Flora had been cautious when Helen would have been hasty. She took her assistant, Luke, to the designated meeting place. They left after twenty minutes. Helen would have waited an hour, longer.

'Do you remember if there was a beggar?' Helen asked.

Flora: 'Was there? Perhaps there was. I don't know. I wasn't looking for a beggar. I didn't notice a beggar.'

Helen: 'Perhaps turning up with your assistant frightened him away.'

After the second card, Flora took Maria, her cleaner. They were early. They waited longer, at Maria's insistence, more than half an hour. Maria was more like Helen would have been. Nobody approached them; nobody signalled to them.

'Was there a beggar?' Helen asked again.

'I don't think so. I don't know. Maybe I do remember seeing one of those homeless placards and a blanket. Did I? I'm not sure. Yes, I did, because I remember thinking the placard was familiar. I don't know why, something about the words. I don't remember a beggar, though, just the placard and a blanket.'

Helen: 'He saw you coming. He saw you had someone with you. He took off.'

Flora said she ignored the other cards. 'Luke said they were probably hoaxes. By then I thought so too.'

Helen asked, 'You didn't tell Kate about them?'

'No, she would have been angry if I had.'

'Angry with you, not angry with the person who sent the cards?'

'Angry with us both, I imagine. Angry with the situation, me trying to find out what happened to our mother, and the writer of the cards for exploiting the situation, my emotions.'

'You were frightened?'

'I suppose I was, frightened of whoever was doing the writing, what he wanted; also, I suppose, apprehensive about what the truth might turn out to be, if he knew the truth.'

'*He?*'

Flora nodded. 'I thought so, yes.'

'Did Kate know you were frightened?'

'No.'

'Once she read the cards, would she have guessed?'

'I imagine so, yes.'

'She stabbed someone once before to protect you.'

Flora rolled her eyes, sighed. 'That was a long time ago. She didn't really stab her. The girl who was bullying me pushed the knife in so Kate's punishment would be worse.'

After talking to Flora for almost three hours, Helen realized there was a crucial difference between a child whose parents had been killed accidentally and one whose parent or parents had disappeared, where the reasons for the absence were unknown to the child. That child, if Flora and Kate were examples, would grow up to be inconsistent, sometimes angry and rejecting, at others longing for the parents' return. The keenness of the hurt and the extent of the anger depended on whether or not that child had ever been loved by one or other of the parents before the separation. Helen had been loved by both;

she loved both in return, still longed for them, the emptiness inside her still a raw and gaping hole that her adoptive mother, despite giving love to Helen and receiving love, had never filled. Flora had been loved by her mother. Kate had felt unloved. Flora was calmer than Kate, less hurt, less angry.

Was Kate so hurt, her rage so strong, she would have stabbed a man without asking any questions if she thought that man might be the father who had abandoned her?

Helen said, 'I haven't told anyone this before. When I was ten, I remember reading about two girls, one six, the other four, whose mother had gone missing, who didn't have a father, who'd never known their father. I read everything I could about those girls because, you see, those girls were like me. They were orphans and I thought I'd like to look after those girls. I used to imagine . . .' She made a sound to show how young, naïve she was. 'Well, I used to imagine all of us living together, a community of orphans, all girls. I used to think I'd look after you, you and your sister. I'm sorry, Flora. It turns out I'm not able to do that. I'm sorry because, when I leave here, I'll have to write a report which will result in your sister being charged with murder.'

Flora watched as Helen removed a folded piece of paper from her pocket.

Helen said, 'I can't withhold this any longer. I'll have to show it to my senior officer.'

'What is it?'

'Do you remember Kate sending you an email threatening to kill your mother if she came back?'

Flora said, 'Yes, but she wouldn't have.'

Helen read: '"I won't even let her open her mouth. I'll kill her as soon as I see her. I will. I'll fucking kill her because I won't be able to listen to her fucking excuses for running out on us."'

Flora closed her eyes and shook her head.

'Is that what happened?' Helen asked. 'Somewhere inside her, when she felt that familiarity she mentioned, did she realize that Louis Dufour or Jacques Picoult was her father? Did something snap in her? Did she stab him before he could open his mouth, before he could make excuses?'

'No,' Flora said. 'No.'

'That's the way it looks. The knife that killed him had a black handle – there are other identical knives in this kitchen. A similar knife with a green handle was found in Kate's coat pocket. You have two others like it too.'

Silence hung heavy in the room.

Helen said, 'I wish we'd met under different circumstances.' She looked at Flora. 'I'm sorry.'

At the kitchen door, she looked back. 'You know Cal McGill, don't you? I gather he's helping you, something about a suitcase your mother had with her when she disappeared.'

Flora said, 'That doesn't matter any more.'

'Let him carry on. He's good. Once he's on the trail he never stops. He'll follow that suitcase to your mother and all the way to Jacques Picoult becoming Louis Dufour and turning up outside Haymarket Station, if that's where it leads. Flora, once my boss has read my report, he won't give me time to look for another killer. Kate will be charged with murder. If Kate didn't kill Picoult, Cal

McGill's your only hope of finding out who did and of saving your sister.'

And then she said, 'Would it bother you if Cal kept me in touch with his investigation? In case he finds out something important?'

Flora answered, 'I wouldn't mind, no.'

'Then please tell him, because he can be a little uncommunicative when he's working.'

Uncommunicative whether he's working or not, Helen thought.

28

At a hold-up for roadworks on the A12 near Chelmsford, on his way to Margate, Kent, where Ruth Jones grew up, Cal read a news update about Louis Dufour on the BBC Scotland website.

Louis Dufour, who was found murdered yesterday in the vicinity of Haymarket Station, Edinburgh, has been identified as Jacques Picoult by former neighbours in the French coastal town of Gravelines, near Calais.

Mr Dufour or Picoult used to be a familiar sight around L'Anse des Espagnols, part of the Gravelines marina, on the River Aa. He kept a boat there and rented a flat nearby. Twenty-three years ago he left the area the same day a pregnant woman with whom he had been having an affair committed suicide. He went to Portugal in his eighteen-foot motorboat, *Bel Esprit*. Despite Dufour's changed appearance – attributed to alcoholism, drug use and a prison sentence as much as to age – the owner of the restaurant beside L'Anse des Espagnols recognized a photograph of Mr Dufour and has told police investigating the murder that he was the man they used to know as Jacques Picoult.

If Dufour is formally identified as Picoult, it could be a significant breakthrough in the case of Christina Tolmie, the British charity worker who vanished in mysterious circumstances two days after Picoult left Gravelines in his boat. The last sighting of

Tolmie was in the vicinity of L'Anse des Espagnols where she was inquiring about Picoult.

Her abandoned and empty van was found parked in a nearby side street. A ferry booking in her name from Calais to Dover was unused.

Tolmie and Picoult were thought to have become friends while working together on famine relief in east Africa about ten years earlier. During the police hunt for Ms Tolmie, Picoult was one of a number of men identified as the possible father of her two daughters, Kate, now twenty-nine, and Flora, twenty-seven. Picoult was eventually found and eliminated from the inquiry, though paternity was never established. The result of a DNA test to discover whether Picoult was the father is expected soon.

Police sources confirm a twenty-nine-year-old woman is expected to be charged with the murder of Picoult/Dufour.

Margate: along the seafront, past the Turner Contemporary gallery, Cal turned right into a terraced street of three-storey houses. Each had identical and protruding bay windows, which gave the properties the appearance of elderly spinsters who were goggle-eyed at having to adjust to another reduction in circumstances. As if the demise of the bucket-and-spade holiday market in the 1970s had not been shock enough, they'd suffered the neighbourhood's decline into shabbiness, rooms being let cheaply to the unemployed, entire houses converted into residential homes for troubled children dispatched from posher parts of southern England. More recently, an influx of strangers, eastern Europeans, made Margate their beachhead. Now (the last straw?) hipster refugees from London were being attracted to this part of the Kent coast in search of a combination impossible to find in the metropolis: period property, faded grandeur and affordable prices. Perhaps the spinsters were also wide-eyed at streets around this one being described in fashionable magazines as 'Shoreditch-on-Sea'. Had any worse insult been directed at the town?

At number eighteen, Cal found a house which had stubbornly resisted change for certainly more than two decades. Above the front door was the same tawdry display of plastic flowers – Ruth's name in white, a heart in blue, and 'Justice' in red – that had been in the background when Mikey Jones was interviewed for local BBC news after his daughter's belated funeral. The clip was still available in grainy, flickering video on the Justice for Ruth website. 'I won't be taking this lot down,' the teenager's father promised then, 'until the police pull their fingers out and arrest whoever murdered Ruth.' He'd sniffled, wiped away a tear and stared at the camera. 'What proof do the police have for saying she killed herself or was drowned in an accident? Show me the evidence. Do they know her better than her dad? Course they don't.' Sniff. 'I'm telling you, she wouldn't have killed herself. She was a good girl, loved life, loved her dad, ask anyone.' Wipe. Sniffle.

The stone steps to the Jones house were tilted, cracked and uneven. A buddleia sprouted at the base of rusting railings. The paint on the door was flaking. The brass bell surround was hanging off. Cal knocked instead and the door was opened quickly by a twenty-something woman with short dark hair. She wore grey joggers, a pale yellow T-shirt and held a wood-handled floor brush in her left hand.

'Is Mr Jones in?' Cal asked.

She studied Cal before speaking. 'You know Mikey?' Her accent was foreign, probably Polish, Cal thought, and her tone direct, demanding.

'No.' Cal shook his head. 'But if he's available, I'd like to speak to him, it's about his daughter.' He glanced at Ruth's name above the door. 'Is he at home?'

She ignored his question. 'I'm Hanna. I live here, work here.' An eyebrow arched to prompt from him a similar disclosure.

He was slow to catch on. 'Oh, Cal, Cal McGill.'

The eyebrow pushed higher. 'Why do you want to speak to Mikey about Ruth?'

Cal replied, 'I investigate cases like Ruth's.'

She nodded. 'Mikey drink,' she said after a while. 'Has funny ideas, lots of funny ideas. Understand?' Her eyes searched Cal's as if looking for comprehension. 'Drink buggered up Mikey's brain. Head buggered. Everything buggered.'

'Can he talk about Ruth?'

'Talks only about Ruth. Talks shit about her.'

'Would he talk to me?' Cal wasn't sure if Hanna was being protective of Ruth's father or contemptuous of him.

Her eyes narrowed. 'You not hear what I tell you?'

'I heard you.'

Her bottom lip pushed out. She shrugged. 'OK,' she announced in the same matter-of-fact manner. 'You don't mind hearing shit, I show you Mikey.'

She turned, beckoned Cal to follow. They went along a narrow passage, stepping round stacks of brown boxes. Some were open and Cal noticed each contained A4-sized colour posters of a smiling teenager with long dark hair, big eyes and wide mouth. Above her face, in bold black, was printed 'Justice for Ruth', and along the bottom, in red, 'Murdered', followed by the date of her death.

The posters on top were faded.

Hanna said, 'Before brain buggered, before legs buggered, Mikey handed out posters every day, Saturday, Sunday, rain, not rain, sun, not sun, every day talk about Ruth. Then, not talk shit.'

At a flight of stairs descending into a basement, she said, 'Mikey down there.' Then she glanced at two open doors beside and behind her. Cal saw one led to a small kitchen.

'Mikey's legs buggered so can't get upstairs. I clean, I shop, no pay rent. This where I live. That where Mikey.'

Cal said, 'You don't live together.'

She smiled, appeared satisfied. Cal having shown sufficient grasp of the domestic arrangements in the house, she banged on the wall at the top of the stairs and shouted down: 'Mikey, there's a man to talk about Ruth.'

Cal heard a grunt, followed by the noise of a bottle falling.

'Mikey awake now,' she said.

Cal said 'Thanks'. As he was about to go down the stairs she extended an arm to block him. 'He talk shit but . . .' Her mouth pulled to one side.

'His only child's dead,' Cal said.

Her arm retracted. 'Remember, OK?'

'OK,' Cal said.

Cleans and shops for Mikey and looks out for him, he thought.

The stairs were wood, covered in paint that had once

been white but with age and use had turned brownish-yellow. They opened on to a small square hallway, which was dank-smelling and dark, and a doorway – with no door – into a big, low room. An exposed steel beam travelled its width. Jagged plaster cracks extended across the ceiling. On the right of the doorway was an old-fashioned cooker, a large sink chipped around its rim and a table covered with plates, mugs and glasses, empty bottles – Cal saw whisky, vodka and beer – and another open box of Ruth's posters. At the other end of the room were a sofa and two high-backed armchairs with torn covers and protruding stuffing. They stood in front of a gaping fireplace in which was a cheap blow-heater. Above the mantelpiece was a display of photographs and newspaper cuttings – Cal recognized Ruth's face in close-ups and blown-up group shots – and a large-scale aerial photograph of Margate on which were Post-it notes, some peeling off, others askew, few stuck-on flat and straight.

The scene reminded Cal of his office. Was he, had he been, would he *be* a similar kind of oddball pursuing an obsession? Would he end up somewhere like this, neglected and ramshackle, and watched over by someone called Hanna who was relieved to be living apart upstairs and who made sure visitors understood the arrangement? Would his Hanna also describe him as 'brain buggered'?

The other reason for Cal being disconcerted at being in this basement was the apparent absence of Mikey. Only when Cal asked, 'Mr Jones? Mikey?' – hesitatingly addressing one half of the room then the other – did Ruth's father make known his presence. Cal heard a wheezing, sobbing sound that emanated from one of the two high-backed chairs. Cal went further into the room. 'Mr Jones?' First he saw more empty bottles, lying where they had dropped, like casualties in war, followed by trousers that were hanging loosely as though there was no flesh, muscle or bone inside them. *Legs buggered.*

Cal carried on until a torso came into sight – rather, a stained, long-sleeved, zipped-up, mushroom-coloured fleece that was torso-shaped – and a shrunken-looking head with a slick of greasy greyish hair and papery skin, the same thin texture and parchment colour that Cal associated with cancer. In contrast to the rest of him – shrivelled, diminished, almost not there – his eyes were large with a surround that was as startlingly white as the pupils were black: oily black and shiny.

Everything buggered.

Not the eyes, Cal thought. *Not the eyes.*

The eyes were as big as his daughter's.

'Mr Jones? Mikey?'

Those large eyes stared at the wall above the fireplace, at Ruth's photographs, with a yearning expression that Cal associated with Old Master paintings depicting adoration. Thin, cracked lips like worm casts parted and a voice croaked: 'She was something, my Ruth, good girl, always loved her dad.' One hand clenched the other. 'Me and her, tight, tight, always were.' His knuckles turned bloodless white as his grip firmed. 'Did the best for her even though it wasn't easy, bringing up a girl without her mum.'

Talks only about Ruth. Talks shit about her. Cal called to mind the few newspaper reports he'd read about Ruth's death. They told a different version of the father-daughter relationship. How Mikey was absent one way or another despite being Ruth's only parent – Rita, her mother, having died from heart failure when Ruth was twelve. Either Mikey was working on building sites in London, staying over at night, or he was at home in Margate, unemployed and usually with one of a series of live-in women. After her mother's death, Ruth found herself being metaphorically pushed out to sea by the neglect of her father. No one was surprised when that was where she ended up, dead. It had almost been expected, tragedy having a way of passing from one generation to the next.

Now Mikey was imploring Cal to go closer to a blown-up photograph of Ruth. 'Look at her,' he commanded. 'Forget about Ruth's dad. Forget she loved him. A girl who looked like that wouldn't take her own life. Course she wouldn't. Ruthie had everything to live for. Go on, look for yourself. Go closer.'

Before Cal had a chance to answer, Mikey began sobbing. Between gasps and stuttering, he managed to complete a sentence. 'Ruthie wouldn't have done that to her dad, not Ruthie.'

'I'm sorry.' Cal was taken aback at such a show of uncontrolled emotion after twenty-three years.

Mikey shook his head slowly. His eyes widened. 'Terrible, it's been; my nerves . . .' He stretched out his fingers. His hands shook. 'See that. Used to be steady as a rock. Before. Before.' He looked up at Cal. 'You tell me, would a girl like that, a girl who loved her dad, have taken her own life when she'd have known she'd be killing her dad too?'

'No,' Cal replied, after looking again at the blow-up of Ruth, 'I can't imagine she would. That's why I'm here.' He introduced himself, emphasizing *Dr* McGill. 'Not a medical doctor, one of marine science. My work involves trying to find out what happened when people – bodies – wash up on a coast and no one knows exactly how they got there. Like Ruth.'

The empty clothes were motionless, so were Mikey's eyes. They were suddenly dry, watchful. Thin lips curled back to show brown front teeth.

Cal carried on: 'A woman was reported missing around the same time as Ruth. She was last seen on the other side of the English Channel. Her name was Christina Tolmie. Her body's never been found. I wondered if you recognized the name, if you knew of any connection between Ruth and her . . . the coincidence of two people going missing like that . . .'

The eyes kept staring.

Cal tried again. 'Could they have been together? On a boat?'

Still staring.

Cal said, 'I'm asking, Mr Jones, because a suitcase belonging to Christina Tolmie was found on the Suffolk coast twelve days before Ruth's body was recovered on Texel. I've tracked back both. At one stage in Ruth's journey – near the beginning – she drifted close to the suitcase. I'm just trying to work out whether your daughter and Christina Tolmie knew each other and some accident occurred, if they were on the same boat, if Ruth and Christina Tolmie went overboard together . . . with the suitcase.'

The eyes stared.

'Or whether Ruth and the suitcase just happened to be

in the same vicinity and there was no connection between them other than, for a while, they were close to one another. I'm exploring possibilities. It's not a precise science.'

'An accident, you say?'

'Maybe. I don't know.'

The head shook, the eyes remained on Cal. 'You haven't been listening.'

Cal blinked once and again to encourage Mikey to do the same.

The voice rasped: 'She was murdered, understand, murdered, not an accident.'

Cal nodded.

A scrawny, clenched hand pressed against his fleece, where his heart was. 'Swear to God.' Mikey's lips moved.

God was being sworn to.

'Do you know who killed her?' Cal asked.

Mikey's other hand slipped down the side of his chair and returned holding a photograph. When Cal reached out to take it, Mikey snatched it back. 'No one touches this picture. Apart from Ruthie's dad.' His jaw jutted. 'Right?'

Cal said, 'Yes.'

Mikey held the photograph towards Cal.

It showed four people and a boat. Two were on a pontoon – a woman and a boy. Their backs were to the camera. The woman had her left hand on the child's left shoulder. Her right was holding a small, familiar suitcase. She wore a light summer dress, a flower pattern of pale yellows with white short sleeves. Her hair was red, shoulder length and disarranged. The boy was old-fashioned by comparison. He wore dark grey short trousers, grey ankle socks, black shoes and a white shirt. Another female, younger than the first, reached from the boat for a rucksack which was on the quayside. She was dressed in black jeans, a turquoise T-shirt and had long auburn hair which was blowing across her face. Behind her, standing straight, was a fourth person: a male. Although the quality of the print was poor, the detail blurry, his features were in focus. He had curly white-blond hair, a straight mouth, a skewed nose as if it had once been broken. He was young, late teens or early twenties, well built, fresh-faced and boyish-looking.

Mikey said, 'The dark-haired one, that's my Ruth. I'd recognize her anywhere.'

Cal said nothing. He stared at the photograph. If Mikey had been observant he would have noticed the colour draining from Cal's face. He would also have seen Cal's eyes darting from one figure to the next, disbelieving what he was seeing but seeing it nonetheless.

Olaf as a young man! Olaf with a woman who had the same hair colour as Christina Tolmie. Olaf with Ruth Jones, the suitcase and a boy.

29

'You listening to me?' Mikey demanded.

Cal managed to stutter, 'Him ... the ... the young man on the boat ... do you know him?'

Mikey replied, 'He killed her, murdered my girl. Six years ago Detective Constable Jane Jarvis stood where you are, told me he was the suspect. She had to say suspect, didn't she? But she knew. She knew all right. Murderer, that's him. Killed Ruth.'

Mikey slapped his left hand against the arm of the chair. Dust rose as he waved the photograph in his other hand. 'Jane Jarvis asked me if I could identify any of them. I said nobody apart from Ruth. Did she know the man, I asked her, but she didn't answer. So I kept her picture, told her she'd have to kill me before I'd hand it over.' His thin lips stretched in a sly smile: *clever Mikey*. 'I took it to the editor of the local newspaper, said I had a big story. The ... man ... who ... murdered ... Ruth ... Jones.' He held his arms apart to illustrate how big the headline would have been.

'What happened?' Cal asked.

'A conspiracy, that's what, a cover-up. The newspaper refused to publish because the police warned the editor off, said there wasn't a suspect and I'd dug up a photograph that could have been of any teenager with long dark hair. An inspector came to the door, gave me a lecture and told me I'd be in trouble for fabricating evidence and wasting police time. I told him to ask Detective Constable Jane Jarvis whether the picture of Ruth was genuine. He said there wasn't any detective constable of that name working in Kent, never was and never had been.' Mikey stopped. 'If you want my opinion, they moved her out of the way because it'd look bad for the others. Hadn't got off their arses for the previous seventeen years, had they? Said Ruth had killed herself or drowned after drinking. No, not Ruth. Murdered, she was.'

'Jane Jarvis, the detective constable, did she visit again?'

'I told you, they got rid of her.'

The head shook. The eyes remained on Cal, who took out his phone and was about to take a picture of the photograph when Mikey snatched it away.

His lips stretched back in a snarl. 'You promise to find out who he is? You tell me, all right?'

Cal nodded. 'Yes.'

Slowly Mikey's arm extended.

Cal took more than one picture with his phone, in case any were blurry. 'Do you know where the photograph was taken? Was it Margate?'

Mikey's head shook.

'Who took the photograph?' Cal asked. 'Did Jane Jarvis tell you?'

Mikey didn't answer. He gazed longingly at the blow-up of his daughter on the wall, then said, 'Take what life offers, Ruthie. Live your life, Ruthie. That's what I'd told her. Drummed that into her.' His body heaved at his part in the tragedy. 'But she wouldn't have killed herself. Not Ruthie, not my girl.'

Rather than watch Mikey, Cal looked at his phone. Using two fingers, he blew up the photograph, peered closer. 'Has Sarah . . . Ruth's best friend . . . Sarah Pauling seen this? Does she recognize any of them or where it might have been taken?'

Mikey's expression hardened. 'That bitch, she lied about Ruthie. The night she said Ruthie didn't turn up for the concert, course she did. Ruthie always turned up, never let anyone down. Ask anyone. Ruthie did what she said, always, just like her dad.'

'Why would Sarah Pauling lie?'

Mikey shrugged and unfurled a crooked finger and pointed at the display on the wall. 'That's her, second picture on the left, with Ruthie. Always jealous of my girl, she was.'

Cal went closer. Sarah was smaller than Ruth, plainer, with black frizzy hair; not sleek like Ruth's. Cal said, 'I'd probably have been jealous of Ruth if I'd been Sarah.'

'Jealous, lying bitch.'

'Does she still live in Margate?'

Mikey shook his head. 'Took off after Ruthie's funeral, went to London with a boy from along the road, Danny Allison. Married him, worked in one of those fancy shops selling women's clothes. Got divorced after a couple of years. Calls herself Sarah Allison still.'

Cal said, 'Do you have a phone number or address?'

'Doesn't live in London any more. When her parents died, she sold their big house in Margate, bought another abroad.'

'Where?'

Mikey's lips stretched in a sly smile. 'Texel, close to where Ruthie's body was found.'

Mikey watched for the effect on Cal.

'Really? Texel?'

'Thought she could run away but Ruthie won't let her go.' Mikey pointed at the wall. 'There, that card on the right. That lying bitch sends me one like that every September, arrives a day or two after the anniversary of Ruthie being found, has done ever since she moved there.'

Cal went closer. The photograph was of a beach hut with its double doors wide open. The sun shone on the back wall, illuminating a mural of a girl with long dark hair, not yet a teenager, playing in the sand by a deckchair in which sat an older woman. In the background of the mural was a beach hut, identical to the one in the photograph.

'Who's the girl?' Cal asked. 'The girl in the sand?'

'Supposed to be my Ruthie.'

'And the woman?'

'That's her mother, Rita, who's long gone, bless her.' After a respectful pause, Mikey rasped, 'Ruthie dreamed about being reunited with her mother, the two of them having a holiday together. There'd be a beach hut, a deckchair and Ruthie would be playing in the sand while Rita slept.' His eyes were hard when Cal looked at him. 'That bitch thinks she'll be forgiven. But she won't be. If she wasn't guilty, why would she have gone to Texel, turn a beach hut into a memorial for Ruthie and send a card once a year?'

'The mural inside the hut is Ruth's dream,' Cal said. 'Sarah's keeping Ruth's dream alive.'

Mikey jutted out his chin defiantly. 'If it hadn't been for her, Ruth would be alive.'

Cal spent some moments pretending to be interested in

228

the other photographs and cuttings, many of which involved cases where police concealed evidence or were reprimanded for failing to be sufficiently rigorous in their investigations.

When he turned round he noticed Mikey's big eyes were once again on the large blow-up photograph of Ruth, the prelude to a replay of sobbing and sighing, the self-pity and the rewriting of history: father and daughter being 'tight, tight'. Cal felt sorry for him: a ruin of a man racked with guilt at having been a bad father.

'Thanks, thank you for your time,' Cal said. 'I thought it was worth asking . . . about Christina Tolmie, whether Ruth knew her. I've disturbed you enough for one day.' He held up his phone. 'And if I find out anything about the man on the boat, I'll let you know.'

Cal crossed the room quickly without waiting for Mikey to reply. Before going upstairs, he looked again at his phone, at the copied photograph. Was he sure it was Olaf? So much time had passed. After enlarging the young man's face, he noticed another identifying detail apart from the crooked nose: a small vertical scar running from the corner of the right eye. It was Olaf. There was no doubt. The curly hair had become longer and silver. The outline of the jaw was now fleshier. But the eyes were the same, so was the scar and the crooked nose. When Cal met Olaf Haugen on Texel for the first time they compared noses. Cal's slanted to the right; Olaf's to the left. They'd laughed together about that. A diving accident in his case, Cal said. Bad navigation in his, Olaf replied. He'd been thrown out of a dinghy on to rocks. His nose had been broken, his eye gashed.

Cal lifted his head. Did Olaf know how Ruth died, what happened to Christina? Was Olaf a murderer? Cal couldn't believe he was. But the photograph was proof he knew Ruth and Christina, also that Ruth's and Christina's lives had crossed. Cal recalled how Olaf, a Norwegian by birth and nationality, had explained his residency on Texel: he'd 'washed up' on the island, he'd said when Cal met him. Cal assumed a woman was involved and the relationship had ended, a period of his life Olaf preferred not to revisit, hence the vagueness of his answer. Now Cal wondered if a dead teenager had taken Olaf to Texel. Ruth? Was Olaf a killer who revisited his victims? Where was Christina? Where, too, was the boy? Did Olaf know?

Was that why Olaf hadn't replied to his emails?

Cal exhaled loudly before ascending the stairs. At the top Hanna was waiting, arms folded, gloves on and brush propped against the wall. 'Talk shit, Mikey?'

'Maybe, I don't know,' Cal replied.

She frowned. 'Some shit?'

'Some,' Cal agreed.

'Told you.' Hanna went along the passage, past the boxes of posters. Cal followed. After opening the front door Hanna turned back. 'Shit happens,' she said. 'Shit happens to Mikey.'

She gave Cal one of her looks.

He said, 'Yeah', but thought, *Shit, Olaf!*

Then he wondered: did Sarah Allison, formerly Pauling, know she was living on the same island as the man who might have killed her best friend?

*

In London, between appointments, Sarah read an email from Lotte.

Dearest Sarah,

You must think me peculiar, disappearing off to Amsterdam without saying anything especially after your suggestion that, one of these days, we should travel together. That old busybody Jan De Vries mentioned you'd dropped by yesterday as you were leaving for London. He said you were surprised to hear I was away and apologized to me in case I hadn't wanted you to know. Silly man!

I'm sorry; I should have put an explanatory note through your door. My behaviour is not as (I fear) it might appear. I wasn't keeping anything from you.

I wasn't intending to go to Amsterdam yesterday until my aunt rang at four twenty-four a.m! She'd fallen on her way to the bathroom and couldn't get up. As you know, she hates anyone else dealing with her apart from me. So I caught the bus at six thirteen a.m. and was sitting her up in bed and having breakfast with her by eight fifteen. Then she wouldn't let me go! After shopping and reading to her, I wasn't back in De Koog until about ten thirty p.m. (as, no doubt, Jan De Vries will tell you!). I'm exhausted.

Are you back tomorrow? Should I put milk in your fridge? That yoghurt you like? Bread? Wine? It's no trouble because I'll be going shopping. Let's meet for a drink or supper. I'd very much like to hear about London.

Lotte XXXX

Sarah read the email again and thought, once she was back on Texel, Lotte might be back to normal again.

*

Helen leaned back. She narrowed her eyes. She frowned. She turned her head to the left, then back to the right. She studied Cal's text message as if it was some sort of visual puzzle and that if only she looked at it in the right way she might spot some civility – there was no 'Dear Helen' or 'Hi Helen' or 'Can you help me?' or 'Please' or even 'How are you?' There was no preamble, not even a question.

> I'm interested in a detective constable called Jane Jarvis who was working in Margate, Kent, six years ago.

You're interested. Helen sighed impatiently. It was typical of Cal. As soon as he was following a line of inquiry he thought of nothing else, of no one else.

Helen texted:

> No, Cal. The rules are: 1. You tell me why you're interested in Detective Constable Jarvis. 2. I decide whether to try to find out where she is and to share information with you. 3. You tell me everything about your current inquiry. Oh, and just in case you're going to claim client confidentiality, Flora Tolmie has no objection to you sharing information with me. You should have a confirmatory email from her to that effect.

Waiting in the queue to board the P&O ferry, *Spirit of Britain*, at Dover, Cal tore a sheet from a notebook and wrote *IOU Flora* and, underneath, *£63.20 diesel* and *£131 ferry*. Next he counted the loose change lying on the front passenger seat, after which he studied a chart of the southern North Sea. Each activity was a postponement of the inevitable, his routine crab-wise approach to having to do anything with which he was uncomfortable, in this case briefing Helen. Having read Flora's email, his reluctance was habit – his default being to give little away to anyone, (in case of what he wasn't exactly sure, though; in his mind, it was a wise, precautionary principle). Finally, after more procrastinations, rubbing his knee, running his fingers through his hair, glancing in his mirror at the queue of cars behind, he started an email to Helen, the opening sentence of which was, 'You know I don't like doing this.' His protest registered, he agreed to her conditions, before briefing her on his discoveries so far, explaining why he was inquiring about DC Jarvis. He attached the photograph Jarvis had shown to Mikey Jones.

She gave Mikey the impression the young man on the boat (looking towards the camera) was being investigated in connection with Ruth's death. Mikey said he didn't recognize him. Nor was he aware Ruth knew him. But I know him. His name is Olaf Haugen. He's a beachcomber, a Norwegian, who has lived on Texel for, I think, fifteen years. When I did some research on Texel a couple of years ago, I met Olaf. We were introduced by my friend Alex Lauder, who met Olaf at a conference on Texel (coincidence?). Alex thought Olaf and I would get on. We did. I bunked at his house (well, shack made of flotsam and tied together with rope) and we've kept in touch since, exchanging information. But I can't help thinking what a small world this is turning out to be.

Alex knew Olaf. Now it appears – see photograph – Olaf (the young man) knew Ruth Jones (long dark hair) and Christina Tolmie (red hair, back to camera). Olaf lives on Texel where Ruth's body washed up. So does Sarah Pauling (married name Allison), who was Ruth's best friend from Margate. Also, Alex, until his death, was the boyfriend/partner of Flora Tolmie. One thing leads to another, and everything and everyone is connected. Odd, don't you think? Is Jacques Picoult/Louis Dufour's murder also linked? Was the photograph taken in Gravelines, which Picoult abandoned a day or two before? If so, I'm beginning to think this is one of those examples of seemingly disconnected events having a common origin. I'm at the Dover ferry, en route for Texel. I'm going via Gravelines. That's why I asked about DC Jarvis. Mikey Jones says she's been moved. Can you find out where? She's key.

Please.

Also, there's a boy in the photograph. Where is he? Who is he? Flora's last words to her mother as she left home for Romania were, 'Bring me back a brother'. Is he the brother Flora wanted? Is he a present from a Romanian orphanage? There's no mention of a boy being missing in any of the many news reports about Christina Tolmie's disappearance. But boys' clothes were in the suitcase, similar to the ones the boy is wearing in the photograph. Any ideas welcome.

As Cal was embarking on the ferry, Helen replied:

Dear Cal,

Thank you. The thought which occurs to me right away is this: if everyone else is connected, what's *your* connection? Why are you involved in this?

Cal swore. He didn't reply. 'Because Alex was my friend, because I owe him,' he muttered impatiently. 'Flora was his girlfriend. Alex would want me to help her.' Helen and her IQ of 173 should be able to work that out.

After embarking, Cal went to the ferry's restaurant, ate fish and chips. He was having coffee when he glanced at the television on the wall to his left. A young woman with red hair was being besieged by reporters and film crews as she emerged from a tenement building. Cal recognized Edinburgh architecture and Flora Tolmie. The sound was low. In his hurry to get closer, Cal knocked over a glass of water. After apologizing to the waitress, he managed to hear Flora say, 'A terrible mistake has been made. My sister is innocent. She wouldn't hurt anyone.'

A reporter shouted out: 'What are you going to do now?'

Flora stopped walking and turned back. 'Fight for my sister.'

Another shouted question: 'Do you wish your father was still alive?'

Flora replied, 'Of course I wish that man was alive. So does my sister.'

'Will you attend his funeral?'

Flora hesitated. 'I haven't thought . . . Really, I don't know. Even if he was my father from a biological point of view, he wasn't ever Kate's or my father while he was alive.' She put her head down, turned away and kept on walking, the photographers and reporters in pursuit.

From Calais, Cal drove east along the A16 dual carriage-way. At Exit 51, he turned off and went north on the D218 towards Gravelines. The close proximity of the town set him thinking again about connections: Christina Tolmie being in the same photograph as Ruth Jones and Olaf. Cal wondered about Helen's last text message. Had he misunderstood her? Rather than questioning his involvement – not *should* he be involved – she was asking him to think about a different, broader question. Everyone and everything else appeared to be connected: how was Cal, and why?

Cal cast his mind back to the beginning, when

Rosemary Lauder had informed him of Alex's impending death. From that moment, Cal was involved whether he liked it or not. No, that wasn't the start, Cal realized. The start had been thirteen years earlier, when Cal was a student at SAMS. Then, too, he was a loner, content in his own company, but he'd been befriended by Alex Lauder, who took an interest in Cal's early research into tracking flotsam, including bodies, *particularly* bodies. Alex always asked Cal to let him know about any interesting cases.

Also, one summer's evening, kayaking on a Scottish sea loch, Alex had extracted a promise from Cal to bury him there.

Now, approaching Gravelines, Cal repeated Helen's question with that different emphasis: 'Why are *you* involved in this?'

A few moments later, he asked, 'Why was Alex so keen for me to go to Texel?'

Cal's trip to research washed-up cargoes on the Dutch island had been Alex's suggestion. He'd introduced Cal to Olaf, had thought the two would get on because of their shared interest in beachcombing. They had. Cal liked Olaf.

Names and connections swirled around in Cal's head: Olaf with Ruth and Christina; Olaf with Alex and Cal; Flora, Christina's daughter, becoming Alex's girlfriend; Sarah, Ruth's best friend, living on the same island as Olaf; Jacques Picoult or Louis Dufour with Christina, also with Kate and Flora; Cal with Alex, Olaf and, recently, Kate and Flora.

Was that Helen's meaning? Not why had he *chosen* to become involved but why had *he* been chosen?

Ahead he saw the masts of yachts in Bassin Vauban,

the largest of three sites which collectively made up the Gravelines marina. He crossed the River Aa, turned left, following the sign to Petit-Fort-Philippe and the beach. Somewhere further along that bank of the river he would find L'Anse des Espagnols, named after the Spaniards who built the channel in the first half of the eighteenth century. It had seventy-eight moorings on three pontoons and was the smallest of the marina sites, the one where Jacques Picoult/Louis Dufour had kept his boat. On Rue Pierre Brossolette, Cal tried to turn towards the river, but no-entry signs were at every junction. Having overshot L'Anse des Espagnols, the road veered right into a square, Place du Docteur Calmette. The name was familiar. Somewhere here, all those years ago, Christina Tolmie's van was found abandoned. Cal wondered if she, too, had driven along Rue Pierre Brossolette, had been frustrated by no-entry signs and had parked, as he had, as soon as she realized the road was taking her away from the river, away from Jacques's mooring.

For the remainder of the evening Cal had similar thoughts about Christina Tolmie's movements.

As he walked along Passage Blondin, the river now in front of him, he imagined Christina Tolmie crossing the road ahead of him, Boulevard de L'Est, and going to the entrance – a locked grille gate – of L'Anse des Espagnols. Had she checked whether Jacques was on his boat before going to the nearby restaurant which he frequented? Now Cal was approaching the restaurant. There were tables outside, families eating dinner. A group of men stood at the entrance, talking. Cal looked at them, then at the river, which was canal-like. Had Christina Tolmie also been disappointed by that or had her mind been on other things? Cal sat at the last empty table outside. He ordered coffee and contemplated the river as though he thought it might reveal a clue to Christina Tolmie's disappearance. After half an hour he returned to his pickup. Before sleeping, he sent another email to Olaf on Texel.

> Will be arriving on Texel tomorrow, making inquiries about Ruth Jones (see previous message). Any chance of meeting up?

*

Helen emailed Cal:

> Louis Dufour/Jacques Picoult has been confirmed as the father of Kate Tolmie. Likely he's Flora's father too but she's unwilling to provide blood or a swab. She'd prefer not to know since he had nothing to do with her in life. For Kate Tolmie, the paternity finding provides motive. At trial, the prosecution will say she realized Dufour/Picoult was her father as soon as she saw him and killed him just as she threatened to kill her mother if she ever reappeared. The evidence all points to her even if my heart would prefer it didn't. One interesting loose end for you: the last Kent police officer called Jane Jarvis died fifteen years ago. She was in uniform, not a detective constable. So, who was the Jane Jarvis who visited Mikey Jones? How did she have the photograph? Plus: we mustn't lose sight of the boy. Who was/is he and what happened to him?

Helen waited for Cal's reply. When none came after twenty minutes she went to bed. Questions were piling up

238

again, her forty-eight hours running out. As she turned off her bedside light, her head hitting her pillow, she sighed loudly. Beacom was under pressure. If she asked for more time because finally there was a chance of clearing up the mystery of Christina Tolmie, he'd respond with one of the contemptuous glares she'd seen him direct at other detectives who indulged in special pleading. He'd say, rightly, Christina Tolmie was not their case, not a priority. Two murderers were running loose in Edinburgh. If she wanted, she could brief Kent Police or the police in Gravelines in her own time. There was other, more urgent work to be done. Helen sighed again. She owed Beacom. She must let go of her childhood fantasy of saving Kate and Flora Tolmie, of looking after them. Cal would have to pursue Christina Tolmie's disappearance on his own.

30

Sarah Allison was glad to be home. Travelling north from the ferry, she enjoyed how the lush greenness of Texel's fields was interrupted by rectangular blocks of vivid colour: the pinks, reds and yellows of commercially grown tulips and daffodils in flower. Soon the bus was entering Den Burg, the island's main settlement. As with the rural landscape, she liked the town for being orderly, human-scale and reassuring. However, as she continued north-west, she experienced a fleeting pang of anxiety. How would Lotte be?

She hoped all right. Her last email had been typical Lotte, normal, sweet Lotte.

In De Koog, Sarah alighted at the thirty-five stop opposite the Lidl supermarket. Her house in Wintergroen was only a distance of a few hundred metres, a pleasant walk after so much sitting. On the way she wondered if her sense of easy belonging came from De Koog being similar in atmosphere, if not size, to Margate where she grew up. Both were places which geared up for a summer season and an invasion of families on holiday. Both lived for high days and holidays. Both were by the sea. Also, both were connected to Ruth.

Not only had Sarah linked up again with her childhood friend, she'd done so in a bucket-and-spade seaside resort. Perhaps that was why she never felt foreign here. The reflection was a temporary distraction as she approached Lotte's house and glanced down the passageway to the annexe, expecting Olaf to be working away at his bench. But no, no Olaf. No tangle of long, blond-gone-silver hair. Where was he? Sarah was taken aback because Olaf was as predictable as the tides. Just after high water, every twelve hours or so, day or night, he would ride his wrong-way-round tricycle – two wheels at the front supported a large wooden barrow – to the beach and gather whatever flotsam had been stranded. Otherwise, if it was daylight at this time of year, he would be at his bench, hammering and sawing, making driftwood men. Sarah looked again as though she might just not have seen him. His stock of driftwood was piled against the wall. His workbench was there. So were his stool and tricycle. But no Olaf, no muscular shoulders or hunched back, no cigarette burning at the edge of the bench. Not a man of habit any more. Judging by the sea's height at the ferry terminal, low water would be in less than an hour. Olaf should be here! She was surprised by her disappointment. She told herself there were any number of mundane explanations – he might be inside boiling a kettle; he might be shopping – but she found herself thinking: what had Lotte done?

There: Sarah's anxiety given expression in four words, five syllables.

Sarah was tempted to ring Lotte's bell. She decided not to because she wouldn't be able to stop herself from asking, 'Where's Olaf gone?' and might sound accusing.

After hesitating, Sarah carried on to her house. As if she wasn't unsettled enough, opening the front door proved difficult. The lock wouldn't turn. No Olaf, now this, what was going on? Had she been trying the wrong key? She examined it. No, it was the right one. She pushed it back into the lock as the door suddenly opened. Sarah made a strangulated gasp of surprise and took a step back. When she saw Lotte, she laughed out loud, 'Oh, that's why the lock wouldn't turn! It wasn't locked!' She gave Lotte a hug. 'I suppose you're being naughty, filling up my fridge with wine and food to last a year.'

Lotte behaved oddly, breaking free from Sarah. Usually, when Sarah went away, Lotte would be the one doing the hugging and Sarah the escaping. Lotte would pull her tight and tell her how much she'd missed her, even if Sarah had only been away for a day. Afterwards, Lotte would sit her down and insist on telling her all the news and gossip. Within half an hour, Sarah's head would be spinning. How had so much taken place in such a short time? Usually, Lotte was a whirlwind. But for this reunion, Lotte was withdrawn, almost rigid.

'Olaf's gone,' she announced to Sarah, giving her a fearful look.

Sarah's hands went to her mouth. 'I thought something was odd when I didn't see him. When? What happened?'

'Oh,' Lotte said, 'you think it's my fault, don't you?'

'Of course I don't,' Sarah answered as emphatically as she could and hugged Lotte again to hide her dismayed expression. 'Tell me what happened. When did he go?'

'Yesterday, I heard his door shut and saw him pass my kitchen window.' Lotte blew air between almost closed lips. 'Pffft.' Olaf had disappeared into thin air, she meant. She threw up her arms. 'Pffft.'

'He didn't come back?'

'No.'

'Are you sure?'

'I looked for him. I sat up all night waiting for him. He wasn't at his bench this morning. I knocked on his door. But he didn't answer.'

'Did you let yourself into his room – you have a spare key, don't you?'

Lotte frowned. 'If he came back . . .'

Sarah understood. Olaf's room was *his* private space, despite being adjoined to Lotte's house. Even Sarah, who had been acquainted with Olaf much longer than Lotte, hadn't been allowed inside, not even when he moved in. Both Sarah and Lotte knew it was a boundary they would probably never cross, never be invited to cross, no matter how familiar they became with him.

'It's not like Olaf,' Sarah said, making herself appear as puzzled as Lotte. 'You don't think he could be sick, do you? Nothing's happened? He didn't have bad news or anything, as far as you know?'

She meant: *Nothing's happened between you?*

Inside Sarah was accusing Lotte but couldn't bring herself to say so out loud because she could see how distressed her friend was.

Lotte said nothing.

Sarah glanced behind her as though hoping Olaf's familiar and shambling figure, hair flying, would be coming along the road towards Lotte's. 'Why don't we wait a little longer? There's not much else we can do. The police won't look for a grown man, particularly a grown man as independent as Olaf, who's been missing for, what, not much more than twenty-four hours. They'll think, *Lucky Olaf: he's found a bed warmer than his own.'*

Their eyes met again. Sarah said, 'They don't know Olaf like we do, that he doesn't drink or have affairs. They won't realize how different he is, how out of character it is for him to break his habits.'

Sarah watched for Lotte's reaction. She couldn't help herself thinking, *What have you done?*

As if in answer, Lotte blurted, 'I'm sorry.'

'Why?' Sarah said. 'You've given Olaf somewhere to live. If he's gone away for a few hours, it'll be because of something that's going on with him.' She gave Lotte another hug. 'You know Olaf well enough by now. He suits himself; he does what he wants and when.'

Lotte pulled away again. Sarah noticed her jaw clenching, as if she was readying herself for an admission. 'What's wrong?' she asked.

'Yesterday, when he was working at his bench, I said some things . . .' The sentence trailed off.

'What things? When?'

'Before he left.'

'You think he went away because of what you said?'

She nodded.

'Oh, Lotte.' Sarah knew she sounded alarmed, cross too. 'What did you say?'

'I asked him about his driftwood men: why he gives them eyes and noses and ears but never mouths.'

'Lotte, you didn't. Why? What did you say, exactly?'

'I said, "Olaf, these sculptures you make with mouthless faces and with their limbs always in motion, legs striding, arms pumping like pistons, are they supposed to be a tribe of little Olafs? Because that's what I think they are. I think they're representations of you because you're always busy —"' Lotte broke off. 'Then I said to him, "Olaf, you prefer silence to speaking, don't you? Is that why they don't have mouths, or is there some other reason?"'

'What happened? What did Olaf do?' Sarah imagined his back arching as though he was a runner on a starting block preparing to sprint off.

'Nothing, he didn't do anything. He listened. He shifted so his left ear was turned towards me. He does that when he's paying attention.'

'What happened next?'

'I told him my theory.'

'Oh no,' Sarah said. 'What did you tell him?'

'I said —' Lotte exhaled loudly — 'I said, "Olaf, I think your driftwood men have no mouths because there's something they can't talk about, something *you* can't talk about, a secret, something that's not very nice, something that's hurt or distressed *you*." I stopped there in case he wanted to say something, but he didn't so I carried on. I said, "If I'm right, Olaf, and that's why you don't put mouths on your little men, I want you to know you can trust me, if ever you feel overwhelmed or want to talk. I'm good at listening and keeping secrets."'

'Did Olaf answer?'

'No.'

'What did he do?'

'He stood up, went to his room and shut the door.'

'Then?'

'I saw Olaf go past the window and he hasn't come back.'

'Oh, Lotte!' Sarah was exasperated. 'It *was* your fault. What made you ask him that? You knew he'd react badly.'

Cal's welcome to Texel came in the form of a diaphanous, damping mist drifting off the North Sea. Driving his pickup from the ferry, the road took him through a flat landscape of sheep enclosures and, now and then, blocks of flowering tulips and daffodils. The different shades were muted by the weather. Cal was similarly off colour. To his way of thinking, islands should be wild and unpredictable places, preferably with soaring cliffs and hills. Texel was flat and low-lying. Also, Cal preferred islands where settlements and inhabitants clung precariously to land, and both were toughened by exposure to extremes of weather. But, on Texel, as Cal was aware from his previous visit, most of the resident population, which exceeded 13,000, had suburban, well-ordered existences. They lived in tidy villages which could be transported in their entirety to the mainland, far inland, without looking out of place. Texel had been domesticated and Cal understood why. Without defences, the island would long ago have been reclaimed by the sea. But, in his opinion, human intervention had resulted in Texel losing its essence, like a wild stallion having been tamed. For Cal, an abundance of beaches and birds were insufficient compensations.

For the rest of the way to Olaf's farmstead, which was a mile south of De Koog, Cal turned over in his mind what he would say. Would he inquire whether Olaf knew about Alex Lauder's death before asking about Ruth Jones? He thought he might. He would say nothing about meeting Ruth's father or that photograph of Olaf with

Ruth and Christina Tolmie. He would observe, listen. He would pretend to know less than he did.

At the back of his mind he wondered if Olaf already suspected Cal knew more than was contained in his last email. Perhaps that was why Olaf hadn't replied. Normally he was enthusiastic, corresponding at length with news, sometimes photographs too, of all his latest flotsam finds on the island's western beach.

Another possible reason for Olaf's silence became apparent when Cal turned into the gates where his farmstead used to be. Instead of stacks of driftwood and flotsam and a house constructed of driftwood and tied together with rope, the one-hectare site was bare, muddy and being traversed by a bulldozer. Rows of pegs had been hammered into the ground. A truck was unloading pallets of building materials. Cal parked outside a portable cabin, left his engine running and went inside. Two men were leaning over plans that were spread on a table. Both looked up when Cal said, 'Excuse me, do you speak English?' Their expressions answered for them – they did – and Cal carried on: 'A man used to live here, a friend of mine, name of Olaf Haugen. What's happened to him? Do you know where he's gone?'

The men looked at one another. Neither appeared to know or care.

'Is there anyone who might know?'

The same look.

'Thanks,' Cal said, 'for your help.'

As he turned away, one of the men called after him, 'Someone mentioned he was renting a room in De Koog, one of those streets behind Strijbosstraat.'

The other laughed and said, 'You'll be able to see where he's living by all the flotsam, rubbish and crap outside.'

After her parting reassurance to Lotte, 'I'm not the slightest bit cross with you, honestly', Sarah entered her hallway not quite knowing what to do next. She *was* cross with Lotte. No wonder Olaf took off after Lotte said that to him. Instead of carrying her bag upstairs and changing into jeans and a jersey, Sarah put on a waterproof and boots. She'd go to the beach. The walk would do her good and the sea air would calm her and clear her head. She'd sweep sand from Ruth's hut – the act of brushing, of caring for Ruth, always made her feel better. Maybe Olaf would be there? After hurrying past Lotte's house, she kept up a similar pace through the village to deter casual encounters. She didn't even glance up as she passed Sarah's Beach Fashions, its window display a sea-blue blind on which was printed in Dutch, French, German and English in white, undulating letters, as though rippling waves, 'Closed until the sun shines'. Then, on the road which climbed the first rampart of dunes, she thought the unthinkable about Olaf. What if he didn't return?

At the top of the second dune, Sarah stopped and, from habit, extended her foot forward, as if testing the ground. Almost immediately, she brought it back before extending it again. Once more, she repeated the action. It was like a dance or a practised ritual, the steps and timing precise. Next she looked over her shoulder, back towards the village, then in front of her, at the slopping, sliding water. Behind, she reminded herself, lay a village kept safe from storms and a capricious sea by a double rampart. But

248

in front, in that oily-looking, shifting expanse, nothing was certain. In front, fortune was arbitrary, fate random. To Sarah, the sea's relentless motion was a metaphor: it was like her guilt, always active, always threatening to inundate her, forever reminding her of the night she was supposed to be with Ruth when, instead, she'd been with Danny Allison, with good-looking, funny Danny. Sarah hadn't been tall, slim or pretty like Ruth. Every boy wanted Ruth. But Danny, Sarah knew, was the best-looking boy she'd ever have. As it turned out, he was the only boy she'd ever have. And that night, while she was with Danny, Ruth died.

Helen was wavering. Sometimes her heart persuaded her, then her head. What should she say? Soon DCI Beacom would look up, the signal for a briefing about one murder investigation to end and the next to begin. Helen had a minimum of three minutes, a maximum of six, before Beacom's sharp little eyes would dart to the back of the room, where he knew to look for her because he was aware of her preference for watching the other detectives' backs rather than have them behind hers, passing comments, pulling faces.

Her head told her to say: *Sir, there's no evidence of anyone else being involved in the murder of Jacques Picoult. In fact, since yesterday, the case against Kate Tolmie has become stronger. She continues to deny stabbing him but there's clear motive. Picoult was Kate's father. The DNA results confirm that. In correspondence with Flora, Kate threatened to kill her mother if she ever reappeared. The prosecution can fairly argue she carried out that threat against the father who similarly abandoned her, Picoult. Also, we know Kate*

249

went prepared. She admits to taking a knife, the one found in her coat pocket. The murder weapon was of a similar type. Others like it were found in the kitchen of her flat. A jury would believe she armed herself with two knives. She has previous for such violent behaviour. When she was a teenager she stuck a knife into the hand of a girl who was making life uncomfortable for Flora at school. History has repeated itself.

Her heart told her to say: *Sir, the evidence against Kate Tolmie is compelling. However, the case is clearly linked to Christina Tolmie's disappearance in ways we don't yet understand. When she was six, Kate's mother disappeared in mysterious circumstances. Twenty-three years later, that mystery remains to be solved. Until it is, until we know everything about Christina Tolmie's disappearance, there's a risk we're missing something important about Picoult's murder. Recently, a photograph has been discovered showing Christina Tolmie going on to a boat, probably at the French town of Gravelines. Three other people were photographed with her, one of whom, Ruth Jones, a sixteen-year-old, had gone missing from Margate in Kent on the same date as the last confirmed sighting of Christina Tolmie. Ruth washed up dead on an island off the Dutch coast and Christina Tolmie was never seen again. Before the discovery of this photograph, nobody knew there was any connection between Ruth and Christina. Sir, in my opinion, it would be safer if we spent a few more days trying to solve that earlier mystery, although, obviously, I understand the difficulties and pressures, given the two other active murder investigations.*

Which one to say? She wasn't sure.

She tuned back in as Detective Inspector Phil Welby was droning on about the investigation into the murder of the Somali waiter in the Grassmarket becoming 'problematic'. Although the marauding gang of youths had been identified and detained, the difficulty was pinning

the murder on any one of them. The speed of the attack –
a single slash to the neck inflicted while running fast – meant
no blood spatter on the killer. Nor had the knife been found.
'Our fallback is to charge all of them with murder, joint
enterprise. At least we've got the bastard, boss; we just don't
know which bastard he is.'

Beacom lifted his head. 'By tomorrow you'll have found
that out, all right?'

Welby replied uncertainly, 'We'll do what we can, but –'

The imminent excuse was cut short because Beacom's
attention had moved on. DI Brian Ronaldsay, a large man
with slow reactions, fluffed his cue by clearing his throat
before beginning his briefing on the faceless, handless
corpse discovered on waste ground in north-east Edinburgh. Helen already knew little progress had been made:
the body was still unidentified; no witnesses had come
forward; no one had reported the sound of a shotgun
being fired; no weapon had been found, nor had the missing body parts.

Quicker than Helen expected, Beacom's head lifted
again. DI Ronaldsay was still speaking when Beacom's
eyes darted to the back of the room to find Helen. In that
fleeting moment, while she waited for DI Ronaldsay to
finish, she knew what she would say, what she had to say.
Beacom was impatient for good news. Helen had arrived
with him to improve the clear-up rate of a lazy and failing
team of detectives. She couldn't let him down.

'Sir,' she said, 'I think you'll be pleased to hear there's
no evidence of anyone else being involved in the murder
of Jacques Picoult. In fact, since yesterday, the case against
Kate Tolmie has become stronger . . .'

At her conclusion, when she said 'History has repeated itself' she lowered her eyes, because she knew if Beacom looked up, he would read her expression, he would know she was telling him what she thought he wanted to hear, rather than what she felt. He would be angry with her, would possibly challenge her in front of the other detectives and they would hate her, hate her even more, if she made the case for taking more time to investigate Christina Tolmie's disappearance.

Beacom gave Helen a quick nod. His eyes narrowed as he looked around the assembled detectives. 'I'm glad someone in this room knows how to conduct a murder investigation. Helen . . .' He searched for her again. 'Now that you have time, perhaps you could help out the others. They appear to be in need of your assistance.'

'Yes, sir,' she said, glancing up. Beacom was going towards the door. Apart from her, no one watched him. Eighteen pairs of eyes turned towards Helen.

Sarah hurried on. Soon tarmac gave way to sand and she was striding in front of a long line of beach huts. Ruth's hut was the last.

Sarah looked out for Olaf, hoping to spot his familiar bulk. The beach seemed so big and empty without him. She carried on walking, a sudden gust of wind causing the sand to blow. For that reason, on reaching Ruth's hut, Sarah didn't open the door. She peered through the window to check everything was all right before turning back. She hunted the beach once more, looking one way then the other. 'Damn, Lotte.' She was surprised by her intensity of feeling. 'Damn you, Lotte.'

A few times during the previous seven years, sitting in deckchairs outside Ruth's hut, often in silence, Sarah had the feeling Olaf was on the point of telling her something important, something difficult. She'd never pressed him or been inquisitive. She'd hoped, in time, he might trust her enough to tell her. Now he'd be wary of her. He'd know Lotte wouldn't be able to resist telling Sarah about the conversation – Lotte's prying questioning – that had preceded his sudden departure.

'Damn you, Lotte.'

A shriek like a gull's cry made Sarah look up. It sounded like her name being called. Someone was running towards her. Lotte? Was it Lotte? Did Lotte ever run? Did Lotte ever go out in damp weather without her hair covered? But it was Lotte and she was shouting at Sarah to hurry, to come and look.

'Why?' Sarah sounded as cross as she felt. Why was Lotte always so dramatic, so demonstrative?

Lotte stopped, her mouth half open.

'Heaven's sake, what's wrong?' Sarah was impatient.

'Olaf's room . . .' She was gasping, not making any sense. 'Come, come quickly . . .'

'Oh, Lotte. You didn't go into his room, did you? Why, Lotte?'

Lotte glanced behind her as though scared at having been followed. 'Two women . . .' She looked back at Sarah with a panicked expression. 'Quickly, you must come.'

31

'Olaf Haugen? He's big . . .' Cal held his arms away from his body to give an impression of Olaf's size and muscularity. 'And his hair, it's white, wouldn't have been cut for a while. He collects wood from the beach. Olaf Haugen?' Cal talked in that fractured, ungrammatical manner people adopt when they're trying to communicate with people who speak another language. 'He lives here.' Cal looked around. 'Somewhere. Do you know where?'

The response to Cal's inquiry was the same whether he asked shoppers exiting the Lidl supermarket or, after crossing Nikadel, at the bus stop where two mothers talked while their children, a boy and a girl, stared sullenly and silently at each other. Everyone in De Koog recognized the description of Olaf.

'Do you mean Olaf the strandjutter?' they replied using the Dutch word for beachcomber. 'Yes, of course we know Olaf. He's very familiar in De Koog and at the beach.'

Also, everyone knew the general direction in which he lived, in one of the streets behind the Catholic church, most likely in Strijbosstraat, though perhaps in Wintergroen or Zeekral.

In Strijbosstraat, a man walking beside his bicycle was adamant. 'Wintergroen,' he said.

'Not Zeekral?' Cal asked.

The man insisted, 'No, no, absolutely Wintergroen. Go past four houses.' His left arm extended, his hand bent further left at the wrist. 'That side of Wintergroen, on the left.'

Wintergroen, Cal discovered, was a quiet, residential street of two-storey houses with small front gardens. Cal imagined the residents being polite, solicitous and neighbourly. Perhaps that was the cause of his discomfort. Living here would be a daily reminder of his differences and failings. How un-neighbourly he was. How careless he was about people. How contentment for him was to be disconnected from people and property, from commitments and obligations, from community.

Olaf the beachcomber.

Cal, the misanthrope.

The only sound in Wintergroen was the thud of his boots. He walked past four houses, counting them off and looking for signs of Olaf. He stopped at the fifth. A drive-in at the side led to a passageway and a covered area – an awning – which jutted from a single-storey extension to the neighbouring house. A workbench was outside, as well as a tricycle with a large wooden barrow. Driftwood was stacked against the gable end of a lean-to shed and graded by length. He was surprised at Olaf being able to live within such constraints, in such a habitat, being able to be tidy.

What happened? Why had he abandoned his farmstead?

As Cal wondered about Olaf's change of circumstances, the door of the extension opened and two women came out. The first was five six, wearing a thigh-length waterproof coat and walking boots laced to her calves.

Her wiry corkscrew hair was tied back. Her face was thinner and her skin better than in the photograph on the wall of Mikey Jones's basement, but there were enough similarities for Cal to recognize a grown-up version of Ruth's friend Sarah Pauling; the difference was maturity. Also, her name had changed. Now she was Sarah Allison.

Cal registered another likeness between this Sarah and her younger version. In the photograph, Sarah's female companion – Ruth – was taller and better-looking. This new companion was too. Her hair was ash-blonde, attractively dishevelled. Her jersey was coral-coloured and she wore expensive-looking black trousers with coral and black trainers. Although older than Sarah, she appeared sleeker, richer, more coordinated.

Another contrast was their expressions. The other woman looked unhappy. She was pulling away, but Sarah held on to her arm as she talked to her. The companion seemed difficult to console. Her eyes were either cast down or darting towards the open door behind them, anywhere but at Sarah. Both women were so involved in their private drama they were oblivious to Cal. When, after a few moments, he still hadn't been noticed, he said 'Hello' and the women looked at him, startled.

'Is this where Olaf lives?' Cal tilted his head towards the table, trike and driftwood. 'I suppose I know the answer to that already. Is he about?'

His question produced another odd response. The reaction of both women was to glance at the open door behind them, then at each other before answering, as though neither knew quite what to say or do. As if they had been caught. Caught doing what?

'Is this a bad time?' Cal asked. 'Should I come back?'

'No, it's all right, we're . . .' Sarah glanced at the other woman, then at Cal. 'You know Olaf, do you?'

'Yes, we share an interest –' he tilted his head once again, at the driftwood – 'in beachcombing and flotsam. I've known him for a while.' Cal took a few steps towards them. 'I'm sorry, I should have said. My name's Cal McGill. Olaf might have mentioned me. Or not, since Olaf's not exactly talkative.'

'The name's familiar, at least the McGill part is. Caladh?' Sarah tried. 'That's what I've heard him call you. You're that sea detective, aren't you?'

Cal nodded.

'I'm Sarah, Sarah Allison.' There was a slight pause as though Sarah thought Cal might say, *Oh, Olaf's talked about you too, some*.

'Hello,' he said.

'And this,' Sarah said, indicating Lotte, 'is Lotte Rouhof. She's Olaf's landlady. We're neighbours. I live there.' Sarah pointed to the wall on her left. 'And friends.' She glanced at Lotte. 'I think we're still friends, don't you, Lotte?'

Lotte folded her arms.

An awkward silence followed which Cal broke by repeating, 'Olaf, is he about?'

Instead of answering, Sarah said to Lotte, 'Why don't you go on inside?' She extended a reassuring arm, but Lotte was already walking away and passing Cal without acknowledging him or looking up.

After Lotte turned the corner of her house, Sarah said, 'I'm sorry . . .' She glanced at the open door behind her. 'Lotte's upset because Olaf's gone off somewhere, disappeared, since yesterday and Lotte thinks I blame her. Which, I suppose, I do, a bit. Lotte said something not very sensible to him.'

She spoke in bursts, as though nervous. 'Look, we don't usually go into Olaf's room when he's not here.' She looked behind her again. 'In fact, we never have before. It's just that we're worried about him and Lotte's upset . . . upset about what she said and Olaf taking off like that. She's got a key. She thought he might have left something . . . a note, an address, something.'

Cal frowned in puzzlement: why was she explaining to him? He asked, 'Why, what did Lotte say to Olaf?'

'She questioned him about his driftwood men . . . Have you seen them?'

'Yes. I've got one.'

'Does it have a mouth?'

'It does, yes.'

'Really?' Sarah looked surprised.

'Not much of one, but a mouth, yes. Why?'

'I've never seen one with a mouth. I wonder why yours has got one. Mine hasn't.'

Cal shrugged. 'Does it signify anything apart from Olaf deciding to give one driftwood man a mouth and another not?'

'Probably not,' Sarah said, 'but Lotte has a peculiar theory that Olaf's driftwood men are really a tribe of little Olafs and that none has a mouth – apart, that is, from yours – because Olaf has a secret, something he can't talk about, something that might explain Olaf.'

'Explain Olaf?' Cal sounded doubtful.

'Lotte's sure she can get to the bottom of Olaf, why he

is as he is, if only he'll talk to her about his past . . .' Sarah let out a nervous laugh as if to say Lotte didn't know Olaf very well if she thought that. 'Yesterday, for reasons best known to Lotte, she decided to ask Olaf why his men don't have mouths. Olaf didn't answer. Well . . . surprise, surprise! Instead he went to his room and, later, he went off somewhere, God knows where, and hasn't returned. We don't know if he'll be coming back.' Again Olaf's open door took her attention. 'We thought . . . Lotte thought . . . there might be something in his room . . . a clue to where he's gone.'

'There wasn't?' Cal asked.

'No . . . though . . .' She looked at Cal as though she was deciding whether to tell him. 'A bed, nothing much else, except . . .'

'Except what?'

'Some driftwood . . . I don't know what they're supposed to be.' A worried expression crossed her face. 'Not like his driftwood men. They're not men. They're not running. Their legs and arms are straight.' Her arms went rigid. 'Like this. And two of them are big, life-size. I think they're supposed to be women.' With a shudder, she added, 'The others are smaller. I think they're children.'

A bizarre tableau confronted Cal. Three driftwood figures were grouped together close to the head of a pale-wood bedstead which was in the middle of Olaf's room. Two were about five feet ten, Cal's height. The third was smaller, less than four feet. All three were clothed. Despite the room being in semi-darkness – the curtains were drawn tight across the window – the figures appeared purposeful but in a different way to Olaf's driftwood men. Their limbs weren't in motion. But they were slightly leaning, their heads hanging over Olaf's pillow. The sight was so odd, so arresting, that Cal halted abruptly inside the door.

'What are they?' Sarah whispered from behind Cal's right shoulder. 'Olaf's family?'

'I don't know.' Cal whispered too, as though he'd intruded on a scene of intimacy and wondered whether he should turn away, lock the door and leave.

Instead he went further into the room. 'Is there a light?'

Sarah pressed a switch by the door. A bare bulb cast a stark glare, revealing two other smaller figures, holding hands, against the curtains. 'Why are they over there?' Sarah said. 'Why are any of them here? What are they? *Who* are they?'

Cal examined the two groups before approaching the two tallest figures by the bed. One wore jeans and a T-shirt, the other a dress with short sleeves. He recalled Mikey Jones's photograph on his phone. The colour of the T-shirt was not quite the same, bottle green rather than turquoise. The style and colouring of the dress were similarly approximate, pale yellows and white, though stripes, not flowers. Were they the best matches Olaf could find? Cal's attention moved to another feature, their hair, long and dark for the one in jeans; lighter, redder, shoulder length for the other. Cal touched each. Both times his hand recoiled. *Human hair.*

'What's wrong?' Sarah asked.

He didn't reply or turn round in case she saw how shaken he was. Did Ruth have hair when she washed up?

Had he just touched the hair of two women who died twenty-three years ago? He looked closer and noticed a mesh. 'They're wigs, professionally made by the look of them.' He managed to add in evident relief, 'You'd be surprised how many wash up on beaches. I've often come across one. Olaf would have picked them up.'

Now he was paying attention to the smaller figure by the bed. The top of its head was made from upturned brushes with the bristles trimmed to give an impression of cropped hair. It was dressed in short grey-coloured trousers and a white shirt – Cal was reminded of the clothes in the suitcase and of the boy in the photograph. Were these the clothes the boy had been wearing or similar clothes?

Cal looked from one figure to the next. They were finer than Olaf's driftwood men. Their limbs were longer, more like mannequins than recycled seaside curiosities, more human in their demeanour. Their faces were less boxy. Their noses were made of colourless thin plastic tubing, which was more elegant than the multicoloured noses which usually adorned the men. Another difference was their eyes. Instead of being made from sea glass, as the eyes of Olaf's men were, they had round black stones.

He glanced at each one in turn, saying under his breath so Sarah couldn't hear, 'Ruth . . . Christina . . . the boy.' His eyes stopped on the boy. 'Who's the boy?'

Cal noticed how each stared with those black eyes at the single pillow. It was still indented with the impression of Olaf's head and the duvet was folded back as though Olaf had just risen. Cal knelt by the bed, placed his head on the pillow. Looking up into the three faces was disturbing. The two with wigs – the females – stared back as though accusing. The boy appeared frightened. Yet, as Cal looked from one to the other, he was unable to identify the feature or features that gave them individual expressions and emotions. Their eyes were similar and the same distance apart. None had mouths.

'What are they?' Sarah asked again as though she would prefer not to know. 'You don't think they could be . . . ?' The thought made her voice tremble. 'Well, you know . . . People he's harmed, his guilty secrets, his conscience? That's what Lotte thinks they are.'

Cal said nothing. He approached the two figures by the curtains. One was smaller than the other, and both had red hair like the adult figure by the bed. Both wore girls' summer dresses, which were water-stained. Scattered around both, on the floor, were wood shavings which had been painted to give the appearance of flower petals. Cal picked up a handful and let them fall. Then he studied their faces: both had longing expressions and looked in the direction of the group by the bed.

Cal remembered Helen's description of Kate and Flora Tolmie scattering rose petals at Gravelines after their mother's disappearance. Olaf would have seen the same photograph in newspapers. Cal said under his breath, looking from one driftwood girl to the other, 'Kate . . . Flora . . .'

Still crouching, he glanced at the far end of the long room. A table, a chair, a bedside table and a chest of drawers, all in the same pale wood as the bed frame, were pushed against the back wall. A rug was rolled up under the table. The room, Cal realized, had been *made* to appear bare. Space had been cleared for the bed and driftwood figures, as though they were exhibits in an art gallery. Except this wasn't an art gallery. It was Olaf's bedroom, Olaf's temporary home.

Lying in bed, all Olaf would see, on one side, were the longing faces of the two driftwood girls and, on the other, three figures looming over him. They hemmed him in, tormented him. They wouldn't let him forget. But forget what? Were they the trophies of a killer or the conscience of a tortured man?

To the right of the furniture was a shut door. 'What's in there?' Cal asked.

'Kitchen, a bathroom.'

Cal went to look. Two dishes and a cup were on a drainer by the sink. Beyond, Cal saw a shower and the rim of a toilet seat.

'When did Olaf move in?'

'End of February, two months ago. I asked Lotte to let him stay, as a favour. The room wasn't being used by anyone else. So . . .'

Cal closed the door. He dragged a finger across the top of the chest of drawers. A line was left in the covering of dust. 'Has Olaf always had the room arranged like this?'

'I don't know. He hasn't asked Lotte or me in. The curtains are never opened. Lotte can't see in from her garden. That's probably just as well.' Then: 'Poor Lotte. I think she might have been becoming rather too interested in Olaf – that's why he took off. Now she's discovered he's been living with two driftwood women and these . . . these children. Do you know what she said to me? "Men like Olaf always turn out to have dirty little secrets."'

Cal went to stand by the adult figure with red hair. 'I wonder,' Cal said, 'did Olaf ever mention a woman called Christina or –' he glanced at the two girls by the curtain – 'or her daughters, Kate and Flora?'

'No, not to me,' Sarah replied. 'Is that who they're supposed to be? How do you know?'

Instead of answering, Cal gave an impression of being absorbed by the three driftwood figures by the bed, peering into their faces, touching their clothes. After studying the female with long dark hair, he asked. 'Did Olaf mention anyone from his past? If not Christina, another woman? A younger woman? Do you have any idea who this is supposed to be?'

'No.'

Cal watched Sarah before turning towards the figure of the boy. 'Or this?'

Sarah shook her head. 'You think they're all people Olaf knew?'

Her surprise seemed genuine, Cal thought. Perhaps she didn't know about Olaf's connection to Ruth. Perhaps he hadn't ever told her. Cal wasn't sure if he should trust her. Not yet. 'Yes, that's what they are,' he said. 'Ghosts from his past.'

32

On the kitchen table were six knives for cutting and slicing food. They were about five inches long and their design was identical. The blades were stainless steel and pointed, the handles rubbery to the touch and in two colours. Three were green and three black. Had there been another green *and* another black? Had Kate taken one or two? Flora stared at the table, trying to remember if there ever had been another black knife. Or had there always been one more green one, the knife found in Kate's pocket?

Flora shouted aloud, in frustration at her bad memory, also in pent-up anguish. Her thoughts flitted constantly between Kate and Alex, her emotions mixed up, worry mingled with sadness that had invaded her bones. Alex! Why hadn't she kept his ring? Why hadn't she worn it? He was dying. She shouldn't have reacted as she did – she was off balance because of his marriage proposal and his disturbing comment about her growing to hate him. In hindsight she realized Cal McGill was right: it would have been the drugs. She shouldn't have left Alex. She sighed. Did she still love him? She didn't know any more because so much had happened. Her attention switched back to the knives. Had there been another black knife? Had Kate taken one of each colour as the police said? Flora stared at the black knives, saying over and over, 'There wasn't another one; there wasn't . . .'

She had to believe there wasn't another. Although it

wouldn't change the outcome for Kate – according to her lawyer, she should prepare for a life sentence – it mattered to Flora. When she was able to visit Kate and Kate said to her, 'I'm innocent, I didn't kill him, I didn't,' Flora had to be able to look into her sister's red-raw eyes and reply without a flicker or scintilla of doubt, 'I know, I know you didn't, I know you couldn't. I know you didn't take a black-handled knife because there isn't one missing.' Otherwise Kate would think Flora, too, judged her guilty.

Flora shouted in frustration. 'Half the kitchens and most of the supermarkets in Edinburgh, in the whole of Britain, have knives just like this. Anyone could have killed him. Just because no one else was seen doesn't mean there wasn't someone.'

But still, in her heart, she wasn't sure.

Perhaps there had been another black-handled knife.

Another cause of anguish was Flora's culpability. If she hadn't breathed life into the long-forgotten mystery of her mother's disappearance, would Picoult – she refused to refer to him as her or Kate's 'father' – be dead, would Kate be facing a charge of murder? No. No, she wouldn't.

Staring at the knives, she made a stabbing motion. If Kate stabbed Picoult her hand wasn't the only one on the knife. Flora's was too. At that moment she picked up her phone and emailed Cal, contradicting Detective Sergeant Jamieson's advice to the contrary:

Please ignore my previous email about sharing information with Detective Sergeant Jamieson. After recent events, I have no interest any more in discovering what happened to my mother. Please stop what you're doing.

33

Cal waited at the front gate while Sarah knocked at Lotte's door. After each rap, she added an appeal or injunction: 'Lotte, please.' 'Lotte, let me in.' 'Lotte, don't be childish.' 'Lotte, for goodness' sake.' 'Lotte, open the door.' Finally, saying, 'I give up,' she pushed the annexe keys through Lotte's letterbox. After a final despairing glance at Lotte's upstairs window, she said to Cal, 'Olaf might be on the beach. I'm going to look for him. Want to come?'

Cal nodded.

On the way, Sarah alternated between being irritated by Lotte and being anxious about Olaf. 'Why does she always have to be so impulsive?' 'Those driftwood figures in his room, the women – they're not what Lotte thinks, are they?' It was as if she was trying to persuade herself of an innocent explanation. 'Poor Olaf, where could he have gone?' 'He wouldn't do himself harm, would he?' She stopped. 'I'm sorry. I'm not dragging you with me, am I?'

'No,' Cal said. *No, because I need to find out if you know about Olaf and Ruth, if I can trust you.*

They walked on, passing a hotel, a café, a steakhouse, another restaurant and, on the other side of the road, a parade of shops with pavement displays of kites, plastic buckets and beach balls in neon pink and green. In almost every window or doorway, the owner or manager was peering out. Cal had the impression of nervous expectancy. 'What's happening?'

'It's always like this at this time of year,' Sarah replied. 'Everyone's fretting about the weather. If there isn't blue sky and sun soon, visitors won't book for the weekend. It's like waiting for a migration to begin. When will the season start? Everyone's being neurotic. Perhaps it's catching. We're all behaving a little oddly.' She looked at Cal. 'Me, Lotte, as well as Olaf.'

Then she pointed out her shop. 'I'm also waiting for the migration. I'm not going to open until there's better weather – not worth it.'

At the edge of the village, a road veered left. Another, Badweg, carried on straight and went uphill.

After giving way to cyclists, Cal asked, 'How long have you known Olaf?'

'Seems like forever. Must be seven years, not long after I bought my house here.'

'Olaf lived on Texel before you?' Cal asked.

'Quite a long time before, a few years.'

'How did you meet?'

'I knew he was Olaf the Strandjutter because that's what everyone called him. But I didn't ever speak to him until, one day, he walked backwards and forwards along the beach, coming closer and closer, until finally he got up enough courage to introduce himself.' She laughed at the memory. 'He's been stopping to talk ever since, once or twice a week. We sit in deckchairs, side by side. We're very middle-aged.'

'So he found you?'

'Yes, yes, I suppose he did. But I'm glad. He's become a

friend.' She gave Cal a worried look. 'Lotte wouldn't have frightened him away forever, would she?'

Cal waited before asking another question. He rehearsed it silently. It had to be delivered in an offhand way. 'What brought Olaf here, do you know, a woman, what?' He coughed afterwards because he thought his voice had sounded tight, unnatural.

'He washed up here. That's all he's ever told me as well as Lotte. And she's turned out to be a lot more inquisitive than me. It's what he tells everyone.'

'Yes, he told me that too,' Cal said.

Sarah sighed. 'Years have passed and none of us, you, me, Lotte, is any the wiser or knows him any better. How does Olaf do that, manage to be aloof, mysterious and pleasant, all at the same time?'

Cal stayed quiet. He'd said enough for the time being. Also, he was making up his mind about Sarah. Did he believe her? Was that how she met Olaf? Wasn't she aware of his past, his connection to Ruth? She appeared genuine, guileless. Her answers about Olaf sounded truthful. Cal had one more question, the last test. He'd wait before asking it, surprise her.

A gully opened up below them. At the bottom, to their left, was a collection of buildings in red and grey with blue doors, the largest of which was a long, low structure – Sarah said it was the reception for a campsite. To the right was an almost empty car park. Spanning the gully bottom was a wooden bridge, after which the road went uphill. At the crest of the next dune were buildings, luxury holiday suites on the left, a hotel and restaurant with a glassed-in eating-out area on the right.

Flags flapped in a desultory manner.

Desultory was the mood of the day. Although the mist was clearing, few people were about – some dog walkers, a family of cyclists. As if no one was expecting much to happen. As if a migration of holidaymakers was still weeks away.

Cal said, 'So what happened to make Olaf move into town? When I first met him, he was outside De Koog in the house he built from flotsam, on his own plot.'

'I don't know the full story,' Sarah replied. 'Does anyone know the full story about anything to do with Olaf? His house, the plot, was sold because he'd run out of money. Even Olaf can't quite live on thin air. He agreed a deal privately with a neighbouring farmer. But he had to clear the site, which was expensive. After paying off the bank and other debts, he only had a few thousand euros left.' Sarah sighed. 'I warned him about being taken advantage of. I said to use a lawyer, but he was determined not to. Said lawyers earned money dishonestly but farmers didn't. The farmer saw Olaf coming. He sold the land to a property company to build holiday flats. He'll make a fortune.

'Afterwards, Olaf tried to rent somewhere but no one wanted him as a tenant or as a neighbour after the mess he'd made at his farmstead. So I asked Lotte if she'd let him stay in the room at the back of her house and, bless her, she said yes. I thought it would suit them both – Olaf doing odd jobs instead of paying rent; Lotte having someone about the place. She's widowed and doesn't really like her own company, particularly at this time of year.'

Sarah's face was set in sympathy. 'Poor Lotte. Her husband was unfaithful to her, even when he was ill and dying.

She said to me once, "Why do I only ever like men who aren't what they seem?" When she saw those driftwood –' Sarah struggled to find the word – '*people* around Olaf's bed, she must have thought Olaf's another one.'

A pause. 'But he's not, is he?'

Cal said nothing.

After crossing the wooden bridge, they continued uphill in silence, Sarah lost in her own thoughts, Cal biding his time. At the summit, they stopped to look at the view. The sea was grey to the horizon apart from three vast black hulks, container ships going north towards Hamburg and the Baltic.

Cal turned to Sarah. 'Where did you live before Texel?'

'London.'

'What brought you here? That's quite a change.'

Sarah's eyes narrowed as she hunted the beach for Olaf. She appeared not to have heard Cal but then, when he was about to ask again, she said, 'It's complicated.'

Cal suggested, 'You washed up here, like Olaf?'

She nodded. 'Yes, I suppose I did.'

Cal cupped his eyes and looked for Olaf too. 'You know, I think you're both here for the same reason.'

'Really? What might that be?' She sounded off balance, not sure whether to be offended or amused.

'Not what but who.' He was aware of her watching him as he carried on scanning the beach. 'Ruth Jones,' he said. 'Isn't she why you're here?'

'How do you know about Ruth?'

Cal walked on.

'Yes,' Sarah said after him. 'Ruth's the reason I moved to Texel.'

He stopped and turned round. 'Isn't she why Olaf's here too?'

'No.' Sarah looked bewildered. 'Why on earth would Olaf be here because of Ruth? He didn't know her.'

'Are you sure?' Cal watched for any change in her reaction. There was none.

'Yes, of course I am.'

Then Cal said, 'You really don't know, do you?'

'Know what?'

The outline was blurry though sufficiently distinct for the shape to be obviously a young woman caught in a moment of time. She was leaning towards the camera and framed by the blown-up, out-of-focus legs of two other people. Her right arm reached forward. Her face was hidden by her hair which was long and dark. She wore a turquoise T-shirt.

'Oh my heaven, that's Ruth.' Sarah stared at the photograph. 'It is her, isn't it?' She seemed unsure, then certain, angling the phone one way and another for a different view. 'It is her. It is! It's Ruth.'

She stared wide-eyed at Cal before being dragged back to the screen. 'That T-shirt . . . I gave it to her for her birthday.' She looked again. 'Oh my God!' She stared at Cal. 'Her birthday was the week before she disappeared!' Each implication or realization brought another exclamation. 'She told me she was going to wear it for the gig . . .! Where did you get this? When was it taken? Was it that night?'

Cal replied, 'I don't know exactly but I think it was around the time Ruth went missing, so the sixteenth or seventeenth of August twenty-three years ago. I was given the photograph by Mikey Jones. He doesn't know who took it.'

Sarah's expression hardened. 'You spoke to Mikey Jones.' It was an accusation. 'Why? What's going on?' When Cal didn't answer, she said, 'Ruth hated him. Why did you go and see him?'

Again Cal didn't react. After manipulating the screen, he handed the phone to Sarah. 'This is the same photograph; a different part's enlarged. See the woman in the flowery dress, red hair? Do you know who she is?' Sarah shook her head. He held out his hand. Sarah was slow to give the phone back.

With two fingers, Cal reduced the photograph. 'Now look. That's the whole photograph, Ruth, the woman in a flowery dress and a boy. The detail isn't sharp, but can you also see the blond-haired young man at the back?'

'Yes,' Sarah said.

'Recognize him?'

She looked closer. 'No.'

'He wasn't one of the people Ruth and you used to know in Margate?'

'No, I don't think so.'

Cal took back the phone. 'I've enlarged his face.' He showed it to Sarah. 'Recognize him now?'

A cry of shock was followed by Sarah exclaiming, 'Oh my God, it can't be! It isn't!' She stared at Cal. 'Olaf? It looks like him, younger but like him.'

Cal said, 'Same slant to the nose. Same scar by the right eye. Same hair, though shorter and curlier, blonder. Twenty-three years ago, he'd have been seventeen. Yes, that's Olaf.'

Sarah's head jerked up. Her mouth was open, her eyes

wide. She scanned the beach. Before, she'd looked for Olaf in hope, wishing his familiar bulky figure to be there, finding his presence reassuring. Now she was alarmed at the possibility.

'He didn't tell you he knew Ruth? You didn't know?'

Her head shook. Her eyes darted from one part of the beach to another. '*I* told *him* about Ruth. *I* used to talk about her and Olaf listened and never, ever said anything about having met her. I thought he was being nice to me, letting me talk, not interrupting or changing the subject. He wasn't, was he?'

Cal said, 'Perhaps he needed to hear about Ruth as much as you needed to talk about her.'

'Why?' She frowned. 'I must be stupid or something. I thought Olaf was different. But he did have a secret. Lotte was right.'

She looked at Cal again. 'The driftwood people in his room . . . Is Ruth supposed to be the one with dark hair?'

'I think so.' Cal nodded. 'And the one with red hair is called Christina Tolmie. And the boy is the boy in the photograph.'

'You mentioned a Christina.'

Cal carried on. 'She was reported missing about the same time as your friend Ruth. No connection was made because Christina was last seen on the other side of the English Channel, in a French town called Gravelines, close to Calais. It wasn't just different countries and twenty miles of sea that separated the inquiries. Christina Tolmie was older, thirty-one, a mother of two daughters, middle-class, who liked to take off in a van and distribute clothes to orphans in Romania. Also, the police in Margate had

Ruth pigeonholed as trouble, as one of life's casualties. They expected her to come to a bad end one day. When she did, they weren't really interested in finding out what happened because they thought they already knew.

'To cut a long story short, there's a connection between Christina's disappearance and Ruth's death. That's why I went to talk to Mikey Jones. Before I saw him, I wasn't sure whether the two cases were linked. Now I'm certain they are. He had the photograph of Ruth, Olaf and the others. It was shown to him about six years ago by a detective constable called Jane Jarvis. She gave Mikey the impression that Olaf was a suspect – the detective asked Mikey if he knew who the young man was or where he lived. Mikey went to his local newspaper about there being a new line of inquiry. Nothing was published. The police warned off the newspaper editor, said Mikey was a fantasist. The detective constable vanished. Mikey doesn't know where she went. It turns out she didn't exist. Jane Jarvis was an imposter.'

Another shock. Sarah stared at Cal, seeming to be in a daze.

Cal said, 'Those figures, in Olaf's room . . . I don't know why they're there, why Ruth's there. Sometimes killers like to have mementos . . .' He stopped and gave Sarah time to understand his meaning. 'But there could be another reason.'

Sarah's eyes registered horror. They searched the beach for a monster in the form of Olaf.

'Sarah,' he said, 'Mikey Jones told me you keep a hut in memory of Ruth. Can I see it?'

*

We. Us. Sarah's version of Ruth's story, their joint story, was of two girls growing up together, who were sisterly, if not sisters, who were kinder to each other and more supportive than siblings frequently were, who shared everything, clothes, cigarettes, make-up, as well as secrets, and who became, to all intents and purposes, a single, harmonious organism. Ruth and Sarah.

With every telling of the story – in summer, when Sarah was in her deckchair, holidaymakers might stop two, three times a day to inquire about Ruth's hut – the merger had taken place.

We. Us.

The erosion of singularity had been gradual, an elision of incidents or anecdotes, or a shift in emphasis. Sarah refined the narrative as she might have polished a stone. But, with each rub of the cloth, the friendship became less as it had been, more as Sarah imagined it might have become, hoped it would.

As Sarah pushed at a pile of blown sand with her left shoe and opened the double doors of Ruth's hut, she experienced a peculiar dizzying sensation. Inside the left door, on the window's wooden surround, were captioned photographs of her and Ruth: 'Ruth and Sarah eating ice cream'; 'In school uniforms'; 'On Margate beach'. Sarah looked at each one in turn, oblivious to Cal. Another photograph was in her head: 'Ruth and Olaf'. It forced her to remember Ruth as she had been, unpolished.

Sarah recalled her parents' home – a big house in a well-to-do street in Margate. Sarah was sixteen, like Ruth, and restless. She was in her bedroom on the top floor. It had gone eleven o'clock at night. Next door, Ruth's room, her off-on sanctuary from a neglectful and drunken father, was empty. Sarah was at the window watching and willing Ruth to appear, running along the street, long hair flying, hurrying to tell Sarah her news: the cafés and bars she'd visited, the boys she'd seen, the ones who'd tried to kiss her, those she liked, those she didn't, those she'd kissed back.

'No Ruth tonight?' her mother asked after looking round the door.

'Uh-uh.' Sarah's reply was offhand, unbothered. 'At her dad's.'

By then the lie was well honed. With each repetition, Sarah suffered sharper stabs of resentment at Ruth for taking her for granted, using her as cover. That night she dreamed up the idea which would change the course of her life. Danny Allison, a good-looking, older and amusing boy who lived in Ruth's street, had asked her out. Her! Sarah! Not Ruth. He'd tried to kiss her after school. The next day Sarah bought two tickets to a gig. A local band called Crazy Stupid Dreams was playing later that week. Her parents said she could go if she went with a girlfriend. In their hearing, she offered Ruth a ticket and made an arrangement to meet up at seven twenty p.m. on Marine Drive.

Instead she went to Danny's house and lost her virginity. She felt changed, grown-up, as she waited at the back of the venue for the gig to finish. Would Ruth notice something different about her?

As the audience pushed for the exit during the encore, Sarah stood on a rubbish bin looking for Ruth. 'It's your turn to lie for me,' was all she'd say. She'd be mysterious.

She'd make Ruth jealous. But Ruth wasn't there. The crowds dispersed and Sarah went searching around town for her. A stab of resentment goaded Sarah. Ruth hadn't been to the gig. Where had she been? Where was she?

Sarah did the rounds of Ruth's haunts and hang-outs – the beach, her favourite cafés. There was no sign of her. No one had seen her. Sarah went home, anxious that Ruth might already be there and her parents would know they hadn't met up.

She wasn't. They didn't.

'Had a good time?' her father asked.

'Yes,' Sarah replied.

'No Ruth?' her mother asked.

'Oh, she's gone to her dad's.'

The following morning Sarah went to Ruth's dad's house. A woman wearing a man's shirt, knickers and a smudge of lipstick opened the door. 'Who the fuck are you, girlie?'

Mikey Jones stumbled out into the passage. Swaying, slurring, he said, 'Only the little girlie who's stolen Ruthie from her dad. That's who the fuck she is. Where's my Ruthie? I want to see her.'

A bare foot slammed the door shut.

Sarah told her mother, 'Ruth didn't go to her dad's last night. She lied to me.'

'Ruthie, as in Mikey Jones's daughter?' the police officer inquired when Sarah's mother rang the local station to report a missing person.

'You know her?'

'You could say that.'

'Oh.'

'Ruthie Jones will turn up in her own good time,' the policeman assured her.

'But she's only just sixteen.'

'Sixteen going on twenty-six.'

Now, on Texel, in Ruth's hut, a few hundred metres from where Ruth's body had washed up, Sarah experienced again that familiar and bitter feeling of being left out by Ruth, of Ruth not really taking her into consideration, of Ruth being selfish and wilful. That night long ago, had Ruth met Olaf? *Olaf!* How had she known Olaf? What had Olaf been doing in Margate? How did Ruth know Christina Tolmie? What had Ruth been doing on a boat?

Why hadn't Ruth told her?

Cal was copying old photographs on the hut's walls, apparently unaware of Sarah reliving the past. Then he was talking about the mural, wondering whether it was a good likeness of Ruth at that age. What age would she have been? Eight, twelve? Next he took an interest in a small rectangular piece of paper, which would once have been white but was now yellow. The print was still black and legible.

Carter Emery Entertainments presents
Crazy Stupid Dreams
Winter Gardens, Margate
Friday 16 August, 7.30 p.m.

He said, 'Is that a ticket to the concert the night Ruth disappeared, the night she didn't turn up?'

Startled by the question, Sarah blurted, 'Ruth could be

a total bitch, a bitch to me, a bitch to any girl, really.' She appeared surprised at what she was saying. 'If a better offer came along, she'd always take it. She liked stealing boys. She didn't mind what girls thought of her. She didn't have girls as friends apart from me and I was more of a friend to her than she was to me.'

'Is that why she didn't go to the concert? She had a better offer?'

'I didn't used to think so.'

'That evening,' he persisted, 'was Olaf the better offer?' She flinched.

'I'm sorry,' Cal said, taking another photograph, this time of Sarah and the beach behind her.

'Don't.' Her head shook. Her eyes closed. She turned around, hiding her face from Cal.

Cal asked, 'Why did Olaf follow her here? What happened? Do you know?'

'No.'

Cal carried on photographing the hut and noticed a reflection in the window, a movement, someone approaching. He glanced up just as Lotte rushed towards them. Her right hand was brandishing some papers. She stopped, out of breath.

'Sarah,' she gasped. 'Olaf . . . he's not Olaf at all. His name's Thomas Larsen. Olaf and Haugen are his middle names. Look.'

Sarah read the cutting, from an English-language Norwegian newspaper, before passing it without comment to Cal. The article was about Thomas Larsen, sixteen, almost seventeen, who had gone missing from home following a row with his stepfather. A small inshore fishing boat was also missing. At the same age, in the same boat, the teenager's late father had navigated single-handed to Greenland via Iceland. Thomas's mother feared he might attempt to do the same. Shipping had been alerted to look out for him. There was a photograph of the boat and another of Thomas. Cal recognized both. The boat was similar to the one in Mikey's photograph. Thomas was Olaf.

Cal and Sarah swapped documents. Now Sarah was looking at a birth certificate. The registered name was Thomas Olaf Haugen Larsen.

'There's more,' Lotte said. 'Under his bed. Come. Come and see.' She grabbed Sarah's arm. 'Sarah, we must hurry.'

Cal stayed where he was, as though he wasn't sure if Lotte wanted him along or not. When Sarah glanced back he shouted, 'I'll search for Olaf.'

Everything about Lotte was speeded up. She walked quickly. Words tumbled out. She was terrified, she said, terrified for them both. After linking Sarah's arm, she pulled her close. 'Hurry in case Olaf comes back and finds us.' A few moments later, her eyes widened as she stared in fright at Sarah. 'What awful thing could he have done? What other reason could he have for pretending to be someone he's not?' Fear as much as self-justification inhabited each remark and question. 'We'd never have known if I hadn't gone into his room. Don't be cross with me, Sarah. You do understand, don't you? I had to. I knew there was something wrong with him.'

Lotte shivered as a child might at a horror story.

'Stop it. Stop it.' Sarah shook free from her. 'Stop talking about Olaf. I can't stand it.'

Lotte reacted as though she'd been slapped. She gave Sarah one of her repertoire of hurt expressions. Without saying another word, she carried on towards De Koog. Sarah followed, walking more slowly, the gap between them widening. Sarah's eyes were cast down in case Lotte glanced back. Her arms formed a cross, left hand on right shoulder, right on left. Her thoughts were not on Lotte but on the previous twenty-three years. After Ruth's disappearance and subsequent discovery of her body, every big decision, every milestone in Sarah's life, every feeling and emotion, could be explained by a single thread of narrative.

Why she'd dropped out of school, aged sixteen.

Why she'd married Danny.

Why she'd moved to London.

Why she'd divorced.

Why, with the money from her parents' house, she'd moved to Texel.

Why she was alone.

That thread was guilt at having lost her virginity to Danny when she should have been with Ruth, at being alive when Ruth was dead, at having lived when Ruth hadn't, at Ruth's chance having been taken away, and violently, because Sarah had been with Danny when she should have been waiting for Ruth at seven twenty that night twenty-three years ago when Crazy Stupid Dreams was warming up at the Winter Gardens.

As she walked behind Lotte, she pulled and pulled and pulled at that thread until there was no more to pull.

That night Ruth hadn't been waiting for her. She'd gone off with a boy. Olaf! Typical, selfish Ruth. Ruth would be dead even if Sarah hadn't lost her virginity to Danny. *We. Us.* How Olaf must have struggled to conceal his amusement at such a fabrication. Was that why he remained so silent, sitting in his deckchair beside Sarah? Was that why he kept on coming back to listen to Sarah talk about Ruth, for entertainment?

At Lotte's front gate, Sarah hurried past while staring fixedly at her feet. 'I'm tired, Lotte,' she announced. 'I'm going home.' And she carried on without attempting to see if Lotte was there or waiting for Lotte to answer. She was feeling dizzy again, this time remembering the first time she'd seen where Ruth had washed up. She'd walked from De Koog, alone and nervous. After the switchback of dunes she arrived on the beach. She saw pale golden sand stretching uninterrupted for miles and a line of beach huts with double doors that were painted blue and had windows. Through the glass, she saw folded-away, stripy deckchairs.

Not only had Sarah cried, she had cried her eyes out. 'Sorry. I'm so sorry, Ruth. Forgive me.' Over and over.

A man had asked her what was wrong and she couldn't answer properly. Was there something he could get for her? Would she like a drink from the nearby beach restaurant, coffee, water, wine? As he hovered, not quite knowing what to do or to say, a woman walked up to her and wrapped her arms around her. It was dark when they let go of each other. By then Sarah had been able to talk about Ruth, about her regret. How Ruth had always dreamed of being reunited with her dead mother on a beach that stretched for miles, had beach huts with blue doors and deckchairs. Just like this beach had.

The woman, Anneka, a visitor from Germany, was as practical as she was maternal. 'Look around you,' she'd told Sarah. 'Texel has sea defences around its perimeter to keep its residents safe from being overwhelmed by the sea. You're being overwhelmed emotionally. Build some imaginary sand dunes around you, retreat behind them when the memory of Ruth becomes too much for you. Tomorrow morning, rent one of these beach huts with blue doors. From then on, that's where Ruth will be. She won't be lying dead on the shore. Don't ever remember her like that. Always imagine her to be in the hut or close to the hut. Think of her as being happy, with her mother and digging in the sand. Look after the hut for her, paint the hut every year, sweep out the sand that will blow in, put out deckchairs in summer, sit with Ruth, talk to her, about you and her. When it all becomes overwhelming, and it will, go back to the other side of the dunes. Keep her on this side, your sanity safe on the other.'

After closing the hut door, Cal replied to Flora's message requesting him to stop work on her mother's disappearance.

Hello Flora,

I saw you on television. Kate's lucky to have you fighting for her. The evidence against her means she's going to need all the help she can get. For that reason, please reconsider your previous message. There have been some interesting developments which might not exonerate Kate but could very well provide context and mitigation.

I'm attaching photographs. Please study them.

Have you ever seen or heard of this young woman before (see Photographs 1, 2 and 3)? Her name was Ruth Jones. She lived in Margate and died when she was sixteen. Her death and your mother's disappearance are linked. See Photograph 4: the woman with her back to the camera is your mother (she's holding your suitcase). The younger woman reaching for the rucksack is Ruth Jones. The young man facing the camera is called Olaf Haugen or Thomas Olaf Haugen Larsen, Norwegian by origin. I don't know the identity of the boy, nor am I exactly sure when or where the photograph was taken. My best guess is around the time your mother and Ruth Jones went missing. Where? It could be Margate but more likely Gravelines in France? If you don't recognize Ruth Jones or Olaf Haugen, do you remember your mother ever mentioning their names?

Also: who is the boy with his back to the camera? Do you have an idea? Could the clothes in the suitcase be his? Who took the photograph? Why?

Plus: see Photographs 5–6: Photograph 5 is of Ruth Jones with her best friend Sarah Pauling, 6 of Sarah (married name, Allison) as she is now. Photograph 7 is of a beach hut on Texel where Ruth Jones's body washed up. Sarah maintains the hut as a memorial to Ruth – the girl in the mural on the back wall is supposed to be Ruth; the woman in the deckchair, her mother, Rita.

Any distant bells ringing, any faces you recognize or names your mother might have mentioned?

Cal

PS: I've spent some of that money you left. I'll pay you back.

Having sent the email, he looked around, imagining Olaf approaching across the sand, Sarah putting out the deckchairs for her visitor.

'We'd sit in the deckchairs and watch the world go by,' Sarah had told him as they walked, before Cal showed her the photograph, 'or he'd tell me about the ships that were passing. He didn't ever say much. He left that to me. I told him I felt guilty about Ruth, about being alive when she was dead. He was very understanding. Talking helped me, talking about Ruth, talking to him. But, I think, listening helped him, listening to someone else's troubles. It wasn't that he didn't have anything to say. I think it was the opposite of that. The thing he had to say was so big and difficult he didn't see the point of saying anything else.'

Cal had had a similar thought about Olaf once. It was the last time he was on Texel.

34

Cockle shells crunched under Cal's boots. The same evocative sound had accompanied him and Olaf when, two years earlier, they'd walked the beach from De Koog towards the north of the island. They were flotsam hunting and, intermittently, talking. At one point, Cal inquired whether Texel was where Olaf felt he belonged, having lived on the island for many years; whether it was home for him and if not there, where? Olaf had rubbed his face, squinted at the sky as though an answer was difficult. To make the question easier for Olaf, Cal said he was interested in the subject of belonging because he didn't feel he did. Anywhere. That sense of 'knowing where to put your pin in the map' had been taken from him, 'not in a single violent act but a series of assaults'.

Although Olaf remained silent, his demeanour changed. He was taut, listening, interested.

Olaf attempted to disguise his alertness by lighting a cigarette. When they resumed walking, Cal elaborated. His mother, a lawyer, had died when he was seventeen. Her death triggered a mental collapse in his father, James McGill. After his recovery, he worked abroad, mostly for charity schools in Africa. He never returned to the scene of his breakdown or to Scotland to visit his son. Eventually, in Mozambique, McGill senior found a new, younger wife, a teacher called Honesty Dlamini, who had three daughters by a previous marriage. A son, Moses Ngwane McGill, was born soon after their wedding. Cal's family home in Edinburgh was sold to pay for a Portuguese colonial-era house in Maputo. Cal and his father were no longer in contact. Cal had not been to Mozambique, nor had he met his half-brother. Cal had been replaced as well as displaced. At least, that was how it felt to him.

Cal's flow of revelation was out of character. Afterwards, he felt awkward, embarrassed. He thought Olaf's continuing silence might be an indication of a similar reaction. Had Cal's confession shut up Olaf rather than encouraged him?

Cal changed the subject. He asked about the cormorants that flew from the sea over the dune to their right. It was a constant and sinister procession, four or five black-clad birds always in the air, one after the other, going in the same direction. 'What's happening?' Cal inquired. 'The forces of darkness gathering?'

Olaf didn't answer. He was lost in his own thoughts, his expression as black as the birds.

They carried on walking to the accompaniment of two different sounds, both rhythmic – the sea's swoosh-splash and the crunch of shells underfoot. One lulled, the other galvanized, like a marching beat.

After a while, they arrived at a breach in the dune. It was three or four hundred metres wide. Through the middle was a channel of water gouged in the sand, draining like a river towards the sea.

'Here.' The word burst from Olaf like a cough. 'That place you were talking about. This is it, here, where I feel I belong.'

Cal looked around as Olaf explained that the area was called De Slufter, a rare example of the wary Dutch allowing the sea to penetrate a sea defence. The result, between the outer and inner dunes, was a system of tidal creeks which regularly flooded, creating a salt-marsh habitat for numerous birds and plants, including purple-flowering sea lavender.

Olaf spoke with an intensity which surprised Cal, with a mixture of awe and affection as well as some emotion.

Cal said he hadn't seen anywhere quite like it and imagined how different De Slufter's demeanour would be with the tide flowing the other way, a storm raging, waves being driven ashore by a north-westerly gale, how threatening that would be: 'Like a warrior horde hell-bent on destruction charging through a breach in a fortification.'

Olaf didn't express an opinion or offer a description of De Slufter inundated by the sea, even though he must have seen it.

Instead Olaf led Cal inland, going round De Slufter's southern flank, following well-trodden paths. They didn't talk. Rather than cockle shells, birds provided the backdrop of sound: shrills peeps of oystercatchers, the base and tuneless honks of geese and, every now and again, the sudden and cacophonous alarms of terns, which scattered and wheeled in fright at the appearance of a marsh harrier: a thousand white wings flapping, De Slufter noisy with sharp cries of panic.

At the eastern edge of the salt marsh, they climbed to a viewing platform perched on a secondary, high and intact sea wall, the last line of defence. They'd stood for a few minutes looking at the view, though Olaf's attention kept returning to the black hulks of ships on the horizon, as sinister-looking as the cormorants had been earlier. Cal made a throwaway remark – 'The big bad world's out there' – and wished he hadn't.

Olaf gave Cal a rare unguarded look, as though he was thinking that too.

Just as Cal expected Olaf to turn back, he took off again, skirting the salt marsh to the north and west. Olaf spoke once. 'This area,' he said, 'is closed off to the public at this time of year because it's the birds' breeding season.' He carried on regardless, finally stopping on the crest of a dune above the beach where a natural parapet of sand had been formed. The interior was scooped out so that, standing up, Cal saw a panorama which included two seas – the North and, to the east, the Wadden – as well as the lighthouse at the northern tip of Texel, and beyond, the next island in the West Frisian chain, Vlieland. Crouching down below the parapet's walls, the air was still, the sea's sound muffled: a discreet, private, enclosed place. Olaf made a gesture – his thumb pressed down as though sticking in a pin.

'Exactly here?' Cal asked. 'This is it, your pin in the map?'

Olaf nodded.

'I can see why,' Cal commented, looking round again with an approving expression. 'And not Norway? There's no sentimental attachment to where you were born? Norway isn't written in your heart?'

'Norway when I'm dying,' Olaf replied, turning in Norway's direction and making a paddling gesture with his hand, as though he would use the last of his strength, his last breaths, to be taken there by the sea.

Cal said, 'Yes, I think I'd like that too, but in my case to keep going north, to drift all the way to the Arctic.'

They'd sat and Olaf lit a cigarette. The smoke eddied within the circular walls of the parapet as though caught in a vortex.

That memory was fresh as Cal, once again, climbed the parapet's walls. He looked for signs of Olaf, but the sand was loose inside. The depressions and scoops that existed could have been caused by a swirling breeze as readily as by the imprint of a boot or foot. They could have been recent or old. Cal examined the heathland and beach to the north and, seeing no Olaf-sized shape, climbed inside the parapet. He sat in approximately the same place as he had the last time, his elbows digging into soft sand as he leaned back.

The re-enactment aided his memory as he recalled what Olaf had gone on to say.

At first he'd rambled, becoming exasperated with his inability to be coherent. He'd emitted a howl of frustration as terns wheeled overhead. Then, addressing the sand between his spread legs, he'd talked about 'an incident' – he wasn't specific and Cal didn't like to interrupt by asking him to be – which had had devastating consequences. In his case it had been a single violent event, not a series as it had been for Cal. He'd been seventeen, the age Cal had been when his mother died. 'This is where I hide away when everything becomes too much for me.' He'd looked straight at Cal. 'One day I'll tell you what happened, Caladh.'

Like Alex, he used Cal's full name.

Olaf hadn't waited for Cal's response. 'Shall we go back?' he'd said abruptly.

The return journey was completed in silence apart from the crunch of cockle shells and the sea's swoosh.

Cal's memory now resonated with Sarah's description of Olaf: *It wasn't that he didn't have anything to say. I think it was the opposite of that. The thing he had to say was so big and difficult he didn't see the point of saying anything else.*

Had he almost said it that day to Cal?

Cal raised himself just enough to peer over the parapet's sand walls. The big black hulks of tankers and container ships going north were silhouetted against the fading pink of the setting sun: 'the big bad world'. Then, as darkness came, he lay back and watched the stars. Finally, he slept, dreaming vividly of cormorants and of black hulks that travelled silently, menacingly. When, suddenly, one of those black hulks loomed over him he woke. A cry escaped from him, his own tern-like call of panic at the threat of a swooping raptor or worse. Was it dream or reality? It seemed real to Cal. He sat bolt upright. His breathing was quick, nervy. His tongue tasted salt in the air and something else – tobacco; not the fresh smoke of a burning cigarette but the stale, acrid and cloying stink of a smoker's clothes. Now he smelled it, now he didn't, now strong, now faint. The stench swirled around him, caught in a vortex.

Slowly, he lifted his head above the parapet. To the east, dawn was turning the night sky grey. To the west, he saw ships' lights. He searched the beach, watching for movement, for Olaf – black shifting against black, like those cormorants and hulking ships in his dream. He registered the direction of the wind. It blew in gusts from the east when before it had been a stiff breeze and westerly.

Could it be? Had a change in the wind caused Olaf to visit the place where his 'pin in the map' belonged, to say farewell? Had the looming black shape been him? Had he known that Cal would look for him there? Was Olaf about to become a driftwood man, his dying act to be taken by the currents to Norway?

Cal scrambled over the parapet wall. Descending the seaward flank of the dune he slipped and slid, a firm footing difficult to find. At the bottom he stopped to catch his breath. A glance south made him rule out that direction. He looked in the other. If he was Olaf, he would use the easterly wind and the ebbing tide. The fastest currents would be between Texel and Vlieland. They would quickly take him out to sea. Running north, the crunch of cockle shells under Cal's pounding boots grew louder and quicker, the prelude to a crescendo.

Flora was exasperated: *Stop! Didn't I ask you?* Please *stop.* Her pleading was directed at her phone on which Cal's email was displayed. *Please stop before anything else awful happens.* When she saw the photographs, her mood changed. She was mesmerized, examining the back of the woman Cal said was her mother. She was like Kate, broad-shouldered, and she stood like Flora, legs slightly apart, right foot turned out. Flora's attention turned to the other people in the photograph, a young man, young woman and a boy. Flora referred to Cal's email for names. How did her mother know Thomas Olaf Haugen Larsen or Ruth Jones? Flora had never heard of either of them. In life, as far as Flora could remember, her mother had never made any reference to them, nor were they mentioned in her papers.

Who was the boy?

She saw how her mother's left hand rested on the child's left shoulder. Her right was holding a small and familiar suitcase. A quick intake of breath. Had her mother been obeying Flora's childish request: *Can I have a big brother, one of those unhappy orphanage boys?*

Was that why she hadn't returned home?

Almost a quarter of a century later, another request had similarly nightmarish results. Flora had appealed for information about her mother's disappearance and Jacques Picoult had materialized, been stabbed to death, and Kate had been remanded in custody accused of murder.

Now there was Ruth Jones. She, too, was dead.

In a daze, she examined Cal's other photographs, close-ups of Sarah Allison, Ruth Jones's friend, also a series of photographs of the interior of a beach hut. The doors were wide open. On the back wall was a painting of a girl playing in the sand in front of a woman in a deckchair. Cal said the scene was Ruth with her mother, Rita.

Flora gasped. In the window of the left-hand door of the beach hut was the reflection of another woman. Although the image was indistinct, the woman was hurrying, approaching. Her face had an alarmed expression, as if she'd just had a shock.

Flora enlarged the photograph. 'It couldn't be,' she said.

Cal blinked away sweat, making his vision blurry. As he ran, he watched the waves rise and fall. On each crest he expected to see Olaf being lifted up, the beachcomber becoming flotsam. A distant and out-of-focus silhouette brought a shout: 'Olaf!' Cal's legs and arms pumped faster until he was close enough to make out a beach-marker post, number thirty. Cal stopped running, threw his head back, gulped air and wiped his face. He shouted once more – summoning the strength to run again. After another hundred metres, he gasped 'Olaf' for a second time. At the edge of the sea was a solitary, still figure, a bulky silhouette. Cal kept running, then slowed to a walk. When he was behind Olaf, a few steps away, he noticed a small raft, a construction of driftwood and buoys, tied together with rope and wrapped around with netting. It was in the water.

'Olaf?'

Olaf's head shifted, enough for Cal to glimpse the plane of a weathered, ruddy cheek edged by unruly long and tangled hair, flashing silver in the early-morning sun.

'Caladh.'

Cal went closer, by Olaf's left shoulder. 'I'm glad I've found you.'

'I've been waiting for you,' Olaf said. 'You wanted to know about Ruth Jones?'

'You knew her?'

'I killed her.'

Helen studied the CCTV from Haymarket Station before Jacques Picoult was murdered, playing it back, pausing it, studying all the faces. She referred to one of the photographs forwarded by Flora: the reflection of the woman in the beach-hut window was grainy but Helen was sure she'd seen someone very similar recently. It stuck in her memory because she'd thought how well the woman was dressed, how simple and stylish, how wonderful it would be to have manageable, sophisticated-looking hair like that instead of unruly curls.

Flora wrote:

I know who this is. At least I think I know who this is. It's Maria, my cleaner. But how can it be? She lives in Edinburgh. This photograph was taken on Texel. Not only that, she looks quite different.

Although Helen was irritated – why hadn't Cal copied her into the email he sent Flora? – she was excited. An unexpected development like this was why she loved being a detective, why she was rigorous in always trying to answer every question, even though sometimes she tried her colleagues' patience, as she was now by detaching herself from the investigation into the faceless, handless corpse. 'Something has come up, new evidence, another suspect in the Picoult case,' she told DI Ronaldsay, who muttered, 'Fuck's sake, Helen.' After apologizing, she raised her eyebrows and said, 'The boss,' as though she'd spoken to him and had his agreement. Now she didn't care about the other detectives giving her evil looks as she flicked from one CCTV frame to another. 'Where are you?' she kept on saying in a whisper. Then, suddenly, she was there, the same woman, the same hair, similar stylish clothes, an expensive-looking, mulberry-coloured trench coat, matching gloves and ash-blonde hair cut in a short bob. Helen put Cal's photograph beside the frozen CCTV. It was the same woman, definitely.

Helen emailed Flora:

Do you have an address for Maria, your cleaner?

Flora replied:

I'm sorry, I don't. I know she lives in the Gorgie area of Edinburgh, but that's all. Here is her email and mobile number.

Helen emailed Cal:

Flora has forwarded your email and photographs. What's the
name of the woman who was approaching the beach hut? She
was reflected in one of the beach hut's windows. It's not Sarah
Allison because you sent a separate picture of her. Cal, the other
woman is not what she seems. Do you know where she lives?

After putting in a call to the Dutch police, she drummed
her fingers on her desk. She was impatient. She played the
CCTV again. According to the timings from different
cameras, the woman disappeared from outside Haymarket Station about the same time as Picoult, but before
Kate Tolmie had reacted to Picoult's absence. Helen wondered if the woman had chosen the dark mulberry colour
of her coat because it would help to disguise bloodstains.

'Maria Fuentes,' Helen said, 'who the hell are you?'

She glanced at her emails. 'Come on, Cal, answer.'
While she waited, she googled 'How to find a Dutch
phone number'. An online directory for the Netherlands
was at the top of her search results. This was a risk. Should
she take it?

Moments later, she was tapping a number into her phone.
'Sarah Allison?' she asked when a woman answered. 'Hello,
Sarah. My name's Helen Jamieson. You don't know me.
I'm a detective sergeant based in Edinburgh and a friend
of Cal McGill's. I think he's in De Koog right now . . .
He's still there . . . Good, good, I thought so . . . This is a

little bit unorthodox but I need some information. Do you know someone, a woman, in her forties, stylish, who has ash-blonde hair, cut into a short bob? You do. What's her name? How do you know her? What's her story? If I send you a still from some CCTV footage would you be able to identify her?'

Twenty minutes later, after telling Sarah, 'Don't do anything, say anything, not even to Cal McGill,' she emailed the same CCTV grab to Kent Police with a request for it to be shown as soon as possible to Mikey Jones. She also sent a request to the police in Paris for information about a former resident called Lotte Rouhof.

35

Olaf's confession began with another death, his father's, a fisherman from a long line of Norwegian fishermen. He was a depressive, a drinker and eventually a suicide who overdosed on whisky and pills. After his mother married again – the second husband was domineering, a bully – Olaf took off, rebellious and aged sixteen, in his father's old boat. He went south, reaching northern France and crossing the English Channel. One August evening, a day after his seventeenth birthday, having tied up in Margate, Kent, he noticed a dark-haired girl. She was waiting for a friend. They were going to a concert. The band, Olaf remembered – he wouldn't ever forget – was called Crazy Stupid Dreams.

'Would you like to go on my boat?' he'd asked her.

'Go with you? On a boat?' Her expression had been scornful.

'We could go to France,' he'd said. 'We could go tonight.'

Then he'd asked if she'd ever had a crazy, stupid dream about running away. In reply, she said she dreamed of being on a beach with her mother – 'just me and her' with sand stretching for miles and miles and a beach hut with a blue door.

Afterwards, her mouth had twisted. 'My mum's dead,' she'd said.

'Mine too.' He'd lied before realizing he had.

Olaf sighed: *If he hadn't lied, if he hadn't pretended to have something in common with such a pretty girl, if he hadn't wanted her so badly.*

After his lie, she'd changed towards him. 'This boat of yours . . . You do have a boat, right? You'll bring me back?'

He'd promised. He'd bring her back the following night.

Olaf fell silent.

'The girl was Ruth?' Cal asked.

Olaf nodded.

'You took her to Gravelines?'

Olaf closed his eyes. *If he hadn't.*

'Was Christina Tolmie there?'

Olaf stared at the horizon. 'She had a boy with her,' he said eventually, the memory haunting him. 'A boy from an orphanage . . . Christina had got to know him on previous visits. The orphanage's director, a friend of Christina's, had asked her to take him away.'

'Why?'

'The boy's mother was unmarried. She'd died in childbirth. The director didn't say anything else except the mother's family was religious and the presence of the boy, even shut away in an orphanage, was distressing. Christina didn't know why – she thought the mother might have been made pregnant by her father or, perhaps, a brother. When the boy was brought to her van, she was given two holdalls. One contained spare clothes, the other was full of banknotes. Christina understood the money was for her and the boy's upkeep. The family didn't want him back in Romania.

'Instead of attempting to smuggle the boy on to the Calais-to-Dover ferry Christina drove to Gravelines where she knew a man who owned a boat. She planned to ask him to take her and the boy across the Channel. But he'd gone away. When I saw her, she was desperate. She offered me five hundred pounds, which was a lot for a seventeen-year-old.'

Olaf's silence suggested a question: *what would you have done?*

His head was angled towards Cal as if waiting for an answer. Then his eyes narrowed as they tracked the black hulk of a ship going north. Another at a distance followed behind, and another; *like the cormorants*, Cal thought, a sinister procession.

'We crossed the Channel at night –' Olaf's voice broke. 'One of those . . . it didn't see us . . . cut us in two.'

Silence: Cal imagined the noise of the collision, the shouts and screams, the shock of cold sea.

Olaf's next memory: 'We were in the water. It was dark. I was holding Christina. Her arm had been broken. I shouted to Ruth to grab the boy. But she panicked and climbed on top of him, pushing his head under water. I had to stop her. I tried to pull her off. But I couldn't. The boy was drowning.'

A heave of his body, a long exhalation.

Olaf said, 'I hit her. There wasn't anything else I could do.'

That same unasked question: *what would you have done?*

Cal said nothing.

Olaf's left hand closed, becoming a fist, the fist which hit Ruth.

'I didn't see her again.'

Silence.

Cal recalled Sarah's observation: *The thing he had to say was so big and difficult he didn't see the point in saying anything else.*

Olaf carried on: 'Later, Christina and the boy were on wreckage. I was half in the water, holding on. Christina said I should change places with her. The boy's chances of survival would be better if I didn't become exhausted. I said I wouldn't swap because she wouldn't be able to hold on with only one good arm.

'The next time I looked she wasn't there. She'd gone.'

Cal asked, 'She sacrificed herself for the boy?'

'For me and the boy.'

Another heave of his body; the same mournful sound. 'When it was night, we saw a light. It appeared to be coming closer. I thought it was another ship. But the light wasn't moving. We were drifting towards it, towards land. When we were close, I swam ashore with the boy. The light was shining from a church. The door was open. The boy went in. I stayed outside. I thought I'd be put in prison for killing Ruth. Years later, I went back to the church because I had to find out whether the boy was all right.'

Had to.

'A woman was arranging flowers – there was a wedding the next day. I asked her about an abandoned boy; was this the same church? The woman knew the story – she said, "You mean the boy from nowhere?" I said I thought so. She said the boy wasn't able to speak. He couldn't even write his own name, nothing. He must have had a terrible shock.'

Cal said, 'Did the woman know what happened to him?'

'He was taken in that night by the priest and his wife. They were childless. They thought the boy had been sent to them by God. They adopted him, moved away, to the other end of Britain, another church close to the sea. The boy was given a name.'

'What name?' Cal asked.

'Alex,' Olaf said, 'Alex Lauder.'

Cal cast back. Had there ever been an indication? Had he known Alex at all?

In the background Cal was aware of Olaf describing his reunion with the boy, with Alex: how he'd located only two Reverend Lauders – one lived in Oxford, the other in north-west Scotland, where Olaf found Alex. By then, he was seventeen, the same age Olaf had been when he met Ruth. Although Alex recognized Olaf and remembered a woman with red hair called Christina, he had no other recollections from that period in his life. Everything that had happened to him, his removal from the orphanage and the collision with the ship, had been forgotten. With Olaf filling in the gaps, Alex's memories flooded back. He became very emotional and kept on talking about Christina. He recalled how she'd told him, as they'd driven across Europe, about her daughter Flora. 'Flora can be your little sister. You'll love Flora. She'll love you. She'll love having a brother.' Afterwards, Alex had become fixated by Flora despite Olaf's warnings at subsequent meetings and in telephone conversations about Alex allowing one dramatic incident to influence his life, one remembered girl's name. Another ten years passed before Alex gave in to his interest in Flora. Without telling Olaf, he found out where she lived, followed her into a shop and talked to her. He didn't say who he was. Olaf wasn't in a position to criticize since he hadn't been able to move on either. He was still trapped by that night, by his guilt, by the easy lie he had told Ruth, by the terrible consequences of that lie. He'd settled on Texel and, years later, encountered Sarah. In her conversation and reminiscing, she brought Ruth back to life for him. Flora would fill a similar emotional need for Alex – he would sense in her the woman, Christina, who had given up her life for his.

For Alex, there was a further complication: he and Flora became lovers.

'Was Alex in love?' Cal asked.

Olaf replied carefully, 'He loved the idea of Flora.'

'Not her?'

'If she hadn't been Christina's daughter, would he have had a relationship with her?' Olaf considered his own question. 'I don't think so, no. He wouldn't ever have met Flora.'

'Why didn't he tell her?'

'Tell her what?'

'The truth, when he knew he was dying?'

'He couldn't. He was protecting me. Also, it was too late. He'd fallen in love with her, or thought he had. If he told her the truth, he thought she would have hated him, for the deception, for Alex being alive when her mother was dead, for her mother sacrificing herself for him. He used to say Flora's love was the only thing which kept him going, which kept him alive.'

Olaf picked up his raft. He looked back at Cal, acknowledgement as well as farewell. 'Alex said you'd know what to say, Caladh, when we were both dead, what story to tell, what was for the best, for everyone.'

He took a step forward. And another, and another, until the sea was lapping his waist.

Cal did nothing. For Olaf, of all people, the beachcomber becoming flotsam, this was the kindest outcome. The alternative was arrest, being questioned by police, prosecuted for withholding evidence, possibly too for causing Ruth Jones's death, manslaughter or murder. Would Olaf's story of accidental killing be believed?

The more Cal turned things over, the less dignified, the more reprehensible he considered Olaf's action. Olaf was fleeing, escaping responsibility for the consequences of that first lie to Ruth, for so many other deceptions since.

Olaf's parting words finally goaded Cal into action, into anger.

Alex said you'd know what to say, Caladh, when we were both dead, what story to tell, what was for the best, for everyone.

Alex and Olaf expected Cal to protect them by lying, to perpetuate the cycle of lies. They trusted him to do so, to be Caladh, because the truth would hurt the living: Flora's love for Alex would turn into hate, as Alex had predicted; Kate would rage at her mother for her final act of abandonment – Christina could have stayed on the raft but she sacrificed herself, sacrificed Kate, for an orphan boy; and Sarah would be dismayed at having shaken the hand which killed Ruth, at having befriended the man.

Now, running into the sea after Olaf, Cal had a moment of clarity. Only one version of the story would protect everyone, the story, the lie he was expected to tell: Ruth, Christina and a six-year-old orphan boy were killed when

Olaf's boat was cut in two by a tanker during that August night twenty-three years ago. Olaf survived, the others drowned. Olaf didn't know the boy's name.

The biggest lies would be Cal's to tell.

Now swimming after Olaf, Cal realized only one part of the truth was possible: how the tragedy had left Olaf damaged. His guilt and remorse, his haunting, were evident by his decision to settle on Texel where he constructed a private purgatory, three driftwood figures – Christina, Ruth and the boy – who loomed over him as he slept, and, at a distance, longingly gazing at their lost mother, two driftwood girls, Kate and Flora.

The distance between him and Olaf closing, Cal thought about the driftwood man in his office. It had a mouth, the only one that did. Why? Was it a signal of Cal's future role, the storyteller? Had Alex and Olaf planned it this way? Had they chosen Cal to perpetuate their fiction?

He recalled Helen's questions: *Why are* you *involved in this? What's* your *connection?* Now he had the answer: not just the storyteller, the arranger, whose role was to cover up, by burying Alex in the sea loch, by lying for Alex and Olaf – Caladh, trustworthy, reliable Caladh.

A flare of rage made Cal swim faster – he must catch Olaf. Other considerations became unimportant or blurred. So when, finally, he grabbed at Olaf's legs it was already too late to turn back. The ebb was flowing through the channel separating Texel from Vlieland. The Wadden Sea was draining into the North Sea, the current speeding up. Cal's weight on Olaf's legs caused the raft to tip just as it was ascending a wave. Olaf fell back. The raft struck Cal on the right side of his head, by his eye.

Then he felt nothing.

The first time he regained consciousness, briefly, he was lying on a raft; Olaf was beside him, in the water, holding on.

The second time – Cal's dulled sense was of time having passed – he was cold, dehydrated and delirious, his head throbbing. Olaf's face loomed, as large as a moon. All he said was 'Goodbye, Caladh.' Then he was gone and Cal felt tightness around his chest as though a rope had been wrapped around him, securing him to the raft.

There was no third time.

36

Drama and intrigue were on the front pages of every newspaper, in every TV news bulletin: 'Race to rescue oceanographer detective lost at sea', 'Christina Tolmie mystery: suspect flees on raft pursued by sea detective; both feared dead', 'Exclusive: lost sea detective linked mystery of missing charity worker to death of Kent teenager'. One subheading announced: 'Suspect's landlady detained on Dutch island'. Going to her departure gate at Edinburgh Airport, Helen found herself unable to look away, or to resist checking newspaper websites on her phone in case of breaking news. When, half an hour late, she took her seat on the plane, she was relieved; there would be fewer distractions. Her phone was turned off. No passengers close to her were reading newspapers. For the next hour and a half, until touching down at Amsterdam's Schiphol Airport, she could focus. Downloaded on her iPad was enough reading for three or four hours: reports and briefings from the Dutch, French and Kent police. Concentration, it turned out, was far from easy. Every time the plane banked, Helen's reflex was to glance out of the window. She prayed for a powerful beam of sunlight to penetrate the clouds, for the surface of the sea far below to become visible, for Cal to be illuminated as if by some celestial searchlight and that she, Helen, might direct the flotilla of ships and boats which had been alerted to look out for him and Thomas Olaf Haugen Larsen to the exact location. But miracles were not to be. Each time the plane straightened, the snow-white cumulus was still unbroken, the sea below invisible, and a sound escaped from her as she turned from the window, a sharp intake of breath. On each occasion the same question sliced into her: *could she have stopped Cal?*

She felt its sharpness in her heart, while she was reading a witness statement taken by the Dutch police. The manager of a beach bar and restaurant close to the lighthouse at the northern end of Texel described two men, one thick-set, with long, silver curly hair, the other slighter with short dark hair, both about the same height, 'standing like statues at the water's edge for what seemed like ages'. Later, when the eyewitness looked again, the slighter man was on his own, having not moved at all, while the stockier one was 'far out on a small raft'. The manager took no action because neither man gave any indication of being concerned. When he went by the same window again, the slighter man was wading into the sea 'deliberately, without looking round', before swimming after the man on the raft, which was 'as good as suicidal, given the tide and the speed of the currents'. The restaurant manager raised the alarm because 'obviously neither of these idiots knew the first thing about the force of the tidal currents flowing through the channel between Texel and Vlieland'.

That presumption, as Helen knew, was wrong. Both Olaf and Cal were aware of the dangers. So why did they decide to go in, Olaf first, followed by Cal?

In Helen's opinion, Olaf's action was explainable, almost

understandable in the circumstances. His past was catching up with him, *Cal* was catching up with him. For twenty-three years Olaf had concealed his connection to Christina Tolmie and Ruth Jones. After travelling the world, crewing on merchant ships, he'd moved to Texel. Moved, Helen thought as she read another report from the Dutch police, not settled. Like some restless spirit, he'd spent his days walking the beach where Ruth's body had been found, searching, but for what? Forgiveness? Also, there'd been a child, a boy, in that photograph of Olaf with Christina and Ruth. Where was he? What happened to him? Helen understood why Olaf might have felt pushed to the edge, beyond the edge, why taking his chances with the sea might have seemed less daunting than the alternative.

But what drove Cal to follow?

Why did he wade into the sea when rescuing or apprehending Olaf and returning to land with him was no longer a possibility because of the strength of the currents? Did Cal also feel pushed to the edge, beyond the edge? Did he also think he had little to lose?

Helen recalled Cal's text message a few days earlier – it seemed like a hundred years ago: *You're a good friend* and he followed that unusual declaration with *To explain, for some reason I was thinking about funerals and it occurred to me no one would organize mine apart from you.*

Helen closed her eyes. It was obvious to her now: the messages were Cal's awkward way of signalling distress. They were cries for help to which she'd been deaf, worse than deaf.

She'd replied, *Fuck, Cal. Is that it? I'm your good friend because I'll organize your bloody funeral. Nothing else?*

No wonder Cal had been off with her. No wonder he'd been odd, more distant and less trusting of her. If she was his 'good friend', why hadn't she been more supportive during Cal's crisis: the social media furore in the aftermath of that Harry Fowler business, the clients of the Sea Detective Agency being scared off and the business having no income? She'd assumed Cal would cope on his own and in his own way. A long time ago, Helen had come to the conclusion that, with Cal, it was always better to err on the side of being distant than intrusive. Their friendship, their *thing*, whatever their relationship was, would survive longer if she waited to be invited in.

Were those odd messages about being his good friend and funerals his oblique way of issuing an invitation? *Had* she mattered to him more than she imagined?

The past tense jolted her. Cal had been missing for a day. According to coastguards on both sides of the North Sea, the chances of him being found alive were diminishing by the hour, minute, second. Hope was fading. *Had faded*.

That slicing sensation in her heart again.

Here she was, with an IQ of 173 and a Masters in criminology, and she was stupid, stupid, stupid. Poor Cal: perhaps he'd tired of being solitary. Perhaps messaging Helen to say she was his 'good friend' was his clumsy way of letting her know he needed help. She imagined how worried he would have been at her reacting the wrong way. And she did. She did. 'Fuck, Cal', she'd written and Cal had walked into the sea.

Helen stared sightlessly at the files on her lap. *Concentrate*, she told herself crossly: other people were hunting for Cal. Her responsibility was to solve the mystery, finish Cal's work, to find out what had happened to Christina Tolmie and Ruth Jones, how Olaf was implicated, what happened to the boy and why, once a week, on different days, Lotte Rouhof travelled this same route between Amsterdam and Edinburgh, departing Schiphol at seven twenty a.m., returning at six forty p.m.; why, between those hours, she turned herself into Maria Fuentes to clean Flora's flat; and why, on the last occasion, she'd travelled from Amsterdam to stand outside Haymarket Station in Edinburgh and had flown back straight after.

One thing was certain: according to information from the French and Dutch police, Lotte was in no need of a cleaning job, of any job, for that matter. The conclusion of both was that Lotte, a French national, was wealthy, an example of which had been her unsolicited bid for a property in De Koog at approximately double the prevailing market value.

Helen was also interested by speculation about the reason for her living on Texel. According to local gossip, Lotte was seeking sanctuary after the ending of an unhappy marriage as well as family tragedy. However, such easy assumptions of cause and effect were not supported by the facts. Lotte's release from marriage happened thirteen years earlier, some seven years before settling on Texel. Her husband, Charles Rouhof, with whom she'd lived in an apartment in Paris, died of a heart attack. He was fifty-four, nineteen years older than Lotte. Apart from being a serial womanizer, he was a serial director of failed companies. Lotte paid off his considerable debts.

The family tragedy occurred soon after. Lotte's father, an invalid in his seventies, administered sleeping pills to her mother before also taking an overdose. Lotte's response was as dramatic as the event. Aged thirty-six, a widow, childless and heir to the family's hotel in Paris which had been under her management since her father's infirmity, she sold everything, her apartment, her parents' house and the hotel – it was advertised at a price of ten million euros and probably attracted a higher bid since the sale was quick. The new owners were announced within three weeks. For the next few years, Lotte appeared to be peripatetic, not having a registered permanent address in Europe, despite frequently passing through airports in France, Portugal, Spain and England. Perhaps, as De Koog gossip suggested, she was running away from the unhappiness of her past, but why, eventually, did she choose Texel as her sanctuary?

Helen wrote in the margin: *Why De Koog? Why buy a house beside Ruth Jones's best friend? Why give lodgings to Olaf? Why fly to Edinburgh to clean Flora Tolmie's flat?*

Then: *What is Lotte Rouhof's connection?*

Helen was so preoccupied, reading emails and reports about Lotte's family history, working out the answers, she was oblivious to the bump of the aeroplane's wheels. 'Oh,' she said when she looked up at the queue of passengers in the aisle, 'have we landed?'

Inspector Andries Bakker was tall, six foot seven, taller than any policeman Helen had met, though unlike others of her acquaintance, not at all superior or high-handed. He was pleased to be of assistance to her, to be working with her, both of which sentiments appeared to be genuine.

He complimented her on her quickness: without her, the case against Lotte Rouhof would have taken longer. Also, he deferred to her; as Lotte Rouhof spoke fluent English, he would let Helen ask the questions. Although she was on Dutch soil, she should consider the investigation hers, though, he added, he'd be surprised if Lotte Rouhof said anything at all. She hadn't so far.

After a few minutes in the interview room, Helen understood Bakker's pessimism. Lotte said nothing, did nothing and displayed no emotion. Helen noticed how she sat, how her arms fell at her sides, her hands on her lap, how simply she was dressed – in a plain blue skirt and white shirt buttoned to the neck – how sparing her make-up, how plain her gold necklet, how constant the blankness of her expression.

After preliminaries, Helen picked a file from the floor, selecting from it two official-looking documents. She pushed them across the table towards Lotte. She did the same with the photograph of Olaf with Christina, Ruth and the boy.

Lotte didn't look up.

'A friend of mine,' Helen said, 'has been trying to discover how the suitcase in this photograph washed up on the east coast of England, at Southwold in Suffolk. He thought . . . thinks . . . it might be a clue to a mystery which has been unsolved for the last twenty-three years: what happened to the two females in the photograph, the one who's holding the suitcase, and the one with long dark hair who's in the boat. The first, Christina Tolmie, disappeared soon after this photograph was taken. She hasn't been seen or heard of since. The other female turned up dead three weeks later. Her name is familiar to you, Ruth Jones. Her body, as you know, was found washed up on Texel, coincidentally not very far from your house. But there's something else about this photograph which intrigues me: not who's in it, but who took it? Why was it taken? And why, six years ago, it was shown to Mikey Jones, Ruth's father, by a woman who called herself Detective Constable Jane Jarvis.' Helen paused. 'You can take over from me any time you want, Lotte.'

Lotte continued to stare at her hands.

'No?' Helen asked. 'All right, let's turn to the two documents in front of you, which have been sent to me from Paris. They're birth certificates. One is yours; the other is your younger sister's.'

Helen opened her file, producing another document, a death certificate. Again she pushed it across the table. 'As you know, Neva, your sister, hanged herself twenty-three years ago. She was young and pregnant, the father abandoned her.'

Another pause.

'If I'd been Neva's sister, I'd have gone looking for the father. I'd have wanted revenge. I'd have watched his haunts. In particular, I'd have kept a look-out at the restaurant he frequented near to his boat mooring. I'd have listened for gossip, some hint of where he'd gone. If I'd heard a woman inquire after him, I'd have followed her too. I might even have taken a photograph of her and anyone she met. I'd certainly have done so if I thought she was meeting up with people who knew where my sister's lover was, who might be taking her to him.'

Helen watched Lotte. Still there was no reaction.

'I think you were the photographer, Lotte. I know you showed the picture to Mikey Jones, the father of Ruth Jones, because he has identified you as the woman who visited him and called herself Detective Constable Jane Jarvis. I'm guessing now, but I imagine you were so upset by what happened to your sister, by your father's subsequent incapacity after his stroke, your mother's descent into dementia, both of which you thought had been caused by Neva's suicide, that every passing day, every year, your desire for revenge became stronger.

'For a while you were too busy to do anything. You were looking after your sick parents, running the hotel in Paris and having to tolerate an unfaithful husband. Suddenly, though, everything changed, didn't it? Your husband died, then your parents. I think you decided then to dedicate the rest of your life to finding the man you blamed for Neva's death and for making your parents' old age so miserable.

'You sold everything. Then, for the next six, seven years you travelled in France, Spain and Portugal, looking for the man. You knew his name, Jacques Picoult. You knew he owned a boat. So you concentrated your hunt on ports and coastal towns. Eventually, you extended your search to England, until one day, in Margate, Kent, you happened upon a stall with posters of a missing girl, Ruth Jones, the teenager you saw and photographed with the woman who asked that question about Jacques Picoult in the restaurant twenty-three years ago. This woman, holding the suitcase. Her name, as you know, was Christina Tolmie.'

Helen put her finger on the photograph. She glanced at

Lotte. 'No, I suppose you don't need to look. So you followed the stall owner in Margate to his house and pretended to be a detective in possession of some new evidence about Ruth's death. You asked Mikey Jones about the young man in the photograph, giving him the impression he was a suspect in Ruth's death. But you were interested in him for another reason. You thought he might have delivered Christina Tolmie to Jacques Picoult.

'After seven years of searching, suddenly there was hope. But Mikey Jones didn't know the young man; another dead end. So when Mikey mentioned Ruth's best friend Sarah Pauling had moved to Texel, to the village near to where Ruth's body was found, you changed tactics. You knew from newspaper reports that your sister's boyfriend had been linked romantically to Christina Tolmie. You were aware of the rumours about him being the father of her two daughters. You decided to stay close to the people who might eventually lead you to Jacques Picoult. That meant keeping an eye on the two Tolmie girls. Also, you went to Texel, to check out Sarah Pauling, now Allison.

'During that visit, I think you saw Sarah with the young man in the photograph, by then not so young, and you decided to stay and to watch them, to make friends with them if you could. Within a few weeks of your visit to Mikey Jones, you'd bought the house beside Sarah's in De Koog. Later, you became Flora Tolmie's very assiduous cleaner, always wearing gloves, always covering your hair. Then you watched and waited, and four days ago, outside Haymarket Station in Edinburgh, you came face to face with Jacques Picoult. You stabbed him using a knife from

Flora's flat, which, of course, implicated Kate.' Helen watched Lotte. 'Which I find puzzling. I thought you'd want to take the credit for killing him, for avenging Neva?'

Lotte raised her head. 'He used to tell Neva –' she spoke softly, calmly – 'about a perfect woman called Christina who was beautiful, who demanded nothing of him, though he was the father of her two children.' Her eyes flashed open. 'He told my sister she should be like Christina. How could she be like that? She was in love with him.'

'Why did you implicate Kate? What had she done? Why try to destroy her life like Picoult destroyed Neva's?'

'She's Picoult's daughter.' Then she made a sound. 'Pfft.'

Helen interpreted the meaning to be: Picoult destroyed Lotte's family; her settling of scores, her revenge, extended to his.

37

They were like ghost hunters: Helen studying each material-izing shape for Cal's easy stride; Sarah, for Olaf's bulk that had once reassured her, which now terrified her. The mist, sliding off the sea, played tricks with their sight and imagi-nations: at a distance, in the swirl, identical beach-marker poles appeared shorter or squatter than each other, one momentarily appearing to be like Cal, the next like Olaf.

After one such mirage, Sarah asked, 'If that had been Cal, what would you have said?'

Helen thought for a moment. 'I'd ask him what was going through his mind in those few seconds before he went into the sea after Olaf.

'And if it had been Olaf, what would you have said?'

Sarah replied, 'Nothing. I'd go in the other direction. I'd run. I'd leave Olaf to you and Inspector Bakker. Do you think he'd tell you how Ruth died, why he settled here, why he walked this beach, why he didn't ever admit to knowing Ruth, why he had a driftwood likeness of Ruth in his room?' She sighed at how little was known, at how painful Olaf's betrayal had been. 'Olaf's gone and he's taken the truth with him.'

'And Lotte?' Helen asked. 'What would you say to her if you meet her again?'

'I don't know.' They walked on and Sarah said, 'Should I thank her? She tried to warn me about Olaf, didn't she?'

Helen nodded. 'She couldn't tell you what she knew. You'd have confronted Olaf if you'd realized he'd been with Ruth before her death. Until she tracked down Jacques Picoult, Lotte couldn't risk Olaf being frightened off. She thought he might let something slip which would lead her to Jacques. But, after stabbing and killing Jacques, she lost interest in him. She threatened to expose him. That was why he ran away. She didn't tell you, did she?'

'No,' Sarah replied. 'All she said was she'd asked Olaf about his driftwood men not having mouths and whether they didn't because there was something they couldn't talk about, something *he* couldn't talk about, a secret, something that wasn't nice.'

'Yes, she did that all right,' Helen said. 'But she carried on and said, "Well, Olaf Haugen, or should I call you Thomas Larsen? Ignore me if you want, but don't you think Sarah deserves to be told the truth about you?" Apparently, Olaf stopped chiselling at a piece of wood and became absolutely still. The only movement, according to Lotte in her statement, was a spiral of smoke rising from a cigarette balanced on the edge of his bench. Then Lotte said, "I know your secret, Olaf. You knew Ruth. I think you were with Ruth when she died. If you don't tell Sarah, I'll make sure she finds out."

'Lotte's intention had been to send you a package in the post enclosing a copy of the photograph of Olaf and Ruth at Gravelines as well as all the other information she had gathered over the years, the cuttings about Olaf running away from home in Norway when he was sixteen, his birth certificate.'

Helen paused. 'Lotte wanted to go on living here. She

liked it here. She liked you. She thought you should know about Olaf. In the end, she found she couldn't be two things at once, an enemy to Jacques and a good friend to you.'

They walked on, the only noise cockle shells cracking under their feet, until Sarah said, 'If I'd been Lotte, I'd have killed Jacques Picoult.'

'Me too.' Helen glanced at the water's edge, at a beached log. She made a wish: if Cal washed up somewhere she hoped someone would protect his eyes and lips, that incipient smile of his, from the greedy thrusts of gulls' and crows' beaks. Also, that someone would kneel beside him and say how loved he was, how missed, would talk to him as he talked to the dead.

'Cal sent me a message recently.' Helen turned to Sarah. 'Telling me I was his good friend. I don't know why he did that or what he meant. With Cal, you never know, never knew. He preferred not speaking to speaking. He enjoyed silence. I enjoyed his silences too. They were . . .' She hesitated. 'I'm not sure quite how to describe them: intimate, trusting and oddly companionable.' She laughed. 'I used to think it was a compliment if I was with him and he didn't speak. It meant he was comfortable.'

Sarah nodded. 'I thought the same about Olaf.'

As they walked on, each noticed a dark shape shifting with the mist, now taller, now smaller, now broader, now not. Before the figure emerged fully, a voice boomed out. 'Ah,' Inspector Bakker said, 'it *is* you, Helen. I have news about Cal McGill. He's been found. A helicopter's with him now.'

'Alive?' Helen said. 'Is he alive?'

38

'A visitor's here, Cal. You know Helen, don't you?' The nurse glanced in Helen's direction, her cue to join in. But Helen was unable to say anything, unable to do anything except manage, just about, to stay upright – her head was spinning, her feet unsteady, the room, too, in motion at the shock of seeing Cal.

The nurse carried on tidying the bed as though nothing was amiss, either with Cal or Helen's reaction at the livid black and purple bruise extending from the bandage on Cal's shaved head, the purple and yellow swelling around a stitched gash on his cheek, his eyes which were shut tight, his stillness, the tubes and flickering monitors which were the only evidence of life. Cal was in a coma.

Helen managed a glance at the nurse. *Is he going to be all right? Is he going to be damaged?*

She answered by nodding at Helen, encouraging her, *Please, you must talk*, before coming round to the other side of the bed. 'Helen's going to be sitting with you for a while, Cal.' Using her foot, she hooked a chair closer to the bed. A peremptory nod of her head followed – an order for Helen to sit. The nurse's right hand slid under the sheet and returned with Cal's left hand. Another nod was an instruction for Helen to hold Cal.

Helen found her head shaking.

The nurse whispered, 'Touch him. Hold his hand. Contact is good for him.' Her eyes arched as if to say, *What's important, his recovery or your British inhibitions?*

The effect was chastening. Of course Cal was more important. Helen occupied the chair by the bed and reached for Cal's hand. 'Hello, Cal,' she said. 'I came as quickly as I could. How are you feeling?'

The nurse's eyes fluttered in approval. No sooner had she left the room than Cal's hand began to feel clammy, cold and lifeless. She studied him closely. Was the bruise at the side of his head growing? Was the pallor of his skin greyer? His eyes seemed to be more tightly shut. *Don't die, Cal. Please don't die.* Suddenly a voice said exactly the same thing. The voice was familiar. *Oh my God*, she thought, glancing around in case anyone else was listening, heard her saying this out loud to Cal. On turning back to Cal, she experienced another shock at the thought he had done this to himself, might want to be dead, might try to kill himself again if he recovered.

Her face suddenly flushed. 'Cal, I . . . Cal, there's . . . Cal, you might not . . .' Whichever way she started the sentence she found carrying on impossible. She scolded herself: *Talk to him. It doesn't have to be important or significant.* Her mouth opened. No words came out. She couldn't do small talk. She couldn't do chatty. She couldn't be inconsequential, at least not out loud.

The next thing she heard was a voice like hers wondering if Cal would be interested in hearing about Lotte Rouhof. 'You'll never guess. She led a double life. She was also Flora's cleaner, Maria.' Twenty minutes later, she was still talking, having filled Cal in on Lotte's background, her sister's suicide, her hunt for Jacques Picoult, how she was in that Gravelines restaurant when Christina had asked about Picoult, how Lotte had taken the photograph of Olaf, Christina, Ruth and the boy; how her determination to avenge Neva never weakened despite the years, how she watched Olaf and Christina's daughters in the hope of Picoult turning up.

Helen had reached the point where Flora launched a charity in memory of Christina and, later on, made an appeal for information about her mother's disappearance. Anonymous postcards started to arrive, telling her where to be if she wanted to discover the truth about her mother. 'The last of these cards came when Flora was missing, around the time of Alex's death. Luke, Flora's assistant, contacted Maria the cleaner, Lotte really, in case she knew when Flora would be home. So Lotte-Maria knew about the meeting and decided to go along. Kate, in Flora's absence, went too. When Lotte saw Picoult begging, she put a note in his upturned cap telling him Flora would meet him in a nearby backstreet. She followed him and stabbed him with a knife she'd taken from Kate and Flora's flat. Picoult was already dying when Kate found him. It looked like Kate was the killer. She had blood on her. Her hands were on the knife. Kate had motive – the abandoned daughter.

'After Lotte killed Picoult, she returned to Texel. She hoped to carry on living there. But she had one piece of unfinished business. Picoult was dead. Lotte had no further use of Olaf. She wanted him out of the way. But she couldn't evict him because she'd fall out with Sarah. So she turned up the pressure. The morning he disappeared,

Lotte told Olaf she knew his real name was Thomas Larsen and that he'd been with Ruth before she died. She gave him an ultimatum: either he confessed to Sarah or she'd make sure Sarah received copies of all the material she'd collected on Olaf, including that photograph of him with Christina, Ruth and the boy, Norwegian press cuttings about Olaf, then sixteen, absconding from home, and his birth certificate.

'By the way, Lotte's the mysterious Detective Constable Jane Jarvis.'

Helen stared at Cal. 'The thing is, Cal, there are all these other unanswered questions. How did Ruth die? What happened to Christina? Is she dead too? If only you could talk, Cal.'

Helen watched his face closely for any movement or reaction. 'Another mystery is the boy. Who was he? What happened to him?' Cal's eyelids didn't even flicker.

'It's just there's no one else to ask . . .' *Now Olaf's dead*, she was about to say. Either he'd sunk or was still drifting towards Norway. Had that been Cal's intention too?

'Would you like a rest?' she asked. 'I mean a rest from me.' She watched him, the heat of the room making her eyelids heavy. Suddenly she felt drained, exhausted.

Sometime later, while asleep, she imagined Cal, conscious.

Later still, she heard Cal's voice and woke with a start. Cal's eyes were open. 'Cal,' she said, blinking to be certain she was really awake. 'You're back, thank God.'

Just then, the nurse came into the room. 'Cal!' She looked at Helen, nodded in approval. 'What did you say to him?'

Helen said, 'Oh, nothing much, just a long and rather complicated story about betrayal, revenge and murder.'

After the checks, nurses and doctors fussing, Helen was left alone with Cal. She flushed. She *always* flushed when she was alone with him. Her heart raced. Her hand felt damp in his, sweaty. Should she remove hers? If she did, could she hold his hand again? Would he hold hers? With Cal, there were always questions, worries, few if any answers or reassurances. But he was alive. Alive!

'Did Olaf tell you what happened?' Helen asked.

Cal struggled to answer. His mouth opened and closed. Helen leaned in. 'What? What did you say? A tanker? A tanker what?'

'Accident,' Cal whispered. 'Accident.'

'An accident with a tanker?' Helen asked. 'Olaf's boat was hit?'

Cal's eyelids flickered.

'Was Christina killed?'

The eyelids flickered again. 'Was Ruth?'

Another flicker.

'Both killed, Christina and Ruth?'

Cal managed, 'Both dead.'

'Cal, what happened to the boy? Who was the boy?'

Cal's eyes closed. His hand pulled from hers, as though he was slipping away.

'Cal,' she said, her voice rising. 'Cal. Don't go, Cal.' She ran to the door. 'Nurse, nurse!'

Four months later

From Place du Docteur Calmette, where her van had been found abandoned, they went along Passage Blondin: two red-headed young women in matching summer dresses remembering their dead mother. They were preceded by photographers and television camera crews who jostled for position to replicate that famous image of Kate and Flora Tolmie, then aged six and four, scattering roses in the French town of Gravelines. On this occasion, instead of their grandfather, a priest walked behind them, stepping carefully to avoid the strewn petals. Once the procession crossed Boulevard de L'Est, he blessed the memorial stone beside the River Aa which had been erected to Christina Tolmie, Ruth Jones and an 'Unknown boy'. After the ceremony, the crowds having dispersed, a young woman approached the memorial. She pushed a wheelchair containing a living skeleton in a stained suit who lamented, 'My Ruthie, good girl, she was, always loved her dad.' Then the school friend of the dead teenager touched her fingers against her lips before pressing them against Ruth's carved name. Later, as darkness fell, a woman with curly hair and a man, a purple scar on one cheek and gripping a newly bought suitcase, emerged from a nearby restaurant. They walked without speaking and stopped by the memorial. After remaining silent for some minutes, the woman glanced at her companion's damaged face and said with more emotion than she expected, 'Cal, you won't ever do that again, will you? You won't try to kill yourself? If you did, I'd be heartbroken.'

For a while he was unable to reply, as surprised by her imagining he'd been suicidal as by anyone being distressed at his dying. 'I wasn't trying to kill myself. I was angry with Olaf,' he replied. 'He should have faced up to his past.' Then, revealing more than was usual for him, he added, 'Why should it be my responsibility to decide what to tell and how much?'

'What?' Helen said, switching from friend to detective sergeant. 'Is there more? Did he tell you more?' Cal's brooding demeanour as well as the quality of his silence told her there was. 'Cal? There is, isn't there?'

He shook his head. 'It ends now,' he said. 'Here, with this.' And he placed his open right hand on the memorial.

Straight after, as if to stress finality, he hurled the suitcase towards the river. It contained a singular driftwood man, the only one given a mouth by Thomas Olaf Haugen Larsen.

Helen watched it splash into the water. When she turned back to Cal, he said abruptly, 'Let's join the others,' which was unusual for him. Normally he preferred to avoid crowds.

Walking back to the restaurant where all those years ago Christina Tolmie had inquired after Jacques Picoult, Helen recalled how, aged ten, she'd imagined herself caring for two orphan girls with red hair, how she'd longed to be a guardian to them, to protect them. And it occurred to her she might at last fulfil that wish if she didn't ask, as a detective sergeant should but a good friend might not, 'That boy, Cal, did Olaf tell you his name or what happened to him?'

Acknowledgements

For his expert knowledge and assistance, I am indebted to Erik van Sebille, associate professor in oceanography and climate change at Utrecht University. If any errors exist in the passages about the sea's movement, they are mine alone. My thanks also go to Joel Richardson, my patient and excellent editor, and Asmaa Isse — both at Michael Joseph/Penguin; to Maggie Hattersley of Maggie Pearlstine Associates, my agent; Colette, my wife; and Rebecca and Rory, my children, all for their advice, help and encouragement.

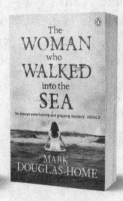
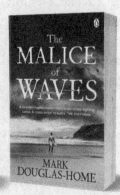